Also by Herbert Gold

Novels

Birth of a Hero
The Prospect Before Us
The Man Who Was Not With It
The Optimist
Therefore Be Bold
Salt
Fathers

Short Stories

Love and Like
Fiction of the Fifties (editor)

Essays

The Age of Happy Problems
First Person Singular: Essays for the Sixties (editor)

The Great American Jackpot

Herbert Gold

RANDOM HOUSE / NEW YORK

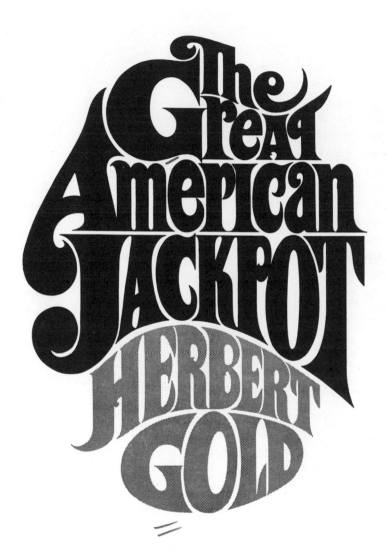

The Great American Jackpot

Herbert Gold

First Printing

9 8 7 6 5 4 3 2

Copyright © 1964, 1968, 1969 by Herbert Gold

All rights reserved under International and Pan-American Copyright Conventions.
Published in the United States by Random House, Inc., New York, and simultaneously in Canada by Random House of Canada Limited, Toronto.

Portions of this novel originally appeared in other forms in *Playboy* magazine and the *Transatlantic Review*.
Library of Congress Catalog Card Number: 71–85612

Manufactured in the United States of America by The Book Press, Inc.

For Melissa

"I am going to foreign parts, brother."
"To foreign parts?"
"To America."
"America?"
Svidrigailov took out the revolver and cocked it. Achilles raised his eyebrows.
"This is not the place for such jokes!"

—DOSTOYEVSKY,
Crime and Punishment

"Eureka, I Have Found It!"

—Motto of the State
of California

PART

I

THE

PLACE

FOR

SUCH

JOKES

1 Al Dooley, graduate student in sociology at the University of California, and bored, sick of being bored, bored with being bored, had thought that his service in the army would provide a nice, unpleasant break in the easy slide of his life. Well, it didn't. He beat the draft without meaning to. Violence avoided him, even the sleek, drilled, institutional violence of a peacetime army, fighting only educational and domino-theory wars.

Dejected, he informed his parents, who ran a travel agency in Santa Barbara specializing in five-day tours to Acapulco. They were happy. They preferred their only child in his studious ease and sloth in the hills of Berkeley. They preferred not to worry about the future, except for the slackening boom in Acapulco. His dad said, "Fine, son! You coming home for your mom's birthday? We're planning a little bust-out—fun!"

Rejected, Al then drove over to Milly's apartment on Dwight Way in Berkeley—his girl Milly Peck with her cable-knit sweaters, her long smooth legs and insides, her pert and perky healthy little face with no makeup at all if you don't count the eye shadow,

mascara, tan-flush foundation, white lipstick, and the
job of combing on her lashes. She was a trifle vain
about her blue-green eyes. She picked her clothes to
match—nighties, sweaters, stretch jeans. She had a
powder-blue Triumph TR4, too. Rejected and dejected, Al came drooping toward Milly's color-
matched pad. "You beat it?" Milly said. "Ooh, groovy.
Let's celebrate. Let's make out."

"First, don't you want to hear?" he asked.

"Ooh, yes, Al. I certainly do." She folded her hands
in her lap to indicate desire to hear. Legs in ski pants
folded under rump on couch to indicate desire to
hear. Desire to hear all over, and she fluttered her
lashes. They caught the mild Berkeley sunlight
through the slats. Now how did it happen? Al told.

He had reported for the pre-induction physical. It
turned out he had suffered a skull fracture as a boy,
and for a whole year, at age eight, he had been mighty
depressed about life. Missed school (third-grade
arithmetic was an ego trip, anyway, really out of
touch with the learning process, which should be a
form of ecstasy), trouble using right leg, double vision. His head was pressing on his brain. Then it
passed. He attended school, used his right leg, saw
single, caught up on non-ecstatic arithmetic. He was
blithe again by age nine, brain nicely floating in head.
But the army doctors had pried, prodded, knocked,
tapped, squeezed, mumbled, listened, and shined
lights at him. No decision. They stared with mild dis-
taste and perceived sandy hair, worried green eyes,
agile slouch, dropout mustache, haircut by Milly,
work boots, Berkeley don't-care clothes and chewed

nails and just another kid who wanted to know the meaning of it all. No wonder it gets harder and harder to defend the perimeters. All the balanced eating and California sun and the nice parents can come up with is this? The good I.Q. and the driver's education class in high school and that sort of decent straight hair (too long) just adds up to this kid, Al Dooley, and they want us to stop Communism with *him*?

They mumbled some more. Then a psychiatrist brought him cannily into a private office and offered him a cigarette and peeled off a whole bunch of shrewd questions: "Wanna be some kinda artist, hey? Wanna live alone? Wanna grow a beard? Wet the bed *and* grow a beard? Ever sleep with a man? Ever wanna?"

Not so fast there, Shrink. Stuffing a fellow in those categories isn't really nice. Al answered No to all the questions. The doctor, sucking furiously on his pipe, shook his head in the grip of mental health agony. His cheeks grew white, then red, then white again. Finally, through clenched teeth, his breath broke: the strain was relieved: the tobacco drew. There was a wet sizzle in the stem of the pipe. He relaxed. He smiled. He took the pipe out of his mouth and gazed approvingly into the bowl. Modestly he inquired, "Ever have a real unpleasant experience, Al?"

"In California?" Al thought that one over. "Well, ye-es," he admitted.

Immediately the doctor looked canny again. "Care to tell me about it?" he suggested. "Course, if you don't care to, that's your business. Course, in this country we trust our friendly army psychiatrist.

Course, aw, come on, Al. I had a sick headache today, one of my Excedrin days, just feeding healthy boys into the machine."

And so Al told him about his unpleasant experience. It was selling shoes last summer, no, two summers ago. *Foot fetishist?* drilled the keen, prognosis-bound eyes of the psychiatrist into Al's dim, remembering, nostalgic, post-adolescent ones. Al shook his head. He was giving a for-instance. There was this woman he sold shoes to. She was trouble, fat, lazy, and playing around. "I have flexible arches," the lady said, flashing a bit of thigh, "flexible fallen arches," flashing upper thigh, "terrible flexible arches that collapse me," flashing ultimate thigh . . . The psychiatrist gazed expectantly at Al. Al looked back apologetically at the psychiatrist.

"Well, and then what?" prompted Dr. Mendel. "You violated the incest taboo? She reminded you of your mother?"

"Naw," said Al, "selling shoes was a drag. That was typical of how selling shoes got to be a drag, and that was the last vacation I took that kind of a job. Now I work in sociology."

A steam of chagrin formed on the doctor's glasses, a compression of lips, a steely foreclosure of Al's case. Al had let him down. He could have hoped for more from Al. The doctor reared back on his swivel chair, pop-eyed; reared forward. He grasped a pencil, using index finger and opposable thumb. Like Cro-Magnon Man, he had made a discovery. The fingers can be used for gripping. He wrote something on a yellow form and nodded to a corporal standing at the door.

The corporal took Al's papers and, with a somewhat swaying tread, led him to the door.

"Well, am I in?" Al asked.

The corporal held his papers by two fingers and merely winced at the question.

"It's important to me, Corporal. Am I in the army now?"

The corporal handed him a folder. "We don't want you."

"May I ask why?"

"Becauth we jutht don't *want* you."

"But why?" Al insisted.

The corporal breathed lispingly, "Thinuth, you crumb. Clogged thinuth. Me with my adenoidth, they took me in for Viet Nam, but you with your thinuth . . ."

"Oh, my, dear," said Milly, plucking at her sweater, "there was a shadow on the bone when they shined the light up your nose, I guess it was."

Al gazed at Milly. She could never understand the man's world, deviated septums from contact sports, continual post-nasal oedipal drips. Her sweater was too busy regenerating itself. On the other hand, he, Al, would never understand cable-knit and the mysteries of a Berkeley coed's world. They met in a failure of communication, temporary going on permanent.

Having run through the human condition, Al explained that the corporal had a point about the injustice. He had a good point there. They had taken the corporal in when he didn't want to go, because of the draft quota for that month, and he had bad adenoids. And his lisping let him in for a lot of kidding from the fellas, not to mention his despair on the days when he didn't get a postcard from his mother. And Al, who really needed a break in the perfect floating of his life, had been set free because of a cloud in his sinus which he never even noticed in this climate. And the questions from the psychiatrist were just for the record and because the psychiatrist was bored and writing a paper for a psychiatric journal on how so many inductees looked peculiar to him. The old skull fracture had nothing to do with it. Nor the psychiatrist. Sinus. Bah, feh; he sniffed and found his passages clear. The army was now less formidable than the Negro problem, but it could still repay attention. He would ask Jarod about it. Jarod was his friend and teacher and one of the most successful sociologists in the country—eleven fellowships and research grants before the age of forty. Five was a good average score. Jarod was a genius, also an original thinker.

While Al explained, Milly was slipping out of her clothes into the true her. She respected him. He was so intelligent. His breath smelled pretty. Therefore she didn't shove any of her various perfumed, cared-for parts at him until he had finished discussing. This took forebearance on Milly's side because Al was a talkative, coffee-drinking, theorizing graduate student. And for her health's sake, Milly needed lots of loving. She furnished her apartment near the Berkeley campus with a Buffet print of a hollow-eyed painter, albums of Montoya playing the guitar in stereo, and lots of athletic loving to supplement her skiing and tennis. She had been used to loving since the summer of her seventeenth year. She didn't count those high school evenings in the parking lot behind the Frosty

Freeze. Addicted to mildly mentholated cigarettes and the prance and squeak of love, she preferred to get the cigarettes by the carton from the drugstore on the corner and the loving by the fireside from her honeybunch, that sweet stuff, Al. He was nice. Though he was long-winded, he was also long-winded, if you get what she meant by that. She liked him medically. "Mmm, honey, let's make out," she whispered when she could forebear no more. She touched his knee and blushed. But she kept her hand there. Still blushing, she stroked the inside of his thigh, but only a little. A girl mustn't be too forward with a really manly man like Al.

Al was good at the whole I-Thou scene. Better'n the Treasure Island ensign, better'n the occasional married instructor she joyed herself with on the evenings Al spent with Dr. Howe and his wife (jealous, jealous). For communication and human relations, she knew no one who could top the young sociologist Al Dooley. It was a meaningful thing, plus soul and funky. Sometimes afterward they had Chinese food, and sometimes, out of pure gratitude, she made eggs or something, cooked them herself.

Honeying with Milly in the honeyed evening, Al did just what he wanted to do. Then he was done. She deposed his king as he kinged her.

Afterward they went for a relaxing stroll because they felt so close. Walking down Telegraph Avenue amid the late idlers of the perpetual mild April of Berkeley, Al tried counting the cable-knit sweaters on the boys and girls clogging the street, tried counting the pretty girls, tried finding a short-legged one, tried to find some variation in the succession of espresso coffeehouses and bookshops and sports cars and sweet California pleasures. *No! Not enough!* he thought. To slip downhill into my Ph.D. and teach sociology in some good Western school and marry a Milly and look slim and elegant until I'm fifty, skiing and art movies and fathering long-legged California children and . . . Oh, no! he cried out, with exhausted, pleasured, Milly-pleasured loins empty.

"I know why you don't feel sexy any more," Milly said teasingly.

"Why?"

"It's because you're so happy, um?"

He wanted to go home alone that night; he needed to think about things. No military service—the future lay before him. Milly, her treadmill health insured once more, sleepily assented. But first she just wanted to confide a little in her best and truest lover. "You know, Al, sometimes I act superficial and I hate myself. I like myself pretty well, you know, but there's something deeper than liking myself. I know that now. There's love. And I don't love myself, Al."

"I'm sorry you have this frustrated relationship with yourself—"

"Now don't be malicious. I'm talking to you as a person, Al. Remember all the dirty rotten filthy nice things we just did. Least you could do is listen. I was reading some of my Alan Watts this morning and I'm in a deeper mood than usual—oh, I know I seem like a good-time chick, just a kicky child of our times—my doctor when I had that trouble, you know, family, conflict, ick, he told me I was trying to prove something to people, punish them, you know? Al? Are you listening?"

"I'm listening."

"With the third ear?"

"Milly, please."

Lip forward and a calm, too-calm face. "Sometimes I think I know myself better than you do, Al. Sometimes I'm silly. But I'm not withdrawn and selfish like some people." And then the pleasured smile, proud of orthodontic attention to teeth. "That's all right, I'll strike back in due time. You'll see how profound I am. In the meantime—" Sigh. "I mean that sigh, Al. I'll just take the fun as it comes, no matter how sad it makes me. It's a force of nature too, I suppose."

Al regretted that he hadn't seized her sincere feeling on the wing. "I know you have a soul, Milly," he said.

"Thank you for that," she said. "I really appreciate it, Al. Thanks a bunch."

"I said I'm sorry."

"The fun isn't going to last forever, Al."

He walked her back to her apartment. She was cooperative. He cooperated with her and she would cooperate with him. Fair is fair. She only added, dropping down to sleep with her sweaters littering the floor and her undies piled neatly on a chair: "Kizmee."

He kizzed her.

The phone was ringing as he tiptoed out in his Tijuana brown-beret boots. It was probably Milly's friend the ensign or her acquaintance the unhappily married young professor. "I won't answer it," she whispered.

The ultimate tribute to Al's I-Thou prowess.

And now, returned to forever April, he was trying to figure out what to do next. So many of his friends

came to the induction center freaked out on speed or
starving (malnutrition due to failure to eat) or clutch-
ing bed-wetted sheets and certificates from doctors or
wearing girls' underthings or chained to Episcopal
priests or waving Maoist banners. A circus of rage
was played for the audience of frowning crewcuts
in the Oakland Induction Center. But Al had gone
peaceably, unwilling and resigned, and his cloudy sinus was quicker and more effective than the holy
hatred of war. Groovy, the folks on the Terrace would
say: wow, groovy, cool, what a heavy trip. Discon-
certing was what Al said to himself.

So what next? If he were a Jew, he could go fight in
Israel, if there were a war in Israel. If he were black,
he could go join the Panthers, if there were need of
him to provoke the integration or protest the non-in-
tegration. If he were an artist or a writer, he could go
art or write. But what could a clever-to-very-clever
grade sociology student find that might make an exception of his ordinary life? This year was the off-year
for sit-ins. And anyway, the State (see C. Wright
Mills and Herbert Marcuse) was in the hands of the
Right; the liberals and the conservatives and the Mao-
ists and the Guevaraists were moiling about in disarray; the action fronts were reduced to coffeehouse
caucuses again. The student leaders of a few years ago
had heroic memories, but no skills. Mario Savio
worked as a bartender and took care of his son.
"Daddy, tell me about the Free Speech Movement."
The Muslims and the Panthers wanted no white did-
dlers. The meaning of life still floated over Al Dooley,
glinting in the California sky, but when he tried to
put his arms around it, there was only air. It was an

umbra by day, a ghost by night. At least with Milly, the air had heft and body, and when he ground his teeth, it was into ripe flesh.

The midnight horrors needed a radical solution. The dawntime longings needed a conservative solution. A personal salvation in joining the oceans of others. A private decision to take nothing but what he wanted right now. Something. An ocean or a desert, earth or space, sacrifice or brutal will, simplicity or contradiction or both or neither. Something more than all this pleasure and vain hope and successful preparation.

Join the Peace Corps? Get rich? Commit a crime?

Now you're getting down to cases. Oceanic longings and the horror of the vacuum are for undergraduates and old men.

Well, the Peace Corps seemed a bit political; Al suffered from that weakness for cynicism which is one of the diseases of the bored. He disliked it in himself. Another of the diseases is melancholia. He disliked this one even more. These maladies led him to ask such questions as: In a time of general disaster, why catch infectious hepatitis in foreign climes? Why teach one Asian to read when a thousand illiterate ones are being conceived every minute? Why not get my jaundice from the needles at home, like the hippies and the yippies? Which only meant that the Peace Corps did not engage him.

Falling in love was another possibility. But once the body is cared for in Milly's or some other Milly's sincere California fashion, love is not an option to be chosen by an act of will. A chap can count on seminal vesicles (one, two, three, four), but this shouldn't be

confused with that magic attention to someone else
as to oneself. No love in sight. Okay.
That left getting rich. Or committing a crime.
Or a scale between.
Or a fantastic and possible life to replace his real
and impossible one.

Hm, getting rational, thought Al, passing the drugstore which sold mostly paperback books and ski
equipment, humming through his cloudy but clear
sinuses. *Crime,* he thought, strolling on past the California Union, a glass-and-aluminum structure devoted to happy times on the old campus. Even at this
hour the leggy girls and their leggy dates lay entwined
on leather couches inside, on benches outside. What
was their problem? Didn't they have someplace better to go or do than foreplay here in the shadow of the
glass halls of learning? Jarod Howe pointed out that
private sex is more personal—*private*—than public sex.
Good idea for a research grant there, developing a
scale of privacy.

Back to Al's major idea. Why not combine the two,
crime and riches?

He could take off the summer to become a rich
criminal in San Francisco or Berkeley. It was more
personal than being a draftee, anyway, or one of
Jarod's assistants. The phrase "heist job" came fizzing
through to his bemused spirit. He liked the sound of
it. Heist, con, strong-arm—an energetic young maestro
of psychopathic behavior! He would have money for
specialties in sex, travel, cars, fun. He could break out.
Isn't free dreaming what America promised?

For Al Dooley, depressed by his comfortable future, revolution within was the moral equivalent of

the Peace Corps. He had a girl and a career and friends and he had nothing. He looked for a way to become bloody and human. Slouching and affable and floating, he was out to make the volcano boil beneath him.

He paused near the little group gathered on the steps of Sproul Hall. An agitated black man in narrow-lapeled suit, narrow tie, was pumping and pumping his right hand into his left hand and calling down the lightning of Mohammad onto whitey, Mister Charlie, and pink men everywhere. The steps led palely up into the halls of administration, deserted by night. The summery air and the imprecations of Wilbur X held a small crowd content. Then a three-wheeled motorcycle, normally used for parking inspections, drove up along the wide walk and the man called Dean Fuzz ambled out, one leg like a cop's, the other like a dean's, the two plump thighs working against each other. "Okay, okay, you fellas . . ."

The crowd groaned. A good-humored, abstract protest. Well, they had won the battle for free speech, but this was nighttime. They had won the battle for the day, not the right to disturb the peace (what peace? what peace? what peace?).

Wilbur X scooted without further protest. He knew the rules. He took two fair-haired coeds with him; they wanted to know more about destroying Mister Charlie, and the three of them would adjourn to the Mediterraneum or the Forum for further discussion. "Tell me, Mr. X, do you hate all white men equally? Do you think some are, well, sympathetic to your cause?" Eventually one of the researchers would drop out, probably the one with the fraternity pin on her sweater.

That Wilbur X is cute, Al thought. But he means it; he's different from Superspade, who carried a copy of *Under Milkwood* about as his ticket to meetings on the Terrace, the same copy until he wore it out and had to buy another; different from Jarod Howe, whose baggage was not simple. Wilbur X had something else going for him. He meant what he said.

Al, too, could learn to mean what he said. A nice little job that would break all the plans.

The student criminal Al Dooley, formerly melancholic, took a hot shower before bed. He left the glass door of the stall ajar, so that it went drip drip on the tile, but before he could get up to close it, he had fallen asleep. Gratification followed by fantasy had worn him out. He was twenty-three years old. He had not suffered very much in his span on earth. The times and his girl friend and his parents seemed to want him to be a diddler, but he felt mysterious stirrings. Sometimes he saw a brother in a word or a glance. Wilbur X could be a brother. Someone else. Or Jarod Howe, the maestro.

Al talked a lot, but he was a loner. He was seldom alone, but he was continually private. He had his problems. He wrote in a notebook. He had a taste for meaning. He wanted life to have meaning. He wanted to be different. This rude ambition breaks molds.

2 Dr. Jarod Howe liked to discuss the meaning of life during those easy moments before the seminar began. The electronic bells of the campanile were chiming and the sandals and sneakers of the top twenty percent of the graduating classes of California high schools were hurrying down corridors and Jarod was telling Al Dooley, his favorite student, his old friend, all about reality, the accidents of reality, and the odd good luck a chap sometimes finds in this bitter life.

"Have you ever come in to find a strange girl in your bed on a hot summer day?"

"No, can't say as I have," Al murmured.

"Sleeping? Pretending to sleep? Curled over naked with her smiling grassy hole uplifted and humid?"

"Nope, don't rightly recollect such an occurrence."

"Ah, poor fellow," Jarod declared sympathetically. "Live a little longer and the chances increase. Well, as I was saying, it really makes a man a poet—me, for instance. All that humidity uplifted and sound asleep. The perquisites of—"

"You are not one of your average fellows," said Al.

"The perquisites of, uh, co-option. Young professor. Young middle-aged," Jarod added thoughtfully, "*black* professor. Young black professor entering early

or is it late middle age?" He wore his hair natural now,
a little full with the burgeoning out of his brain.
Sometimes he wore gold wire-rimmed glasses.

"You're more colored, not black," Al said.

"And you know what I did to that sleeping girl?"

"—that's what you're more."

"What I did, I folded my clothes very carefully, as
I recall. The game she played was pretend not to
wake until the end when she started to come, come,
come. She stuck it up and came, came, came. And
then she rolled over and smiled and whispered 'rape'
and told me her name. I told her I enjoyed raping a
sleeping girl. And so it goes . . ." He measured Al,
laughing. "Until the novelty wears off, my boy." He
composed himself a mouth and eyebrows that said
philosophy. "And so it goes. They look at us and point
their bellies to the moon. We trombone them a little,
oom pah pah. And by the way—black is a way of
thinking. I'm going to call my autobiography 'Born
Funky.'"

And then he nodded and said, "Come in, come in."

Shuffle of notebooks, rattle of papers, slide of tennis
shoes, slap of sandals. Everyone was on time, as usual.
This was not a class to come late to. The students
were proud and chosen. It was the best show on campus, and probably the weirdest one, despite the conventional sociology professor's office—prints of
Auguste Comte and Durkheim, piles of opened and
unopened mail, the homely debris deposited by a
man who has settled in. He had covered the glass door
with a poster showing the rape of the Statue of Liberty
by a mob of cops ("With Freedom & Justice for All").
There was a rug, his own, and a folded army cot, his

own, and the rest was UCB issue of the University of California at Berkeley.

Dr. Howe passed around his pack of cigarettes and the little box of Schimmelpfenninks. He settled into his swivel chair, picked a pair of eyes to near-focus on, made of the seminar one great pair of eyes which he might transfix, and played a few flirty warm-up notes:

"Today, group, we tell how you can positively smell it when someone wants to start an ethnic conversation. Oo-ee, it don't smell black and it don't smell white. It jes' smell *gray*, man."

No, that wasn't the overture. He was still tuning up. The graduate seminar, gathered onto folding chairs around Dr. Howe's desk, individually groaned, snickered, sighed, licked pencils. The subject of the class was supposed to be Individual Psychology as a Function of Mass Psychology, but everyone understood that today they had been chosen to make the wall against which Jarod would bounce his points. More and more it was Advanced Facetiousness 601, Dr. Howe having his put-on of whitey student, some peculiar and out-of-step game he was working out. The man was funny, charming, smart, oh very smart, friendly, capable, an honor to the university, a fine sense of syncopation, a credit to his race. But his race was turning out to be the race of wiseguys and the only people who liked him were those upon whom he turned teeth, eyes, and charm. And they liked him very much, of course, and all the more because of his tricks. The younger undergraduates just lay down with their four paws in the air and he scratched their bellies and they loved it. They sighed and stretched and made preening, cooing noises. These graduate

meetings had different students and a different effect.
The seminar was in a state of reluctance. Even his
good friend Al Dooley was wondering what to make
of him.

Jarod was practicing the consumer arts of unrelia-
bility, vanity, and petty comforts. Perhaps his lifelong
wars and the great days of protest had worn him out.
Perhaps being forty and his work only half done, worn
out, Jarod was having his breakdown by passing it on
to the world.

"Gentlemen and sweet ladies," Jarod was saying,
"today once more we intend to make a speed run on
the nitty-gritty of the Weltanschaung—"

There were two girls in the group, Fran Rosenbloom and Debbie Wills, and four men besides Al.
Al did not necessarily think that Jarod had necessarily
been to bed with either Debbie or Fran. Fran had
straw hair, sparse over pink scalp, and a ball-point
pen always working in her fist. Debbie was pretty,
with a cute way of pushing her glasses back up her
nose, and sharp little teeth and a soft, knowing voice.
Just now Debbie was peeking at the turbulent vein on
the back of Jarod's hand, and the little quiet tributary
veins, and she was smiling. Both Fran and Debbie
peeked at Jarod instead of staring like the men. The
men were all sociology graduate students, but they
were interested in different matters—cultural anthropology, statistical studies, Levi-Strauss, C. Wright
Mills, Max Weber, reform and intuition and teaching
and research and getting good jobs in them later. It
was not part of all this to listen to the distinguished
professor rap, but it was part of all this to have the

distinguished professor remember them well and write the correct letters.

Yes—as Al came to think of it—Debbie's smile curved in that shape of knowing which knows. Oh, it was in touch okay; possession is nine-tenths of the pleasure. A quick one after a Mexican dinner on Dwight Way, and a pat on the rump, and Jarod left her happily dozing, fulfilled, dreaming of letters of recommendation which would make the social work agency's head whirl.

"Your problem and mine are similar in some ways," Jarod was saying, shoes off, feet in desk drawer (cunning little professorial idiosyncrasy). "I know your other profs hand you that line. They want to communicate, too. But you're having the GSIC—Graduate Student Identity Crisis. So you find love, you look for love, you find it again, you swear love, you lie awake over her body—" He rattled the drawer at Fran and Debbie: "Over his, or perhaps under— You eat pears and say you'll never forget. She forgets. He forgets. You want to do something personal. So you rob a bank, say: good. You've done something personal. You're on the right track, you're not into promises—"

"You were saying about the anomie and isolation of the blacks," Al reminded him.

"We have two hours, don't we, Mr. Dooley?"

"Yes, Mr. Howe."

"We've both read the Moynihan report?"

"Yes, Jarod."

They grinned, enjoying the little game.

"All right, then I will proceed at my own pace. Black is the Avis race in this country—only second. So

we have to try a little harder. First we tried keeping
nice clean ashtrays, then we try burning down the
cities. Take me, for an instance and example. I built
my personality on a small foundation of virtues. I
wasn't a litterbug and I didn't pick my nose in public.
By extending these qualities gradually toward neat-
ness, generosity, and kindness to others, I built up a
character. At some point along the line I found I could
litter again, however." Gesture toward pileup on desk.
Busy vein on hand. "Since this course is offered for
credit, let me offer you a citation from a great histori-
cal thinker: Power corrupts, and democratic power
corrupts democratically."

He waited. No applause.

Al was thinking: If Jarod is in trouble, then what
chance is there for me?

And then he thought: Maybe he's not in trouble,
just showing off. Then he's in *trouble*.

Last year Jarod and Al had moved in a warm groove
together. Al did good work for him; Jarod praised his
good work. They strolled through the campus to
lunches at the faculty dining room and lounged by
the fireplace on Jarod's barge and Jarod had suggested, when they finished the school bussing survey,
that they backpack through the Los Padres forest to
Tassajara. "We can talk about the pollution of the
earth by hydrocarbons," he had said, "meanwhile
breathing clean air." But they had left ecology and
melancholia and the city behind. They sweated under aluminum and canvas packs and studied ranger
maps. They camped out and cooked freeze-dried
steaks. They ran into a nest of Minutemen daddies
drilling with their Minutemen sons, carrying Sears

walkie-talkies and sporting rifles. In the California
forest voices rang out in dewy dawn: "Daddy—this is
Stevie. Daddy—do you read me . . .?" "Stevie, this
is Daddy, I read you loud and clear. Get me a Fresca,
roger and over . . ."

The encounter with Al and Jarod stimulated the
little camp of toy soldiers into paramilitary gabble and
drill, marching to and fro and drinking their emer-
gency Frescas. In case of atomic attack from the East,
they kept an extra supply of Frescas packed with dry
ice. The two hikers took off, not having left ecology
and melancholia and the city behind. The Minutemen had littered the piney paths with spent shells.
But it was reality; it was not depressing; they could
live with reality. They climbed down the trail to the
Tassajara River and followed along the bank, hopping
from rock to rock, feeling lithe—and there were silvery
trout quick in the pools, and deep fat slow trout beneath them—and then there was another pool and
they had stripped off pack and clothes and they
swam, whooping and groaning with pleasure. It was
fine. It would always be there, the city, the forest, the
chance to hike in them, and friendship with Jarod. If
the world is very odd and history peculiar, well, it
makes the basic matters that much more important.
No matter what, they would always know where they
were.

Al no longer knew where they were. Trouble fore-
closes the future; everyone knows that; but it can also
foreclose the past, roger and over.

"Love of self," Jarod was saying, "is the model for
the love of others. It begins like that. Adolescents
haven't moved that far yet, and the character disor-

dered—the psychopathic personality—the streetwise
kid may burn himself out before he becomes human.
Life is filled with these little ironies. The sexual and
the racial are all confused, as we know—see Fanon,
Sartre, Ferencsi. Someday you'll meet the perfect girl
on the airport limousine, and you've both got two
hours till flight time, and there's the Pan Am Airport
Hotel, but you'll have dirty underwear. And when
you're out with some frightful old bag, you're horny
and ready to go in your nice clean boxers."

Fran was blushing. The word "boxers" really got to
her. Little dots of ball-point ink stained her fists.

"Sir?" said Sherwin Shapiro. He had an expression
on his face which declared that the seams of his underwear were not relevant. Tongue ballooning out one
cheek, bubbly pout.

"What happened to the American dream? Is that
what you wanted to ask, Sherwin? The dream is gone
now but if you stretch out your hands for the pretty
faces, good exercise, nice money, all the power and
dominion you can get in conquering bodies and souls
and the folks that put a fellow down, Sherwin, well,
you can still catch the jackpot. Some of that might slip
through your fingers, too, Sherwin."

"*Sir*," said Sherwin Shapiro. That *sir* was the bell
that tolled.

"What does this have to do with the course?" Jarod
asked.

"Yes, sir," said Sherwin.

Since Sherwin was one of the campus leaders of the
Maoist group, this yes-sirring was intended for an an-
gry bit of ironical and existential and one-dimensional
Guevaraist nay-saying to a professor who was wasting

his time. It was a way of commenting: Get on with it,
Uncle Stokely.

"Didn't the whole Movement have to do with
greater intimacy between student and faculty, Sherwin? Isn't that why we're here like this, Sherwin, telling it like it is?"

Oh, man, Al thought; and followed the impulse
where it led. He threw himself out of his chair, onto
the floor at Jarod's feet, polishing his shoes with his
sleeve, murmurring Yassuh, yassuh. Even solemn Fran
and Debbie laughed. A joke for Sherwin, too—criti-
cism. Al played at submissiveness, though of course
he really was a graduate student and therefore somewhat submissive to his advisor, counselor, and mentor, and he was also getting the shoe nicely clean.
Nice, nice joke. Until Jarod, with a cackling savage
roar, leaped up, turned, grabbed Al from behind, and
pressed his belly against Al's back. Al tried to raise
himself, but Jarod was leaning hard.

"If you're going to present yourself like a slave,"
Jarod said, "be prepared like a woman, too."

And now his laughter topped them all. And un-
easily the others laughed, too, except for Fran and
Debbie, who were frowning and trying to remember
from books what this might signify.

Jarod let Al up. He shook his hand. Good show, congratulations. He winked. Al felt peculiarly shamed,
but also exhilarated. Somehow his joke had turned
out badly and right. And Jarod seemed pleased with
him for taking chances, so he had gained what he
really wanted—take chances and get Jarod's approval.
His heart was pounding.

"What does bowing mean?" Jarod asked. "Now we

see. Bowing means presenting your exposed neck to be
slain. It means throwing yourself on the mercy of
your opponent, acknowledging defeat. The performer
bows to the audience."

Sherwin Shapiro led the applause. Everyone
clapped but Al. Jarod inclined his head a little.
Words, words, words, and cleverness, and topping
everyone else, these things grew out of him as hair and
fingernails grow, almost without effort. They continue
to grow out of the dead, Al thought. But Jarod had an
answer to everything—that was his real cause. When
he made a frank remark, it was a part of National
Negro Frank Remark Week. His deeds and his self-
congratulation for his deeds were simultaneous trans-
actions. He was his own best audience and he
sought to discipline the world until it approached his
standards. Discipline meant doing what he had just
done to Al; discipline meant what he wanted it to
mean, dominating and controlling; topping. Others
doubted themselves; he also doubted the others, but
not himself, or not at all in the same way. At the level
at which he doubted others, he was absolutely certain
of himself. Perhaps because there was another level.
He could grow a white skin if for some reason he
wanted it. He did not need it. It no longer occurred to
him to want it, since life treated him so cozily as he
was: the model black make-out genius, expert, that
clever and interesting Dr. Jarod Howe, consultant to
the President, advisor to the Supreme Court, chiefest
cocksman at several major universities.

"Look, since the session has begun this way, sort of
group dynamically, groupy-dynamic, let me show and

tell this time," Jarod said. "I'll give you my story and you can draw your conclusions. Show and tell—okay?"

"Hear hear," said Sherwin, whose first child was named H. Rap Shapiro.

But he doesn't polish the shoes, Al thought. On your knees, Sherwin, and I wanna see my face in it.

"Sarcasm, friend, is pointless," Jarod said, "and besides that, you really want to hear my story, don't you?"

"Yes," Sherwin admitted.

"Okay. All right. I'll think out loud . . . Never aged a day after my twentieth black year. Was my own son, and spoiled him. Keep my mystery intact. My blackness works for you, too." He grinned at Ron Thorpe, the only black member of the group. Ron shrugged. This didn't work for him, it seemed. It was only *supposed* to work for Jarod. Ron had organized the Black Students Union, and he wanted ghetto kids in the school, and he worked in A Better Chance, and he liked the Panthers, and he and Jarod were strangers to each other.

When Jarod smiled, he was a boy, he looked like a boy in his smooth satin envelope of skin, but when he opened his mouth to smile, the gums were retreating over the sockets of teeth. An invisible ill health was being brewed in the cauldron. Age was steaming and cooking away. Ron Thorpe was looking at his pink palms; he was either listening very closely or was deeply ashamed. Fran Rosenbloom was enraptured. She stared at Howe. Debbie Wills sat with the half-smile of future gossip on her face. "If God had wanted me to be married," Jarod was saying, "I'd have been married." His eyelids looked slightly raw, like his gums, pinkly turned out, two pink slashes in the satiny skin. "And I am married."

No, man, this is not soul talking, Al thought.

"I want to lead you to seriousness. Follow me, class. Come. No generous impulse ever goes unpunished."

Smartass Jarod.

"Let's talk about the trickle-down theory of relieving poverty; for example, tax cuts. Whitey has more money in his pocket, and our boys can relieve him of a percentage of it by hitting him over the head as he passes by looking for the Snick office, and that's called trickle-down. Of course it's a funny thing, but since all you nice college kids and everybody got interested in civil rights, the gap between white man and black man has widened—you noticed? Not the lunch counter gap, but the money gap. Not the Jim Token gap (that's my game) or the Upward Black gap (me again), but the real mass thing. I say I'm a black, but I'm a sports car dropout. It pays very well. Get rewarded for being strung out. Jealous, Al?"

Al supposed he was jealous.

"You all know I'm absent from the campus half the time. You're all so proud to have a word with me, you too, aren't you?"

He's out of touch, Al was thinking. He is singing his own aria. He isn't high. He is just playing games.

"Well, when I'm sixty, I'll have a face like the map of an emerging African state, a Moslem coast and jungles in the interior. That's the price, if I live. The teeny-bopper pays the price of transmitting the clap when she's young and boring everybody when she's twenty-five. It's cute at eighteen and yak-yak seven years later, if she lasts that long. It's because she has no personality—she's just teeny, as the Negro is just black—and so she is an efficient nothing, good for certain purposes. Personality begins when one man plays a role no other man can play. He—or *she*, Debbie—has carved his niche in the universe and in time. Unrepeatable and unprecedented. Does something which cannot be classified. Doesn't work like other people. He is a wastrel, a destroyer, socially inefficient, and absolutely all that makes civilization worthwhile. And so," he said, grinning, "we have the inefficient black race doing its thing, making the rest of the world sit up and see dreadful reality. The black people is useless? The black *people* has personality. Can you imagine some fanatic composing 'The Protocols of the Elders of Madison Avenue' or some professor collecting 'An Anthology of White Anglo-Saxon Protestant Folklore'? We are *needed*, children—"

Ron Thorpe was waving his hand. "Hey, hey!" he said. "Hey!"

"I'm not finished yet," Jarod said.

"What does this have to do with the course?"

"Don't you need to be more intimate with your teachers? Isn't it what the revolt was all about? Well, I'm giving it to you."

"Mr. Howe," said Ron, "you are giving us the old shuck."

"Yes." He considered this. "Uh-hum. That's what we've got here. Would you rather do subject matter, class? Is that what you'd prefer?"

"Is that the choice?" Ron asked. "That or this?"

"Seems so. Seems I'm a show-off."

"Seems like something else to me," Al Dooley said. Jarod had abandoned him.

"That's right, Al," said Jarod. "Class dismissed for today. I hope you can learn these lessons. Dismissed."

He swung back in his chair. He was smiling as they filed out. Fran carried a bit of torn Kleenex in her hand. She had broken her ball point. Debbie was in a hurry. Sherwin lagged to watch her; no, to watch Jarod watching her. Jarod was not watching Debbie. Ron had disappeared already. There were heels in the hall and chimes from the campanile. Al stood in the doorway. Jarod's eyelids seemed to be bleeding. The smile was gone. Swift jerks of his eyebrows, like a man busy forgetting an immediate petty annoyance. Then he winked and said, "Close the door, please, Mr. Dooley."

And he began: "I've left out a few things. Something more I need to say. I feel I want to talk to someone, but there's no one out there and there's no one in here."

The voice had no tone. The eyelids were raw.

"By the way, Al—"

Al wanted to kill this man he admired. He wanted to love this man he wanted to destroy. For a moment more he would wait and listen to him.

"There's nobody else where I'm going, Al. Nobody. And by the way, thanks for the nice clean shoes."

3 As Al Dooley entered past the display of Tapered Surf Boy Sportshirts, with rawhide tie fronts and side zippers in blue ("will evoke compliments"), he overheard a conversation between a Polk Street slicker and a Haight Street hippie. It was a fine sunny morning in the cool, blue and white and gray city, San Francisco. He noticed two, not one, but two pregnant women picking out tight-crotch clothes with their husbands. One of the pregnant women had an already born child in a carriage alongside her partner. She also wore a Chiquita sticker on her knit dress, shielding her naval from radiation.

The Polk Street slicker, in new white bell bottoms, with striped turtleneck dickie and virile olive Dutch Boy cap, was saying: "Did you hear what the Russian astronaut got asked by the first man he met on the moon?"

The Haight Street hippie in psychedelic-ecstatic paisley silk shirt, wide-wale corduroy with wide belt, trim seat, tapered, and top pockets, and boy scout mountain boots, replied with interest: "There are men on the moon? They got a place to go? The fuzz don't give 'em a hard time?"

"Hey, up tight, listen," said the Polk Streeter. "And answer my question."

"What the Russian tripper got asked by the first stud on the moon?"

"Cool."

"I don't know, man."

"This moon stud come up to him and ask him in perfeck English: *Is it true Lenny Bruce didn't write his own material?*"

With a laughter like subdued grumbling, the two pals pushed past Al Dooley into the sanctuary of stitch and thong, the citadel of far out and way in, the delight of the well-dressed San Francisco stud, Ye Sworde and Casual Whippe, purveyor of clothes in the happy world of men's fashion on Polk Street. One of the pregnant ladies was chatting with the other pregnant lady. They were not discussing morning sickness. They were discussing their husbands vinyl jackets. Vinyl is *out*. Further than madras. Paisley is sort of in. Goodwill is really in. Costumes is in. Nehru and Mao and medallions—used to be in, now beyond the horizon.

Al drifted out of earshot.

"Hey, what's happening, buddy?" asked a slender young man in a tangerine plush velour pullover.

"Fine?" Al said, wondering where they had met.

"Lookin' sharp," said the plush velour boy encouragingly.

"Thank you," said Al.

"But not sharp enough, thinks I. Thinks I: you need you a fire-patterned mind-expanding sportshirt to jazz up whatever downtown outfits you got hanging in your closets next to the old Murphy bed."

How does he know I use an old Murphy bed? Al asked himself. How does he know I call the fall-in,

fall-out, fall-down old bed a Murphy and not a California bed?

"How do you know?" said Al.

"I can tell. Judge of human nature and nurture,"
the men's wear psychologist admitted briskly. "First
place, up front, and for openers, you got that studenty
look about you, oldtimey studenty. You got that
apartment-off-campus look. You got that look doesn't
live in the motely, swimming-pooly type digs. You got
that Free Speech Movement, Cadillac Sit-In Blues.
You got that turn on, tune in, and drop out charisma
to you, kid. Second place, and what's most important:
so what if I'm wrong? *So what if I am wrong, buddy?*
The ice is broken and I can talk clothes and you can
answer back and in the end I get my commission,
which is what made America great, aside from coon-
skin caps and moccasins and dressing right for the
times. Now the times is different-o, trips festivals,
psychedelic-ecstatic shirts, up-tighty expressions of ye
olde zeitie geistie. But remember—Speed Kills.
Which is why I am here to aid and counsel you,
Fred."

"Al."

"Whoops, *Al*. Little slip in there someplace. My
name is Buck Burford—gimme a piece of skin. My
father came out here like an Okie, he *was* an Okie, all
his belongings toted on Ford flivver, my mother had
the pellagra, if only John Steinbeck could see me
now."

"Lookin' sharp," said Al.

"As white men should, too," said Buck. He was
wearing a button that said: KILL A COMMIE FOR CHRIST.
"This is a great country, where in one generation a

man can go from being a long-jawed Okie, his ears
full of Depression dust, to a granny sunglass-wearing
fagola. In appearance. Actually, honey, I'm as straight
as they come. With my oxymoronism corrected—and
the bad bite, too. Had to remove a bicuspid, though.
I've just adopted this dykey manner to keep the ave-
nues of communication disparate."

"Wha?"

"Confused. I dropped out of Berkeley because oh,
man, the square world. Yecch. You're still in Berkeley
—" He darted toward Al. "Right? I'm *selling*, Butch,
you buying?"

"What?" asked Al.

"Well, for instance, this mojo vest in soft cotton
suede. I believe we have your size in olive, blue,
blood, black, and brown. Thirteen dollars and it'll
make a gear new man of you. Or a pair of see-through,
mesh sides boxer trunks, very trim."

"I think I'll just saw off an old pair of blue jeans."

"Listen, don't think our stylists aren't inspired by
the new casual manner—surf. Also the new Victorian
manner—teddy. Tiffany's my maiden name, Al. And
the mind-expandex trip—op, right? We are inspired
by *manners*, kiddo. So how about starting yourself
off in the authentic Sworde and Casual Whippe style
with a letterman boating jac in regimental, excuse it,
naval red. With competition accent stripe. After-swim
jac optional."

"Actually, sir," said Al, "I was looking for a friend I
thought I'd find here."

"You'll find lots of friends here. Browse around and
about. All your friends'll be here. You don't have any
friends, you'll make friends here. This is the *club*,

man, and none of your transvestite horrors, either. It's
men, man to man to girl, all three ways. The ones who
buy fag clothes, buddy, are *straight*. It's life that's
gone kinky. It's the universe in which our leaders
stand waist deep in garbage, shooting missiles at the
moon, which seems a little odd to us. So how about
a Dutch Boy cap?"

Shoppers were browsing among the bins and racks
like Jews in a bakery on Sunday morning. They
tasted, they felt, they compared, they sucked in their
bellies. They had good appetites. They looked as if
they could gobble up these clothes. They were fam-
ished for dress. The thin voice of Bobby Dylan filled
the cracks between wide-wale corduroy and thickly
packed velour. "You're just a rollin' stone . . . You
ain't got no home . . ." There was a speaker between
the hi-boy shirts and the lo-boy pants. There was a
speaker between the free Moroccan espresso and the
Fat Max ties. The folk-rock swing of the cash register
interrupted the trancelike turning before full-length
mirrors, trying on footwear, neckwear, wristwear,
dickies and hickies and watchamacallits. *Just a rollin'
stone . . .*

"You like it?"
"You like it?"
"You like it?"
"Well . . ."
"You *like* it?"
"I guess I like it."

"Well, don't decide in a hurry. Have some moka
first. You want to make sure it's a perfect fit." The
customer tucked a cup of Moroccan blend under his
cowboy belt, trying it on for size. *Leave me all alone*

. . . And it was true that the friendly smell of Moroccan coffee emerging and wafted by a little fan from the pin-striped blender added a new floating to the floating feeling of the clothes. A voice from the fitting room floated out, over Bobby Dylan's blowin' in the Moroccan wind: "Well, you see, sir, why I am here is, well, you see—"

"Out with it, man."

"I'm a knee-grow, sir, and I want to see how the white folks dress."

"It is recommended," replied a cool voice, "that you make your selections quickly, as many of the items are limited in quantity."

"I'm colored."

"All mail orders, for example, will be shipped within forty-eight hours."

"I'm black."

"In order to expedite mail orders, it is suggested that money orders or cashier's checks be mailed, rather than personal checks. Or come in, soul brother, and pay cash, hey?"

It was Wilbur X, playing games. Al recognized him from the Sproul Hall steps. But Wilbur wouldn't recognize him. Blue-eyed devils all look alike.

Another new customer came out of the fitting room, gingerly, as if he were carrying a cucumber between his legs where it might hurt a little. The salesman smiled sympathetically, crinkling up his eyes, and then bent suddenly and straightened things out. "Excuse me, sir," he said, "but a *gentleman* wears his jewels on the left."

"Ah, that's better."

"Well, if you're new to long pants . . . I didn't

mean that, sir. Sometimes my kidding gets out of hand." His right hand, which had done the adjusting of the jewels, still held its pattern, as if it were still straightening some future or imaginary gentleman's jewels.

The man with the jewels on the left did three steps of a little dance and said to Al, "You don't recognize an old friend? You lookin' at the basic part of his anatomy, too?"

Al said, "Hello, Jarod. What you gettin' ready for?"

"Ellen," Jarod said. Jarod's wife came out of the little dressing booth where his old pants were hung. She popped out like a Swiss toy. "The family that buys clothes together—" Jarod said.

Ellen Howe said politely, "I'm glad to see you, Al."

She was dressed in Saturday Polk Street mod. With two children and handsome brown husband at home on their barge at Gate 5 in Sausalito, she looked like a beautiful woman. Here on Polk Street she was an overage white chick with a slightly protuberant belly behind the buckle of her pants, and a smooth-skinned dark cat for a husband. The other white chicks with black husbands could do their takes—lines of fret in her face and the stretching of her middle—and think: Well, she's one or two ahead of me. And since she's here with her stud, good, they can afford a sitter.

"Man, this is a junction central," Jarod said.

"We travel in small circles."

"No sociology on Saturday afternoon," Jarod said, "unless it's a conference. Listen, you come out to dinner at our place Monday, hear?"

"Please do," said Ellen.

"You hear?" Jarod demanded.

"Yes."

"Cause now we got to be wheelin' home," Jarod said. "I promised my wife a day to ourselves." He turned to Ellen with mock apology. "I didn't plan it. How could I know he'd have the bread to be poking around here? I thought just us two, Ellen, out to the boutique together."

She blushed and pulled him by the arm and Jarod did a wide vaudeville turn. Al hid near the coffee machine while they paid for Jarod's pants.

An old friend was talking with the owner at the cash register, or perhaps it was a friend of the owner, or a trusted companion, or a bonded cashier. The old friend was shaking his head. "Look, I knew my marriage was in trouble when we moved from New York to San Francisco and we had the same milkman . . ."

Al Dooley's salesman was smiling expectantly. This was his life. Al must have hauled himself there for some reason. The reason would emerge in due course. Nothing in this life is done without good reason. Al asked, "Do you have any socks? Argyles? Jockey-type shorts or even Jockey shorts? Golf shirts with alligators on them?" With each word the salesman seemed to die a little. Al bombed him with these sneaky attacks on attire. "Bow ties?"

"Oh, stop," weakly spoke the salesman, whose name was P.J.

"Nylon dress shirts? Two-tone shoes? Leather cord ties with silver dollars imbedded in them, like the Las Vegas prospectors wear?"

"Okay, I dig, chuckle-chuckle, but honest, what can I do you for?" P.J. asked Al.

"I'd like a pair of shoelaces," said Al Dooley. "I just broke my shoelace out there."

"Whalehiding?"

"No—shoelacing. To keep my shoes tied."

"I have just the things for you, *thing*," said P. J., with a touch of malice. He took a box out of a drawer. Shoelaces.

"Thank you so much," said Al Dooley.

"Twenty-five cents the pair," said P. J.

Al inserted the lace, first removing the frayed ones. A Roger Miller record played. Moroccan coffee filled the air. A faint tang of velour and corduroy to sweeten it. A touch of moka stretch fabric. A soupçon of peacock dreams.

He heard a voice making a declaration: "That cat is truly righteous and brave. He used to be on this scene all the time, but he got hip—his making-the-scene number was cramping his people number, so he shucked the thing and got real."

My God, thought Al, he is talking about me.

"Look how he ties that shoe. Class."

Al straightened up. He walked.

Al stepped out into the world to settle the wars of Asia and Africa, to win fame, riches, and the love of beautiful women, and to answer, like everyone else, the matter of inevitable time and alteration. Like P.J., for openers he needed to put on some raiment that could enable him to master his own mortality. Soul requires disguises; soul moves in secret ways, toward Milly or some other girl or toward more trouble with Jarod or some nice little bank just asking for it.

Just to see if he would find Jarod or the bank or the girl in the oddest place that came to mind, he walked up Polk to Union and the long way back up Union, up and down Russian Hill, up Telegraph Hill to Calhoun Place, where steep Union toppled off toward the old quarries. He sat on the wooden steps looking out to the bay. He retied the shoelaces. Those new waxed laces always slip. There was a tangle of frame houses, firewood piled at doors, shrubs and pine and willows nestled in the hollowed-out wounds of Telegraph Hill, and then, just beyond, suddenly the docks, the freighters bound for Japan, the Bay Bridge, Treasure Island, and far away across the hills of Berkeley, Mount Diablo, with snow at its peak. And then near at hand again, the wooden steps on which Al sat, feeling splinters, embracing splinters, the steps cracked and crumbling, and the drainage pipes growing like roots out of the slope, and the smell of coffee and chocolate from the plants down at the waterfront.

Blue and white San Francisco bounced down the hills and wound its way up again, ladders of streets and legs and clicking tracks, acid-rock music courtesy of Big Tom Dominant and the various Good Guys, and Al hurrying until exhausted, then brooding down to drowsiness over a cup of coffee in North Beach. It's supposed to keep you awake. Thinking made him sleepier until it was night and he was supposed to sleep and then, brainflash, worry, scurry, he was anxious and metaphysical and his legs filled up with steam. And then he would seek out conversation or the truth or a girl. Oh no, Milly wasn't real enough—she was an absent soul. And his heart wanted more than this, the fun, and even more than the joy of suntime longing on the wooden steps of the quarry side of Telegraph Hill.

If he found a magic lady here now, a thing with long blond hair, say, a weird and lovely and lonely little lady, and he would say something deep out of Frantz Fanon or Kahlil Gibran and she would answer with something whimsical out of Rod McKuen or Jimi Hendrix, and off they would go, arm in arm, soon to be leg in leg.

But most of those girls had already found somebody. And wasn't that just Milly all over again?

A better chance back at Ye Sworde and Casual Whippe.

The dreamy, dropout drug culture of Telegraph and the Haight, Tilden Park and Hippie Hill was not for Al, and the frantic anger-world of politics seemed another form of speed or stupefaction (oh, I'm selfish, I'm on an ego trip). He was locked into his own will about things, an intention to have a will about things. He sought to make his choices. Jarod made choices. He thought the rigors of graduate school would do it—papers and journals, texts and research and employment on Jarod's projects. Eventually Jarod would get him a good job. Maybe Tuskegee or Hampton Institute for a year, to fill out his credentials in race—"Join Howard University and Study Uncle Tom," Jarod had said—and then straight on up home to Penn or Michigan, and then back to Berkeley or Harvard, tweed, pipe, mustache, green bag. The schedule was not precise, but it was clear. And it made his stomach churn.

Well, unearned gains should cause doubt and nausea. Perhaps it was just that. It was irksome to be rejected by the army. To evade, to run away, to protest, to tear up his draft card was a part of things;

okay. But rejection is a lonely matter. Even a plea of bed-wetting or bad-tripping would seem closer to the nerve of things. But sinus. Al feared he had incurred a debt. He was not straight with himself and the world. The horrors and the lonelies validate nothing. A cloudy passage got him free of the draft, but it did not get him free. He would have to pay the price.

Al wanted to be ready. He would put his arms around the clouds in his head and he would grasp everything, clear as air.

When he got home that evening, he discovered that Milly had been in better touch with his feelings than he ever suspected. There was four days' mess of letters in his flapping mailbox—the free coupons, electric bill, telephone bill, check from his father, vitamins from Gabriel Heatter (this 25¢ special offer), and a handwritten letter from Milly Peck:

> You don't really love me, Al. I know that now.
> Besides, I believe there is more to life than love.
> However, I will always be your friend. Do not try
> to find me. I am dropping out of school, but I
> know what I'm doing. Think of me sometimes. When
> we next meet, I hope to be a finer person. Adieu,
> or should I say Adios?

Did this mean she had found a Mexican lover?

Well, she didn't know how to say it, but Milly had a sense of the job to be done. Good for Milly. Poor Milly.

Al slept with his own sense of burdens being lifted and a way being cleared.

4 A happy airplane snarl, roar of many non-jet engines; the Grateful Dead were also expressing their gratitude by tripping out. A horror trip—music, *sound*, NOISE—but it straightened heads, it strung them like beads on the same string, it made a community. In a space without meaning or Milly, the Fillmore Auditorium was the good place for looking around. Within the electronic universe there was a drifting, floating, contact high for everybody. Good times for all in the midst of Al's bad time. The communicants sifted through grassy minds, jittered and flitted across amphetamine souls, orbited into acid heavens, bumping and flying, keeping in touch at the Fillmore.

Al Dooley dropped in to see what he could see and hear what could deafen him. He said hi to the green-clad private cop who let him in without paying, assuming he was still working on Dr. Howe's project. He laid some affable on him. He put down some skin and jaw. He stood and talked with the cop a moment, giving him full value for his illusion. Also it took a moment for the thunder machines and strobe lights to be tucked down inside. He made room among his vital organs for chaos volts. He liked to enter the Fillmore a toe at a time. Moog organs inflicted brain lag on

him, but maybe that's the truth, too. Other communicants were squatting near the door in Yoga positions. The jolly green cop, star blazing on his bosom,
used toe and friendly persuasion: "Move on, Mr.
Guru. I know you bring us the wisdom of the East,
but you're a fire and insurance hazard for Mr. Bill
Graham, my employer, please."

The guru's girl friend, a straw-headed bopper from
El Cerrito High, blue-rinsed eyes and her undevel-
oped kid sister's striped jersey, turned her little face
up to the cop and said, "Wow. Groovy."

"Thanks, man," said the fuzz, very cool.

"Hey, sir," she asked respectfully, "can I soulkiss
you, may I? Really dig your style, officer."

"You got a nice clean tongue," said the cop, "but
Mr. Graham don't like me to go soulkissing the little
underage customers."

"Aw, okay, if you don't wanna," she said. Her boy-
friend stood entranced by a flight of unidentified flying objects between his eyeballs and his brain.

"I wanna," said the cop, "I really wanna, honest I
do, but I just can't. And listen, when you find somebody to love, remember it's a crowd in here. No more'n
an inch and a half of tongue is the house rules, you
hear me now?"

"Spades," said the girl to Al as she drifted off toward the light show walls, "I really dig spades, they're
so groovy."

She had taken the words right out of Al's own
mouth, and also out of everyone else's mouth. But Al
wanted no proof of the eternal human condition from
this little underage El Cerrito chicklet. He covered his
lips. He burrowed into the crowd, which was hustling

reality to a rock formulation. A few moved and touched, swayed and wiggled. There was a little knot of dancers under the strobe lights. Al wondered what Milly would say if he met her now. She'd say, "Heavy, man. Say, this is my friend Al Dooley—" The strobes would blink and she would be here in a silent movie. Al would blink—he had already blinked—and she would be gone. During a break between sets he heard the flower children murmuring to each other:

"He's on a bummer . . ."

"America is on a ego trip . . ."

"He is on a bum ego trip . . ."

"Where? where? they got a new one?"

"I came to San Francisco with Flowers in My Hair, and I starved."

"You came with a ego trip, that's why."

"I want an answer to my question: Why is the Monkeys a bum fuck?"

"You mean they're poor musicians? You know them personally?"

"It ain't the amplification, I mean the words. They made 'em of fish oil and pork fat. Yecch."

"You are on a ego trip, too. They're slim, they're slender. Who cares what you like?"

"Sweet. Sweet thing to say to me. And you're talking to a man who's found God. I don't go on no bummers."

"Hey," a girl asked, putting her head between theirs, "you got an upper or a downer? Or a sideways? I got the nervousness again. I wonder what it all means. You think maybe I'm pregnant?"

The man who had found God reached into his sheepskin pocket and pulled out a linty pill and put it between her teeth. She smiled radiantly, gratefully. She moved off to await developments.

"Okay, so you're not on a ego trip . . ." The argument blew wisps of smoke back and forth between them. "You're a gentle soul with flowers in your hair. Then what?"

"I starved."

"Peace, brother."

"No peace! No peace! Ommmmm. Ommmmm. That means a finer, better peace—top of the top ten peace signs. Them other peace signs is a bum trip. Fuck inferior peace signs, brother."

The lights were beginning to throb. Watts, amps, beleaguered transformers. The new band had finished setting up. The kids waited, crouching in corners and hunched on the floor. When Al did the Teeny-Bopper Anomie project with Jarod, three graduate students making the survey and Jarod certifying it, the kids were still dancing the swim, the curl, the private reverie. Now they were standing and sitting and lying down; a few hypothalmic types were doing all the moving for everyone. There had been rock-and-roll and San Francisco folk rock. Now there was acid rock, raga rock, shock rock, shlock rock, and soul music, too—surf soul, blue-eyed soul, and flower-power-psychedelic soul. The T.-B. Anomie paper was barely published, and already it was history. Al remembered a poem:

> The danger is
> to moralize
> that strangeness.

Or perhaps he had written it in his notebook. He was in the land of joy and it would be wrong to make it moral. He was in the country of the mind-expanded and it was wrong to think lineally. He must hold himself ready for what might come, which did not seem to be Milly Peck, which seemed to be the girl with whom he was suddenly wiggling as the new band went crashing into rebirth. Incense all around. Fluorescent-painted chicks and blinking strobes and it was epilepsy time again in San Francisco. But there was this still unravished bride of quietness with whom, somehow, someway, because the tides of music had swept them together, Al was doing a fairly inventive acid rock bougaloo spastic strut.

"Would you have dinner with me one night this week?" he asked the girl at a pause in the foaming, churning breakers of sound. It rose, it rose again, it fell, it rose, and then there was a pause.

"No," she answered, smiling sweetly.

"But I thought—you seem—that look on your face —" She had a way of fixing her eyes against his as they danced. She had a way of moving against the way he moved.

"Sure, I grok you," she said.

Slightly comforted and emboldened, he nevertheless gave up and thought he might as well be a scientist about it. "What did I do wrong?" he asked.

"Nothing," she said. The amplified sitar, the electric violin, the wired harpsichord, and the pyramids of rhythm weapons were being launched to another victory against the stoned and the stunned. There was a willingness to be overcome.

"You have a friend?"

"Nothing special," she said. "I got here with a group
—all righteous friends."

"Then why not?"

She stood a little sideways, gazing at him with her
clear sweet hilarious smile as the music crested. He
liked her eyes—smile wrinkles at the corners of the
eyes of a girl who couldn't have been more than
twenty-two. He liked the healthy slim California look:
silk blouse, checked Carnaby pants, slouching healthy
spine—a gutsy teasing funny chick. Good style.

"Then why not?" he asked again.

"Don't make dates. Don't make that scene," she
said.

Nothing to do about it.

"But I'll go home with you now," she said.

He had her by the elbow and was pushing through
the crowd toward the door. He was thinking: Both of
us smell of smoke. He was thinking: Oh, man, let's get
out of here, and lucky the wheels are nearby, before
she changes her mind. He was thinking: Thought I'd
find Milly, but do I really need to find her? Think a
little less, please. Time to shut it off.

The Anonymous Artists of America, a heavy acid-
rock group, was pouring its ardent heart and amplified soul into a song called "When I Was Worried."

> When I was worried
> You made the stars turn pink
> When I was worried
> You taught me not to think
> You said you'd make me feel real fine

And then you made me love you
Dr. Swain.

Or maybe the song was called "Dr. Swain." The evening had not yet come to its feature attraction: silent Zen contemplation of stones, pennies, and corn cobs by everyone seated in a circle. However, in the meantime, while waiting to draw up legs in the Mandala posture, there was pop and op body painting, there were strobe lights changing everyone into stop-action dancers, there was the band, there was the drip, bubble, and bounce light show, there were two projectors doing bits of film, there were Hell's Angels and Berkeley students, there were free apples, free licorice, there were posters and petitions to sign and costumes and the dreamy joy-making of people in every known variety of high. Including horniness. The previous number had been introduced by the leader of the band as "an oldie but a goodie, a dusty diamond, a pearl of some kind of price . . . Some a you folks out there might remember gettin' pregnant to this song, 'way back in nineteen and sixty-six." He had an Afro beard, blond and kinky. He was wearing ecstatic dress—swirls, spangles, silks. The crowd included all sorts, even clean-shaven gawkers. Including Al Dooley just hanging around, trying to hang loose and finding not Milly but this girl, this sweet funny radiant girl. He would get her outside before he would ask her to repeat her name. He hadn't been able to hear it over The Anonymous Artists of America. It would be better to ask when they were already on their way.

"I only," she was saying. "I only," she was explaining. "I only," she murmured, "go with people I grok by accident. Dating is a stone drag."

"Yeah, sure," he said. This was a time to emphasize the areas of stone agreement.

"Sometimes it means you're lonely. Sometimes you're going home with Dr. Swain, say, or nobody else, and that's *something* else. I'd rather make it by myself than play that girly-girl-girl game—cop-out sex game, you know?"

"Sure, yeah," he said, being on the safe side. He would disagree later. This was still the time to be agreeable. "Jeez, they're a good band," he said.

"Coming up strong. Write their own songs, communal 'em together, too."

"Who's Dr. Swain?"

She gave him her first puzzled and disappointed look. Well, girls do that. It crossed the charmed, pleased, sinewy face like a cloud; it made her body bend another way, backward and looking as if she were wearing bifocal granny glasses, octagonally dubious. What had he done wrong? How had he let her down? "You don't know Dr. Swain?" she asked.

He walked on without answering. He would not compound his sin. Better wait and see if Dr. Swain came to mind. As a matter of fact, he knew lots of doctors—surgeons, internists, Ph.D.'s in various fields, particularly sociology, anthropology, socio-anthropology, anthro-sociology—but how could a chap know everybody, such as Dr. Swain? It's a big country —the scene is very heavy. She seemed to forgive and forget his failure, for a moment later, emerging out of the convolutions of put-down, he found her still by his side.

Out through the crowd; out into the crowd waiting on the sidewalk, the kids without the two-fifty to get past the guards, the kids selling revolutionary buttons (Yellow Power, Support Viet Rock, Nihilism for Credo), the musicians from the next group, the Margin Account, unloading their cargo of horns, strings, and fuse boxes from a hearse painted all over in night-glo Latin script, the astonished winos, relics of pre-mind-expansion, stunned in the doorways, an urban renewal expert with an amplified clipboard, counting the traffic, the cops watching, the idlers noticing, the pileup of cycles and Vespas and Hondas, the sports cars slowing down, the teeny-boppers giggling in duos, hoping to be invited in. Air, blessed sea drift air of San Francisco. Al took a deep breath. A noise of revving entered with the air, but it was oxygen all the same. The lungs can take vibration. The girl—*his* girl —was smiling at a spade cat in spats, opera slippers, and a long white double-breasted parking attendant coat with the words Rent-A-Trip stenciled in psyche-delic-ecstatic non-Spencerian above the pocket. Al's lungs suffered from bad vibrations.

Uncool was his spirit.

An effort. Wars are won by the steady. A moral equivalent of war must be fought with new forms of steady by a man rejected by the draft.

Uncool to cool, *over*, he thought.

Abruptly Al Dooley had one of those ideas which provide a turning point for an evening or a life, depending on energy of decision and the richness of deposit after combustion. He swung around on the crowded sidewalk, a sidewalk like a Turkish bazaar, put his arm about the girl whom he was leading off to his apartment, and instead of asking her name, he took her chin in his hand, pressed it upward gently, and kissed her; and then, not dislodging his mouth, he slipped around and they slipped together and kissed deeply there amid the murky crowd. Someone nearby was saying mumble-mumble-mumble. Al did not care to listen. He was kissing. When they separated, the girl said, "It does good now and then."

"Yes, good," he said.

"I didn't expect that," she said.

"Neither did I."

She smiled sweetly. Gently she touched a finger to his silky new mustache. It was new to her. Well, it was new to him, too. "You probably didn't hear my righteous name," she said. "Sue Cody."

"I'll tell you my righteous name, too," he said, and told her. She moved her lips as if she had trouble remembering names, though she could always recall the face of the man who had kissed her. She looked as if she had not very often been kissed; felt, squeezed, taken home, rumpled, jumped on, yes, but not, like this, just kissed on the street by a man delighted with silk blouse, narrow pants, graceful dancer's slouch, well-articulated spine. He had thought until kissing her that she was a slender, willowy colt of a girl. Well, she was slender and willowy, but she was also opulent. And smart. And funny. (You can tell all that from a kiss? he asked himself.) And crazy. (From a kiss? you can tell? Al?)

"Mumble-mumble-mumble," she said, and smiled radiantly. "And just think of Buffalo Bill, that way you can always remember my name," she said.

"Wha?"

"Think about it, Fred. It'll come to you."

Erk-erk, said the motor (ignition again), and erk-erk, and started (mighty battery). Droplets gleamed on the streets of San Francisco. They had wheels.

She slid over as close as she could. She liked his dropout mustache. She took a hold on his arm. She was humming "When I Was Worried." Well, that's a hard tune to keep. She was clever, she had music in her, probably mathematics, too; or she had heard it a lot.

It was one of those easy drives home to Berkeley, knowing across the Bay Bridge that the mystery is to be unraveled and no fright at the toll booth. There was a nimbus of fog about the streetlamps. A few deep baying notes reverberated from the Golden Gate—freighters, fog. Joy in the certain slide of present and coming events. Tonight Al liked himself. This was a pleasure, too.

It does good to kiss a girl not Milly, he thought. And a strong acid-rock bird is used to going home with strange men, maybe so, but not used to being kissed first on the wide space of sidewalk in front of the Fillmore. Oh Sue Cody, I like you. That's a nice way to begin a friendship and end an evening.

It sort of occurred to Al that like maybe they would just head on up to his place and scramble some eggs in wine and talk and drink a bit of wine or smoke a bit of grass (he kept it in a leather case marked 14 Transistors on a shelf with his collection of Durkheim, Weber, C. Wright Mills, Frantz Fanon, Herbert Marcuse, and Che). Just that. Not answer if Milly calls.

Maybe no more. A girl who took to a kiss so sweetly
might understand. It was a way to dissolve nervousness: go slow. Sure, she would understand, but then it
was not necessary to go slow, she had understood so
well already, he had understood her so well, it was not
necessary to understand—he was not nervous—not,
not, not nervous—well, not very nervous.

"Let's kiss again. I grok that," she was saying.

"Can't. Driving."

"Mind if I—?"

"Go right ahead. I'll keep my eye glued to the road
and my mighty hands on the wheel. My iron will en-
ables me to respond without moving."

He paused at the intersection. Her breath was upon
his cheek and her eyes were examining his jaw line. In
the throbbing neon of a corner bar (Das Gupta Sutra,
did it say? Could it say that? Could a bar get away
with an Indian raga neon sign?), she was acquainting
herself with his profile ("Al Dooley, not Fred," she
was saying), and then she was tenderly pressing her
lips to his cheek, she was leaning over the gear shift,
her hands were exploring, her . . .

"Wait!" he said.

She pouted.

"About to become a mere statistic in the annals of
sober driving if you keep that up."

"You don't love me," she said.

"I want to stay alive in order to get you home and
jump on your bones," he said.

This sentimental observation consoled her.

"What's my name?" she asked. "Quick!"

"Suecody-as-in-Buffalo-Bill."

"Right. Very good. I don't have a phone, it's a drag. But we're here, aren't we, 'cause you stopped the wheels, and that's what counts in transportation."

"We're here," he said. The top of Panoramic Drive lay shrouded in wisps of fog, thick rolling stretches and then layers of clear mountain air. They were washed in the damp ocean currents slowly drifting through the Golden Gate on a mild evening. Smoke and noise and confusion were being rinsed away; her hair would smell good; he took his time leading her up the walk to the hairbrained wooden steps. It was a house broken up into apartments—a dental student, a secretary who voted to the right but bounced on her bed with hippies, the shrewd old lady who owned the building. Al's apartment was the lucky one with a fireplace and a view of the cool city. Hang up the painted bodies, he wanted to tell her (Sue Cody, he would remember the name); hang up the rock bands and the strobe lights, hang up the Goodwill Industries' clothes, hang up the hang-ups, we're home. The rent was ninety dollars a month.

"We're home," he said.

"I grok it here," she answered.

"You're not here yet."

"Close enough. I like it."

He switched on lights and lit the fireplace. He burned oak logs, not pressed sawdust. He was pleased that she could see his books and papers on his desk. He was hoping she couldn't hear the rhythmic sound of the right-wing hippie upstairs. He had met her in such a frivolous way, he wanted her to think him seri-

ous. If he had met her at school—a graduate student,
a secretary—he would have tried to come on frivolous.
"Play against my type, whatever it is," he said.

"What?"

"Mumbling to myself. I live alone and get to talking
sometimes."

"Well, you're not alone now, are you? Let's kiss
again."

Hand on tight pants and nothing beneath them.
Hand on silken blouse. Gentle mouth and hard right
hand. Gentle left hand rubbing and hard mouth. "Oh
good, good," he said.

She broke away. "Do you know what you're doing?"
she asked.

"Trust me."

"But I could feel your heart pounding."

"That's all right, trust me."

"Al, you're a funny person. Again."

And they kissed and he made a sweet slip-slip-slip-
ping sound as he pulled the blouse out. He tugged, it
caught, it gave, she greedily explored him. "Would
you believe I never kissed like this before?" she asked.

"Don't say would-you-believe," he said.

"I never did. More, more," she said.

Later, he thought, he would try to figure her out.
Now was not the time. She was shameless without
clothes. He switched off the light and she stood at
the window, looking out at the dim and deserted
street. No one could see in, but still, how did she know?
She stood naked in the window, musing over the
bushes light-limbed in night wind, night fog, while
he fled to the bathroom. He spent a few minutes there.

She called to him: "What's that noise upstairs?"

"Thump-thump?" he asked.

"Right."

"Never mind," he said.

"Groovy," she said. "I like your house."

He waited before returning. He wanted a space of silence. Let her look out the window; let her absorb the quiet of the hills and being with this man, Al Dooley, who he was. He wanted to bc easy with her, all organs easy and relaxed, ready to ride. When he returned, she was still naked in the window, in the light of the street, bathed in a bluish suffusion which seemed to come from within rather than from the fog-softened glow.

"You look blue," he said.

"You've heard about bions? My bions are glowing."

"It's the light off the street."

"You don't know what bions are, friend, that's why I tell you. Dirty, dirty, *dirty* talk—in a way. It means I like you." She said *like* instead of *grok.*

"Bions?" he asked.

"Let's now," she said, suddenly hoarse, tugging at him, "right now, oh you're sweet, and I like you."

A hullaballoo of greeting as if she had been looking all her life for a man to put an end to loneliness and to dwell in Sue Cody.

Returning to himself by her side, Al wondered if it would be all right to ask for her company, a date in, say, five minutes. Meet again in this bed in five minutes. Or would that be uncool? Or should he go all the way and propose also meeting tomorrow, no matter what she felt like tomorrow? Dare he make a plan with her, ask her to make a plan?

Here he was, her body opened to him, joyful to him,

and he could do anything with it, with her—right now —but tomorrow was the person who lived only by impulse and we'll-see.

"Would you?" he asked.

"Would I what?"

"Never mind. Later."

"Do you like music?" she said. One toe moved as if to prod him off the bed toward his rig.

"Yes, sure."

"You got any raga rock? The Four Tops' freakout of 'I'll Be There'? Any folk backlash soul? Jimi Hendrix?"

"Uh," he said, "the Jean-Paul Kreber Ensemble doing *Chants de la Renaissance,* songs of the Renascence? There's *'Perdre le Sens Devant Vous,'* there's . . ."

Silence. "Well, any old Beatle record is okay. 'Rubber Soul.' "

There would always be the danger of her taking over. That was the second danger. The first was that she would just disappear like Milly Peck into thin unamplified raga rock in the distant air. Danger made Al's nose itch. He was looking for danger. The moral equivalent of war was suddenly this gear-laden, eyes-aslant, body-greedy young lady. He wanted to open her up to the world beyond tripping and Motown records: to Al Dooley.

He was not sure he could manage. To persuade her that she needed him, but for what? To learn sociology? About Jarod Howe? What else did he know that she didn't know?

Maybe he could just give up. Senator Eugene Mc-Carthy, he thought, plays it Cool . . . Well, he would follow his nose, and where his nose led him—ah, that was nice.

She was sighing. "Nice, nice," she was saying, "oh yes."

He forgot his ideas and plans. She was delicious.

An hour later she sat up suddenly and pulled the sheet over them both. "You don't have to take me home," she said, "if you don't mind my spending the night here."

"*Mind?*"

"Well, some men, they like to be alone afterward, I don't know, I met a boy one time he had to change the sheets and all. You never know when you'll find a freak. You know, a sex freak—they're the worst. He had all sorts of ideas, but afterward—clean sheets, no me."

"Sh."

"Another one, he wanted a full meal sent up by the Chinese Chinkaroony Kitchen. Wow. Not a snack—*food* food. And then he had a frozen pizza, it was more like a waffle with cheese. I'm used to a stud he wants his morning gruel before he wends his weary way out into the rice paddies, but—And then the *real* freak, he—"

"Never mind, I don't want to hear."

"Yeah, I suppose. Maybe you're sleepy. I'm losing my feminine charm, talking so much?"

He rolled over upon her and kissed her cheek, licked her cheeks, kissed and butted her gently, and she giggled and sang, "When I was worried, you taught me not to think," and pretty soon they must

have both been asleep, because he heard a dawn bird
twittering. The fog lay heavy outside. They had never
drawn the curtains. He should get up or the sun would
wake them. He would get up soon. He would get up
right away to draw the curtains. He was sleeping.

Hours later, when she saw his eyes open, one at a
time, it turned out that she had been waiting for his
two eyes so she could say, "You know what? You
taught me to sleep with a man, to *sleep*. I was comfortable. I was lying there in the crook of your elbow—"

She had been lying there, warm and obedient.

"It's not bad," he said, "to do that."

"No, not too bad."

She didn't make dates, but she would stay home
with him now. She didn't make plans, but she would
search in his eyes with the love-me-look, the love-you-
look, feeling for real, desire for real, getting in touch
right now. No, she would keep silent about who she
was. ("Well, you know . . ." she said.) No, she would
make no promises for the future. "It's so beautiful
right now, let's not think ahead, let me, let me do that
now, let me, oh let me sweet—"

It's not so bad to do that.

It was nearly noon.

What if she was right and he was wrong? What if
her way, no plans, was the right way, and his way,
think ahead, think about protecting her, think about
the future, was the wrong way? He had taught her to
kiss, true; he had taught her to sleep sweetly, tightly
rolled against him, all right, yes; but what if she could
teach him about snatching joy on the run? He would

be grateful. He traveled his hand over her body, thinking this over. He rubbed her narrow belly. She was saying shyly, "Can we kiss again?"

Yes. She tasted good. Her skin shone with good health. "Wild rice," she said, "no sugar, but honey, no candy, fruits but not too much, whole-grain cereals, good things like that, what's grown in the area—corn—"

"It's a good thing, that's all. It's not the macrobiotic eating," he said.

She giggled.

"I make people laugh," he said. "Should we get up?"

"If," she said, sighing, "you want to."

It was that reluctant sighing remark which led him into his false step. It was his own fault, but it was her sigh that led him. Was she tired? Was she disappointed? "Was I . . .?" he asked. "Was it . . . ?"

She smiled with that bright alertness of the stranger he had met yesterday. "Well," she said, "I've known boys who came more often than you"—she marshaled her ideas briskly—"but I don't know, it's nice with you."

"You're the second best in that department I've ever known," he said maliciously, furiously. "You're the third or fourth prettiest girl I've ever met, and in the sack, you know, making it, you're fairly close to the top—maybe even second, as I said. Or third, anyway. You like that? You like that, kid?"

"Oh," she said.

"Use a little imagination. Look: other person here! Other person!" he shouted.

She stroked him gently. "You nice boy," she said.
"Sh. All I meant was—oh, I hate to go stone out on a
limb about anything—*I like you.*"

He worked on his heartbeat. Okay, he had been
bored with girls—Milly—okay. He didn't really want
to rob banks. He was inexperienced at it. He had
found this girl in the crowd on the dance floor. What
did he know about her? What else did he know about
her, Buffalo Bill Sue Cody whatever-her-name? Take
it again, okay. "I like you very much," he said.

"I like you very much," she repeated.

And they laughed together.

"It sounds like hypnotism," she said "but it feels
good. Oh, it do."

"It isn't necessary to tell the whole truth," he said.
"Let me explain this situation to you—this sort of situation. You can tell the good part, that's enough."

She looked hurt. "But weren't you asking me? I did
say something wrong, Dr. Swain?"

She poked him. She wanted him to giggle along
with her.

He said, "They let me out of the army. There's this
spade professor I work with, I think he's cracking up.
I'm considering robbing a bank."

"Uh-huh," she said.

"You hear me?"

"Sure. Why they let you out?"

"Sinus," he said. "They didn't let me in."

"Oh," she said. "That's lucky. So long's you don't
get a deviated septum. I know a fellow got one of
those. Snores. G'night, honey."

So everything was settled, past and future put into

order. They knew everything they needed to know about each other.

Well, she was right. Tasted good, even mixed with smoke. Goodnight, Buffalo Sue. If he could sleep, which he couldn't. Maybe hyperthyroid was his game, too.

He swung his legs down to the floor. He sat, slightly slumped, on the edge of the bed. She stroked his spine. He was sulking. He was disappointed. He was wondering what had got him into this. He was jealous. He was thinking about a future of deception. He was going to ask her to be kind. He was about to ask her to be loyal and faithful. He knew she needed him; why didn't she know it? He was about to try to make her forget everything but him. He was making trouble for himself and for her.

She was following his eyes avidly. She was ready for the new stage. She was obedient to him as she had been obedient to her Negro, her Mexican, her hip non-painters and media-mix experts. She was a sweet girl. She grokked him for more than the moment.

And so she could learn to be miserable; that is, to fall in love. The afternoon sun lay aslant on their still, willing bodies.

When they got up for the evening, she said to him, "Shouldn't you go see Milly, um, that girl of yours?"

"No," he said.

I don't know where she is. I don't care.

She sighed. "Or your spade friend? Or rob a nice little bank?"

So she did listen, or at least she heard. "Not tonight," he said. "It's after hours."

She said, "I like your eyes." But she kissed his mouth and tongue, not his eyes.

He sighed. Milly might be in trouble someplace. His body meant to do something about it and what it told him to do was stay right here. Glad his body was so smart.

Sue reached for the spiral notebook on the painted orange crate by his bed. "What's this?"

"My notebook. You can't."

She shrugged and didn't. "I have a private life, too," she said. "It's not all animalistic. It's not all what you think I think."

"I don't know what you think."

"I have thoughts. I am only I and all alone, too. Death, time, the future, the past. Why, where, wow. Oh yes, and who. Isn't that what you write in there, Al?"

"You can't see, Sue. Take your hands off the note-book."

She grinned and winked at him. "Well, I did my best to help you, son. But if you won't let me pry in your innermost thoughts after all we've been through together, wal, you'll just have to fend for yourself."

"I been doin' like that these many a year," he said.

She put her long cool arms about him. "I know," she said. "You're great, too." She lay there a moment, but she was thinking. And then she said, "Hey, listen, you know L.A.? From the air it looks like they rolled the dice and didn't pick them up, and then rolled another pair, and they didn't come out right either, so they rolled another and another and another, and look at all the mistakes together in One Big Mistake."

"Yeah," said Al sleepily.

"Well, listen," said Sue Cody. "That's where I got to go right now. Hey, rise, I didn't pack yet. I got a job down there in the movies. This fellow wants me for Girl Friday. I get to be an assistant in this job. Hey!" She stroked his hair out of his eyes. "Hey, this has been a righteous farewell and I'll sure hurry back fast as I can." He was too tired to feel anything and the feelings he was too tired to feel were angry, hurt, and sad. "Hey," she said, "but you don't have to drive me to the airport. But how'm I going to get home otherwise?"

5 Milly Peck. Waiting for her strong pressure from someplace, she liked to sit in the Minimum Daily Requirement, formerly the Friendly Persuasion Ice Cream Parlor, known as the travel agency ("Take some ice cream on your next trip"), formerly the Hot Dog Palace, known as the Methedrine Palace. It was a coffeehouse dedicated to quick takeoffs and smooth landings ("Give me Librium or Give me Meth," someone had written on the wall). Basic sitting plus coffee and basic protein—roast beef, one leaf of lettuce—was the best news it brought the surviving beatniks, flower children, electric Tibe-

tans, and the people around the corners. Grassy pots
hung from ceilings. The sub-economic set met and
greeted. There were good sounds from the speakers,
KSAN, Walpurgis Nacht FM, and KMPX, a personal
friend to many jug bands and tape-meshers.

The Minimum, in the below-stairs angle between
Columbus and Grant in North Beach, is sometimes the
last stop before the bridge going east to water and the
bay heading west to more water before the swimmer
reaches Hawaii and Japan. The lower part of Telegraph Hill, sunny and Italian, was still devoted to an
idling and dawdling village life, morning and afternoon at least, despite the night given over to selling
piecework anatomy, topless and bottomless, to cul-
ture-lovers bound for the Paris of the West. Bohemia
still had possession of its little enclave between har-
ried Chinatown and the abrupt elegance of the Hill. It
was shaken into a warm hollow and good enough for
Milly.

As she had written to Al, she was beginning her
patient search for the finer, purer, more Zen Milly.
She didn't care if it took a whole lot of sitting, waiting,
and coffee-drinking; she was ready for any sacrifice.
Her eyes glowed. They were banked fires. She had
made a promise to herself and to her former truest
love, Al Dooley. She felt sure she had explained it
clearly to him, but what did it matter now? What
need had he of explanations? Milly and Al, that was
only a superficial sex groping relationship. Well, it
was kind of nice. But ahead of her lay a deeply Eastern erotic love of the universe or maybe somebody
else. She couldn't be sure at this point. Those were

details. She couldn't be bothered with details. She was sitting there, waiting to be seized by reality in general.

Milly's equipment for sitting were cigarettes, black coffee, and a good supply of concentration for the speakers which used to play cool jazz, Ray Charles, and Bossa Nova, and now played Bobby Dylan, the Grateful Dead, and the Juke Savages. They helped her wait for that strong pressure from someplace. Sound helped a lot. KSAN, flower power all day long, helped. Her eyes, alternately blackly inward or blackly demanding, gazed out over cup, saucer, ashtray, and tapping finger toward the invisible pressure surely due her, not from Al Dooley, who was just a graduate student, just an old friend, but from someplace, some unheard music out there in electric space.

One man, Paul Cola, came to the Minimum almost every day to watch her. They never spoke, but he kept up with things. He made sure she heard his name; he sat nearby with friends, young men with narrow, pared-down skulls, tight continental pants, Banlon shirts, expando boots, or with girls who were pouting and attentive under Afro frizzes or ropes of all-hair extra hair from Korea. The men emitted a steady grinning, teasing banter ("Hey like wow! Man!"); the girls seldom spoke—they stared, and went where pushed, when pushed. The banter had firm foundations. Paul sometimes used his hands on the girls, humorously exploring them ("Groovy! Hey, beautiful!"), but then turned with elaborate courtesy toward Milly's table, winking to ask permission. He let her know she was first on his list, but he would not meddle with the process until the proper time. That was as it should be. He had a list. His friends called him Poopie. He also waited.

Milly patiently made herself ready for the strong pressure. It might come at the Minimum Daily Requirement, it might come at Clown Alley; maybe amid the rockquakes of the Condor or Pierre's; maybe from a black man with a Russian fur hat, maybe from an ofay with no hat at all; maybe from no place, maybe from no one. But yet rich America, gentle San Francisco, youth and hope could not all let her down. They gave her so much—why couldn't they give her the rest? Give me Librium, she meditated, or give me Meth. Where had she heard that before? What did it mean? It was in the air, like love, and what did love mean?

Without other goals in mind, she put her trust in coffee and cigarette dreams about love. Love was still the Golden Gate, ambition and power, the huge free mating of her unused and waiting body with her yearning soul. Oddly enough, Milly, who thought this strong revelatory pressure was due her from an ethnic man—"ethnic" meant color, folk song, beard, Zen, hip, in some way a piece of strange—had never yet known a man. Al was just a friend from Santa Barbara and didn't count. The ensign, the married professor—*ick*, she now realized.

And yet, impossible as it seemed to her, she had squirmed hotly in back seats; she had wriggled messily on beaches and in grass; she had found ways to make do and bring the boys to a peaceable gasping by her side, not bothering her too much. Ooh, ick, she had

said the first time with Al Dooley behind the Frosty
Freeze in Santa Barbara.

Now she was passing a cool season in San Francisco,
drinking coffee, learning some of the words to Janis
Joplin and Grace Slick songs, and waiting. Once Janis
had entered the Minimum and Milly had watched her
handle a cup. Once Milly had seen Grace on Haight
Street. Outside the Free Clinic, but she was probably
just walking by.

About nine different types tried to pick Milly up.
She had never classified the types; they seemed more
like a mob to her; but she could list their mild variety
in style and attack.

"Reading?" (She kept a paperback book in her
purse. It was fraying with its use as ballast.)

"Haven't I seen you someplace before?" (The answer to that one: "No.")

"Hey, mind if I join you at this table? The place is
kind of filled up." (The deep freeze froze it.)

"Kind of funny art work, collages I guess they are,
huh?" (There were abstract photographic prints on
the wall. She took up purse, dark glasses, and sweater,
and trailed out onto the street, leaving cigarette, coffee, and art lover behind.)

"Aren't you in the theater at San Francisco State—
the   Interplayers—Berkeley—Stanford?"   (Wrong
again.)

"You look like the sort of girl I can tell my lies to.
Want to discuss me?" (That was a troubling one.
Sometimes she talked awhile, until he started pushing
his pad nearby, the great view it had.)

Although she was off for the season, and she could

use an entire forever to discover her design, Milly
knew she could not take that forever for her search.
America offers chances, but gives a limited time
only. Her parents might come to find her in San
Francisco. She was living in the Swiss-American Hotel and getting rid of a few hundred dollars from
selling her old Triumph. The year would be over and
something else would come to delay the finding of her
line. She needed to find it this year, right now, here in
North Beach, though it could not be hurried. Hurry,
but hurry does not help. She was ready. Waiting, she
would drink her coffee, smoke, watch and be watched,
absorb the good songs.

Milly did what she could. Her legs were tanned. She
didn't wear tights. She spent an hour every morning in
the sun on the roof, clearing up her complexion, putting a bit of tan on her legs; then she showered and
plunged into the day. The North Beach meddlers
stared at the frowning, complicated, delicate reddish-
blond girl as she strolled down Broadway, down Columbus, past the City Lights Bookshop, past Vesuvio's
and the Discovery, and then back on the other side to
her perch—just waiting—at the Minimum Daily Requirement. Meddling was their word for watching,
waiting, and trying—the Grant Street thugs, beatniks,
hippies, idle salesmen, students, sailors, the wounded
Viet Nam veterans on leave from Letterman Hospital,
the larkers and drinkers and melancholic in this last
stop on the way east to the avid crabs under the
Golden Gate Bridge. "I meddled me up a sweet little
trick last night," Larry Something, a space salesman
in an Italian-cut suit, murmured to his friend as Milly
ambled by. "About four ayem made me wish I hadn't,

pal," he said. "That's how good it was, know what I mean?"

Larry had an office in the Columbus Towers, which was owned by the Kingston Trio. He used to live in Belvedere, with a wife-and-three, but he preferred the deep-pile carpet of his office, with a view of the Ferry Building and the bay, Telegraph Hill and Coit Tower, the great western city of hope and chagrin. A booking agent who had meddled Milly one night— tried to, up to a point—had briefed her on this man. Larry liked them sweet sixteen, or at least still looking it. He liked the complicated, pale, childish look which had rapidly become Milly's in her new life. Probably it was the coffee and questing that did it. She was ready for anything.

At the City Lights Bookshop, Milly picked up the new LeRoi Jones. She would carry this one for a while. Perhaps it would hurry her luck. The Ionesco plays in her purse had brought her nothing.

And what else could she do but hurry her luck? What else did she hope for? Husband and child and miseries and boredom? Her mother's luck? Her father's? A job to make do while she waited? What her parents in Santa Barbara wanted, what the girls at school wanted? Al Dooley, the young sociologist making a career as Jarod Howe's disciple? No, she would settle only for exceptional fortune and wait for the pressure to come searching her out.

On the way out of City Lights she met Al Dooley, coming in. "Milly!" he cried. "What happened?"

She let four inches of the strap of her handbag slide between her fingers. "Well, you know," she said.

She had just disappeared from Al's world. She had

him pegged, an artist in make do and make out, planning ahead, instructor, assistant, associate, and finally a full professor, with research grants and travel to Europe and blah-blah-blah. He skied, floated, and took the easy way. Milly had once asked him why he didn't take the hard way, service to mankind, and go into business; dry-cleaning, say. This was in her witty, social-comment period—she had been studying contemporary civilizations.

"Naw, I want to get rich through academia," he had answered. "Not so easy to do research, you know —time and a lot of three by five cards."

Now Al grabbed her out of the bookshop and rushed her down the street to lunch. He babbled, delighted to happen upon her like this, trying hard to take over. He was having a peculiar reaction about the army, really interesting, he promised her. Funny things were happening—he'd met this disastrous girl who called herself Buffalo Bill—a stone disaster—he wouldn't bug her—he wanted to tell her all about it as soon as they ordered lunch. "Let me take you to my favorite place!" Oh, he was a bit excited. The restaurant was an Italian family-style restaurant on Grant, with acoustics that saved every sound and all the cheap-livers yelling at each other through an atmosphere of spaghetti and San Francisco Neapolitan. *Cute* was the word Milly would have used for it back at school: house wine, house accents, pick-up informality. "This is a cute place, I always like it, but it's getting noisy," Al said.

"What?"

"Cute! Like! Noisy!" he shouted.

She bent to her minestrone.

A little later, feeling polite, she added, "I usually don't have a large lunch."

"What? What?"

"Usually! Don't! Lunch!" She spoke almost loud enough for him to understand.

"Me too," he said. "I really think it's better for dinner, is that what you had in mind?"

What she was saying to herself was *Help*. She must escape, waiting only for a little politeness, and if necessary, no politeness at all. She must get away before she was dizzied back into the comfort which was killing her, the Al Dooleys, the Berkeleys, the cute restaurants and darling lives of America. Hands demurely folded in her lap, with downcast eyes, she meditated her immediate problem—to flee before she drowned.

As he paid the check—now!—she suddenly whispered to him, "Oh God! I forgot! Call you soon, I'm late!" And ran.

How simple when you make up your mind.

She took off. She imagined him watching, aghast, her little rump fighting itself under her skirt as she ran. Sandals clacking, patter of heels. She slowed down around a corner, smiled, and swung her purse. She liked what she imagined.

Now she continued on her way to the Minimum Daily Requirement Café, which seemed like that home toward which she had struggled in her childhood dreams of anxiety and home—that safe harbor toward which she swam, toward which she climbed over jagged roofs and chimney pots, that dangerous sure port and place of waiting. Al Dooley and his cute future in Berkeley or some mini-Berkeley darkened her sun, darkened her eyes, as the cool emptiness of

the Minimum never did. There was the freedom of
possibility in that place. In Berkeley there was only
comfort.

A good start for a day. She sat at her table beneath a black paper-mâché construction which de-
picted an angel, a horn, a black angel, a black trumpet.
She turned the pages of her book, she ate a sandwich,
she drank coffee, she went to the Ladies. She was
washing Berkeley and the Al Dooleys of this world
out of her body, but it and they remained; sports cars,
French classes, mixers, term papers, and a little pot
on Saturday night. It was like a relapse of dreadful
normality; she could do nothing against her past but
deny it.

Men stared at Milly's book, tried don't-I-know-you,
tried hey-cute-stuff. They watched and speculated.
Even Hold-the-Mayo Ferd, the sandwich-maker behind the counter, devoted to icy evictions of squatters,
had his curiosity raised by the pretty girl with the
calm, too-calm face. Especially Poopie Cola noticed
her once more. He was in and out during the day,
noticing. She was reading the same page most of the
afternoon. His time was close.

Toward evening there was an escalation of the fun
surrounding Milly. Poopie came in with pals. They
drank coffee, played their transistors, and practiced
jokes and happy abuse of each other. The jokes were
shouted toward Milly. They were aimed at Milly. Still
she did not leave. She felt the shiny pinballs bouncing
against the springy posts. She felt the charge beginning, the payoff. She went to the Ladies.

Someone—a young man with a flat face, bleak eyes,
a duck cut of his yellowish hair—plucked at her as she

returned to her table past the boxed ferns. "Let me go!" she said. He smiled, dodged, shrugged, and begged pardon with an ironic upward heave of shoulders. His hair was bleached. He smiled. His teeth and hair were of the same color. *Get your hands off me, let me go, get away from me, leave me alone* ... Her head was ringing with what she might say, what she might do, as she walked between the indifferent and the humorous of North Beach, passing the time. Despite all her thinking, it was only a second later. His hand, she realized, was still on her.

"Let me go!" she said again.

"Leave her alone, Carlo," Poopie called from the next table. "Don't meddle that girl. That's my Milly."

How did he know her name?

Another young man said, "Aw, Poopie, she's just waiting for it. I think I'll just shake it off the vine."

How could he see what she was waiting for if she did not know herself?

But as if to prove the word, he ran over and sat at Milly's table, putting his hand on her knee and another on her arm, fixing her there. "Hiya, honey."

Milly found herself unable to move or shout. With all those eyes on her, all she could do was spread her mouth, but no sound came; it was a stiff, deathly grin which showed her teeth.

"Nice girl. *Nize* girl. Now you and me is friends."

He was a very short, very slim young man, wearing a Banlon shirt and black ski pants and high boots, with elastic tops secured by a metal snap.

"You're a nice, nice, *nize* chick, huh Milly? That really your name, chick?"

Her face seemed to want to smile. Inside there was

a shriek of protest, but the lid lay closed upon it; she smiled; her body was frozen and hot, with narrow fingers and a stranger's fingernails cutting into her thigh beneath the skirt.

Suddenly there was someone standing by them. "All right, that's enough, get going now, buddy." It was Poopie.

"Aw, Poopie, I was just talking to the nice chick."

"Can't you see she don't want you? Can't you see she's waiting for me? Split!"

"Aw, Poopie—"

"I said"—and he leaned forward, showing teeth— "I said split."

In an instant the man was gone, out, disappeared, and the door shook behind him. Poopie was standing by her table. He did not sit down. He turned in a little half circle without looking at her, very careful not to look at her, and said, "All right you creeps, get off, don't you dig? Poopie's chick."

And only then, hardly glancing at her, he smiled, he murmured gently, "Come on, kid, this is pure trouble. I'll toddle you home."

She arose and followed him. She was as tall as he was, but he led her, protecting her, past the grins and the nudges. On the street, he held back a moment to let her catch up with him. He took her elbow and steered her across Grant, up toward Vallejo.

"Where are we going?" she asked him.

"To my place," he said.

"Oh, I don't think I can," she said.

He took her elbow more tightly. He steered her without argument. She wondered what to do next.

"I don't think I can," she said again.

"Oh, I really do think you can," he said, "if you try."

They walked silently up Grant. From the pressure on her arm Milly understood that they were now crossing toward the door where Poopie aimed to enter, a stairway next to a pizzeria. She abruptly had a sense of someone following her; she was frightened; the man following seemed to know she was about to be pushed through a doorway, and tapped her on the shoulder. "Milly! Where are you going? I've been looking for you all day."

It was Al Dooley. He stared from her to Poopie and then back to her. Poopie kept his hand on her elbow. A cunning look of understanding possessed Al's face. He knew she was in trouble. He was determined to rescue her. "We had our date tonight, Milly, did you forget? Do you remember now?"

Al's eyes looked into hers. He was telling her he was on her side. He was intelligent. He understood about Poopie's hand on her arm. He was ready for trouble. He was willing to fight for her; he was willing to take his chances with this North Beach thug. He was afraid, but his fear gave him life.

Poopie didn't look at him. He stood negligently, spraddle-legged, whistling softly, not asking to be introduced. He kept his hand on Milly's elbow. He slid it up her arm, squeezing, and then back, locked in.

"Come on," Al said, "we were supposed to visit the Howes this evening, you remember? They're expecting us. We're late."

Poopie turned her away almost as she spoke; she turned with him as in a dance, with a deeply satisfying following step. "No, Al, I had a date with Paul tonight," she said. "We're going home now."

6 How can a wholesome young man, with a father in Travel in Santa Barbara, enter the life of crime? It's not easy. It's harder than that. Perhaps because of long association with students bucking for Monsanto Chemical or Civil Service, Al considered becoming a Mafia trainee or an apprentice gangster in some modest, unassuming racket. But where were the advertisements to answer, the references to offer, the curriculum vitae or resumés to prepare? Where was the trade journal called "Safe-Cracking Today"? Where the Prentice-Hall text on how you too can learn to pass counterfeit bills in your spare time? It seemed that they were trying to make things difficult for a young fellow finding his own way in the world. They favored their own. You had to have pull—like for appointments to West Point or the Naval Academy. No smiling and crewcut recruiters from The Black Hand visited the campus to talk with seniors and graduate students in the social sciences.

The Bible says to do whatever you do with a full heart. With a full heart Al Dooley had been doing nothing. He had been doing Milly with a nearly empty heart. He had done Sue Cody with a fantastic heart. He knew little of his heart, only that it was filled with de-

sire, with empty desire, a contradiction; with shame
that he had escaped the army which he had sought to
escape; with love of Sue, with ignorance of her; with
confusion of Milly; with deception in Jarod Howe; with
trouble that had no good reason.

He would prefer to do something brave and useful.
If he didn't, he would do something foolish, violent,
and useless. He would go to his private war. He had
marked himself out for a piece of strange.

And so Al moped, trying to find a dishonest way in
life. Something special, if he couldn't find something
good. He sought to leave the dense ruck of the easy
and ordinary. Hanging around the Tenderloin, just
north of Market, he met a nice criminal called Rough
Ronnie, who took an interest in him. Ronnie sat with
his hard belly close as he talked. He had a taste for
steaks with an order of scotch on the side, no veg,
but extra fries. He told stories and picked up the fries
by the tail. He let Al buy him drinks at the Leather
Trade Bar. But when Al asked to join in his heist or
other activities, Ronnie just said, "You thirsty? I am.
It's all this sitting around and talking makes a man
thirsty."

Sometimes Ronnie paid, too. He wasn't greedy. He
just liked company and took a fancy to Al. His beard
came in grizzled five-day slivers and his eyes glittered
cunningly with the wisdom of stir. He was cheerful.
He had been locked up too much. He patted his belly
and tapped Al on the belt and said, "Have some of my
fries. I love those good fries they make here." In his
prison years he had picked up reading and writing
and he enjoyed talking to a boy who reminded him of

trustee librarians and teachers he had known. "Oh, I
have a story to tell," Ronnie said. "Want to hear it
sometime?"

"Sure, but I'd like to learn some of the things you
know."

"You've got something in your mind, kid."

"That's right."

"Guessed it. I'm a judge of people."

"I'd like to learn, Ronnie, or go along with you—
maybe I could drive a car, or meet you down here
some night—"

"What I learned mostly, son, is crime don't profiteth
a man if'n he loses his whole soul. Someday I wish to
explain this more fully. You still drinking beer? Jeez,
that'll blow you up, skinny fellow like you. Drink
something else."

Al appreciated Rough Ronnie's shy discretion before making his grope, but make his grope he finally
did, and Al was unwilling to commit hung-up prison
acts in the hope of being allowed to come along on a
job. Sorry, he said, and Ronnie understood. "Go,"
Ronnie sighed sadly, "go and fuck women, see if I
care."

It kept occurring to Al to visit Milly Peck in her
upstairs pad on Grant Street, but maybe he shouldn't
involve Milly in his problems. Still, with a little help
from Poopie, she had gotten close to the felonious
world. She had dropped out and turned on; had she
tuned in? But Milly would not mean a clean break
with his past. It was a compromise. He would look
around by himself a little longer.

He took to hanging out in pool halls, but all he
found were admirers of Jackie Gleason and Paul New-

man. No nice hustlers, no heist men, just a few creepy geezers, killing time, licking their cues and looking in the yellowed mirrors, calling each other Oakland Fats and Slim-from-Richmond. In the Golden West pool hall down on Market, beneath the ancient smells of gambling, green baize, and spit, there was a smell of, well, classroom. Al moved on.

Next he tried sleazy nightclubs in the Tenderloin—whores of both sexes, trying to take him, suggesting a hotel room or a Turkish bath. But without going through the unnerving sex round, Al saw no way toward satisfying illicit enterprise through the people he met behind the violet neon martini glasses in the Winners, Gimpy's, or the Whazzat-Lounge. "When I die," said a grand queen in Compton's Cafeteria to his audience of cowboys and Pinkertons, "I wanna go to the Great Gay Bar in the Sky." The Tenderloin seemed to be staffed by office boys, waitresses, runaways, or welfare clients, and hot sheets stamped National Linen Supply was not Al's idea of lying down with crime, washing himself with madness. Al saw a promising type in a dime arcade on Market Street, looking at the sex films—three minutes of a girl all by herself for a dime, for a quarter in color—and he said, "Hsst, I'm looking for a job—"

An answer was shot back, requesting that he do to himself what the man watching the film strip was doing all by his lonesome in this popcorn-scented corner of the lonely arcade.

"Hey, Louie! Here's a winner!" shouted a sailor with his eyes pasted to the machine.

The man to whom Al had applied for a job repeated his invitation to the sailor. He sought beauty, not

fortune. The promising type stood gloomily satisfied
by his three minutes in color of a Mexican lady wriggling out of a black girdle, still wearing her pumps.

Wriggling up from the ooze of Market Street was
not the way for a man of ambition and intensity to
evolve into a life of crime. He would still be a lizard,
dry on shore. He needed to employ the connections
with his fate. He was tired of brooding over cheap
whiskey and waiting to be addressed by a weary
second-story man looking for a sidekick to give him a
boost to a balcony. Even the water in these bars where
he bided his time tasted of whiskey, bad whiskey,
and the whiskey tasted of bad water, and finally people did talk to him, but only about the ball game,
about Fidel Castro, or about the sunny or foggy climate of the Bay Area. They were worn out and goofy,
like Ronnie. Ronnie looked rough, but he was just another talker and groper. Extreme measures were
called for. Milly Peck. She would help.

Milly had joined forces with Paul A. (Poopie) Cola.
She was making a new life for herself and it improved
her complexion. Dermatology and her parents' intelligent trial separation for six years because they had
these problems in getting along and French by the
conversational method in good schools and learning
to play the guitar ("Blue-Tail Fly," "La Paloma")
hadn't done enough for her. She had tried talking
with Al, but he wasn't mature. He was all involved. He
was kind of related to his lonesome. But under the
constant care of Poopie, the hickies went away all by
themselves. She was clearing up nicely. Her hormones
fell into line. It made Al a little jealous, since she had
suffered from skin trouble continuously during the

years of their going together, but of course Al was inexperienced and Poopie had never been young, never
inexperienced. "He's so considerate, Al," she said. "It's
like a little folkway he learned. Great in the sack is a
little folkway among his people, the semi-dark races
—the Mediterranean Sea is near Africa, did you know
that?"

Maybe Milly was the type that just outgrew skin
troubles. She was growing into her new type—a graceful, slow-moving, long-haired girl friend of a Grant
Street pander and retailer of medium-heavy drugs. He
liked her to wear ski pants and her hair in a single
braid. It did something for him. It reminded him of
old times—1962. In return, he wore elastic pants he
bought at the Sworde and Casual Whippe, Mens
Sport Wear, on Polk Street. He had once bought a
leather bikini at the S & C W, but when it shrank and
locked on him at the beach and he had to go screaming to be cut out, Poopie retreated to more conservative haberdashery. He only wore his flaring black
leather cape on chilly evenings. He looked a little
peaked in it—pinched white face, delicately molded
lips, bad teeth yellow at the roots and widely separated. He was self-conscious about the teeth, so he
kept his mouth shut when he talked, also when he
didn't talk. When he shouted, he looked like a ventrilo-
quist. Mostly he didn't shout at Milly. He abused her
quietly. When a fellow uses a closed hand, he doesn't
have to waste words.

Poopie had given up pimping for love of Milly. He
had given up two wives and three children for love of
Milly. He truly loved Milly. He just liked to stay
around their apartment above a pizzeria, occasionally

beating her up to keep his hand in, cashing the stock
from her small inheritance, getting to know each
other. All this and more he did for love of Milly. For
love of Poopie—but only when all the stock was sold—
Milly would hit the street under Poopie's guidance.
Until then, Poopie was a sort of rentier, loafing in
loafers, loving on the love seat, wearing the cape, entertaining Milly in a way she had never been enter-
tained as an undergraduate at Berkeley. Later he
could really earn his keep, selling Milly's mouth and
thighs in the clubs of Broadway.

Poopie yawned in Al's face when Milly said—a formal introduction: "Al Dooley, you remember, I told
you all about him the night you broke my front tooth,
darling."

"Yeah. Hiya, sport."

"Come on in, Al, I'll put the tea on."

"Why thanks, Milly, I'd love it. Brr, that fog."

But it was Poopie who made the tea. He rolled it in
a little piece of paper, licked the cylinder, and passed
it around. The fog had billowed through the Golden
Gate, across Twin Peaks, across Russian and Nob
hills, and now even this cozy little apartment above
the V-Day Pizzeria & Zen Coffeebar was enclosed in a
dense warm muff. They sat cross-legged on the rugs
Milly had brought around from the family retreat on
the Russian River and enjoyed the traditional Grant
Street Tea Ceremony together. Al decided that Poopie
wasn't so bad for a criminal type. He was a sadist and
a parasite and a cheap crook, but he was friendly.
And that's what counts in this world of difficult contacts, where every man is an island entire of himself.

Poopie passed the tea from hand to hand. He was

nice. He was sociable. He made conversation. "There's a funny thing about me," he said, "I never did like a toothache. Funny. And a foot infection—I never did like a foot infection. And a guy who makes trouble neither. I'm a funny guy that way."

He was thoughtful. He meditated his goals in life, no toothaches, foot infections, or trouble-makers. Al reminded himself not to have cavities and to dry carefully between his toes.

To get to know Poopie was to get to accept him. He was the greatest little complexion-clearer-upper of all the petty thugs on Grant. He was sweet, though he did have that death's head grin. He was nice, despite his habit of wearing a sweater without a shirt underneath and his way of laughing in your face without telling why. He was a great guy, really up there, one of the best. Easy to see why Milly picked him when she wanted to let her mother in Santa Barbara, her father in Hillsborough, know they had somehow failed to communicate with her, really communicate, and dermatology and guitars and stock in her own name were mere materialism compared to the love of a fine, upstanding little sadist.

Al inhaled deeply, held, gasped, and passed on the joint. He smiled at Poopie. Poopie frowned back. He had a slight head cold, infecting both Milly and Al, but that wasn't his fault. Anyway, as the army docs had said, Al's sinus was susceptible.

Milly made conversation. "How's Dr. Howe?" she asked.

"Who Doc Howe?" Poopie demanded.

"Just one of our most prominent sociologists in this country," Al explained. "He helped to advise on the

Supreme Court decision concerning desegregation of schools. He did a study showing how segregation adversely affects the psychology of Negro children— black. Also he was a full professor at thirty-four, due to his pioneering studies in urban race relations, and he developed objective criteria for measuring—"

"I don't know him. Shut up about him," said Poopie.

Millie looked reproachfully at her friend and declared, "But Dr. Howe is a Negro."

"He's sort of a social psychologist," said Al.

"He's Al's advisor," said Milly, "and he's colored."

"He's letting me run some of the data in his new book," said Al.

"He used to play football at Harvard and he's an American of the African tradition," said Milly.

"I don't suppose there's another professor in the country who has so much influence in Washington. Outside Harvard, that is. But of course he went to Harvard, undergrad," said Al.

"Did his mother take in washing?" Milly asked. "No, I remember, his mother taught at Tuskegee."

"He's not just a great social-psychologist and my advisor," said Al. "I think he's my best friend."

"He's Al's best colored friend," said Milly, "dig?"

But Poopie was asleep. That is, he had retreated into judgment. The judgment was whether or not to hit Milly for putting him down with all this talk about a couple of guys he didn't know. Milly understood the sleepy, eyes-hooded, teeth-covered shyness of her friend and said abruptly, "But let's talk about someone Poopie knows. Hey, Poopie, when's that nice friend of yours, Rough Ronnie, gonna get out of stir?"

"Out," said Poopie.

Milly smiled happily. "Oh. You never told me." And she turned to Al: "Poopie has lots of friends, but he doesn't brag about them."

Al fell silent. He was not so good at silence as he was at talking. Poopie could beat him easily at silence.

Later, while a quiet little Bossa Nova longplay filled the spaces, Al finally asked Poopie's help in his quest for an introduction into the life of crime.

"Hah?" said kindly, friendly, post-nasal Poopie.

"A heist team. Safe-cracking. Burglaring, you know," said Al.

"Oh Al!" Milly cried, slapping at his wrist. "That would be a really awful mess with your parents. Listen, you should know the trouble I get in with my daddy over just *living* with Poopie, much less if I went to work for him. Parents are so square, honest. Daddy thinks I'm going to peddle my ass—oops, sorry, Poopie doesn't like me to use that language—sell it to the johns. Poopie wouldn't ask me to do a thing like that, would you, Poopie? Remember, you promised, Poopie. Poopie? Poopie?"

"Yah, I promised," he said.

Milly smiled gratefully. "You see, I told you. But if bubble comes to squeak and it's a question of taking good care of my sweet-talking baby, well, there's nothing I wouldn't do for my very own Poopie."

"Count on you," said Poopie, showing his gums.

"Daddy says I'm just going through the stage of parental rebellion, but *I* know better. It's purely true love and economics. I'm going on twenty-one pretty

soon and it's time to live my own life. I wish Dad
understood, he'd like him if he saw him the way I do,
in his cape and all. Poopie's so nice, I mean."

Al interrupted this moment of connubial bliss.
"Help me out?" he asked nice Poopie.

"Naw," said Poopie with that frankness for which
Milly loved him.

"Sometimes he's cross as a pickle," Milly said.

"Just give me some advice maybe?" Al asked.

"Yes and no," said Poopie with that tactful devious-
ness for which Milly loved him. "What's in it for me,
sport?"

An appeal to responsibility for his fellow man
would be inappropriate, Al believed. And yet hatred
of his fellow man also failed to ring the proper bell. Al
shook his head doggedly. It was so hard to communicate. Sometimes he could talk with Jarod or Ellen
Howe; sometimes there was a moment of lonesome-
ness, followed by excitement, followed by lonesome-
ness with a girl. Sometimes there was a bit more.
Today there was less. He got up to leave with a sense
of having spent just one more pleasant evening in a life
of pleasant evenings. It was Sunday, the sky was
fogged in all over the Bay Area, the kids back in
Berkeley were having their last espresso of the weekend and getting ready to do a bit of studying after the
day's hard fun. But somehow fulfillment had not yet
come to Al Dooley. He stood up shyly to say goodnight.

"You leaving so soon, sport? Aw, gee."

"Well, gee, Poopie—"

But Poopie was just grinning, showing the gold
teeth at the back of his mouth. Apparently he had

planned to beat up Milly in front of Al as an audio-
visual method of showing disapproval of her colle-
giate associations, she should have outgrown all that,
but Al's abrupt decision took him by surprise. "So
soon?" he repeated. He clucked his tongue. "Nice
talkin' to you, sport."

Milly also stood up to say goodbye. "Goodbye, Al,"
she said. "Come again soon."

This was a wrong move. Naturally Poopie flew into
a rage. He was no longer like a pickle, cross; he was in
a fury. "You stand up when he leaves, but me? Nothing! And what you mean asking him to come again?
Come again soon, she said,"—he mimicked her shrilly,
appealing to justice at the tangle of wires on the ceiling where there had once been a chandelier. "Come
again soon! Come again soon! You putting me down to
this college spook? Why you little bitch and twobit
whore—"

And he slammed her across the room. Her head hit a
bookshelf filled with her old freshman textbooks.
Cushioned by soggy, worn-out, educational material,
she dropped to a group of satin floor pillows and cried
out, "Poopie, please, honeybunch, we have a visitor."
A tassel fell on her nose. She sneezed.

Before Al could move, Poopie was at her again
slapping her face with his open hand. "Ooh, Poopie,"
she said in a wee voice, looking surprised.

In an instant Al came fully alert. He would not put
up with this, even though it meant interference in the
family life of the underworld. If she was a twobit
whore, it was Poopie who had guided her in that direction and set the price. He had no right to ridicule
her. Tease, yes; but Poopie was going too far. Al-

though Al had a lot of respect for folkways, he leapt
at Poopie and pulled him off. He was surprised at how
easy this turned out to be: Poopie was a very small
and slender man, with a figure like a pre-adolescent
girl's. In Al's imagination he had been a thick criminal
with a menacing heft. Instead, when Al yanked him to
his feet by his leather sleeves, he found himself gasping into the limp face of a blinking, unhappy little
pimp. Al started to say something when the furies
struck. It was Milly protecting her male. Shrilling and
screaming, she leapt at Al; she scratched and kicked;
she was all over him, a crazed she-panther in her den.

Al dropped Poopie. He also slipped free of Milly's
claws. He escaped down the stairway and into the
foggy street with her shrieks pursuing him: "Leave
Poopie alone, you brute! College creep! Monster!
Mother—"

Al shut his ears. This was plainly false. His mother
lived far away in Santa Barbara and was devoted to
her husband, Al's father, even sometimes working late
with him in the travel agency, helping arrange tours
to Acapulco.

Al limped down Grant. He was happy to escape.
He had lost a shoe in the battle with Poopie, followed
by the assault by Milly, and trivial though this seemed,
compared to the deeper issues, it preoccupied him.
The street was damp and cold. One shoe is worse than
none. His quest of certainty was hard on his bruised
and wet feet. Walking through the fog with one shoe
on, one shoe lost, leads to bitter thoughts.

Fortunately, an army-navy store remained open
late on Sundays and Al could buy a pair of Japanese
war surplus tennis shoes. His luck was good. The glue

started to come unstuck from the soles before he had gotten a block further on, but the basic foot shelter would last until he reached home. He felt like unstuck surplus merchandise himself. His car was parked in a red zone, but there was no ticket. He climbed in. Someone had thrown a half-empty can of Seven-Up onto the front seat. His luck was good, but not really superb. It wasn't very refreshing to sit down there with the Seven-Up. He had also brought a package of navy surplus mints to take to bed with him. It was time for some serious thinking. A man cannot expect others to solve his problems. He can raise the sugar level of his blood and do his own problem-solving. Al and the melted-together mints would work together now. He pried them apart with his fingernails. To hell with Poopie and Milly. To hell with Milly and Sue Cody. On the way across the bridge, through the stream of yellow lights, he wondered what had happened to the basis of his life—Jarod Howe and the maestro principle and all he had hoped to learn about really getting straight with America, California, the Bay Area, and real life.

He parked in the dead-end silence of his corner of the Berkeley hills. It was late, foggy, and there was this persistent unease. He hung his pants to dry near the gas space heater in his hall. Seven-Up. He removed the little stack of paperback books nearby on the floor. They were getting singed at the edges. Sometimes it helps to do a physical cleaning and careful inventory. You look at the bank statement to see if what you spent last month came out even with the fellowship money and the check from Santa Barbara. You line things up for tomorrow.

He had received a personal letter. He hadn't expected that from her. It lay among the messages to Occupant and he recognized her handwriting without being told.

> *The Shire*
> *Middlearth*
> *Hobbiton*
> *1 Aquarius 4*

You are awfully sweet stuff Mister Dooley though it isn't necessary to work so hard at everything. Aquarian Age means ne get too wet pas.

> Buffalo Bill.

Another teasing girl. No return address. He never thought she'd write to him from Los Angeles. Just as she didn't make dates, she didn't explain very much. Then go away, Sue.

Oh-oh. He finished the mints and still couldn't sleep. School and the army and his mother and his father and finding a decent job and finding a work he liked and Milly and Poopie and Viet Nam and Cuba and why Johnny can't read and suburban sprawl (which is destroying our great cities) and the plight of oppressed peoples everywhere (including the human race) all got on his nerves. Plus Sue Cody. He tossed and turned. Expecting to go into the army, he had left some papers unwritten. This would be one of those nights. Why did Sue have to do the old teasing thing? The point was: It wasn't supposed to be her way. What did Dr. Jarod Howe say? *When troubled by desire, drag it into the House of Study.* A quotation from Dr. Moses Maimonides.

He sat up, blinked in the dark, and lit a cigarette. Crocker-Anglo is the name of a bank in San Francisco. There are many neighborhood branches of the Crocker-Anglo Bank. The House of Study wore the Crocker-Anglo shield at its door. Milly didn't know as much as she thought she knew about him.

He was thinking: With a note. With a toy pistol. I could do that all by myself and not have to complicate things. Just dollars to fly free with.

And where did I get those scratches on my face? he wondered.

From thinking. From getting beat up and thinking.

7 Al decided to visit the Howes anyway, without Milly. He needed to touch home, something like home. He wanted to see these friends.

Jarod lived on a beached barge at Gate 5 in Sausalito, within sight of the Golden Gate and the musical skyline of San Francisco. There was a continual silent conversation between the mud flats and the yellowish sky, the souvenirs of marriage and money and the lazy accretions of this elegant parody of a sharecrop-

per's shack—china and steel and a sepia photograph of
a very black Southern grandmother. Perhaps it was
she who bore the first mulatto in the family. In the
stained photograph, restored and restained, she was
old and clumsy. Once she must have been thrown low
by a healthy, pink-faced, land-holding son.

Ellen Howe was the daughter of freshly minted
Swedish immigrant parents—long-legged and sweet-
smelling blond hair and the water-dweller's squint at
her blue eyes, edging the health with a lining of fret.
When she tanned, she looked even more beautiful,
though she knew it wasn't good for her.

This young California family deviated, as Jarod
liked to put it, from the norm. He was an elegant professor with green eyes, a taste for Philippine cigars
and English clothes, a conventional California taste
for sports cars (Morgan, leather strap on the hood),
and a great love of deep tanning in the sun. It seemed
not to harm his skin to bake for long hours at his typewriter on the deck of the barge, writing his reports,
squinting at San Francisco and the bay. It was unusual
for a griffon, a medium dark-skinned mulatto, to love
the blackening sun.

Al's life was racketing meaninglessly about him. He
would take a season off, he would figure out something else—he wanted to talk to Jarod. He might or
might not discuss his idea about investigating crime
from the inside. Jarod had investigated the color problem by being a Negro.

Al Dooley understood the difference. Jarod had not
chosen. He was committed by birth, not distraction.

But if Al had been born to do damage to America?
Maybe that was his mission.

Good luck. He drove through North Beach, below Russian Hill, and then out along the Marina, shiny houses facing the shiny bay. The bridge stood out of the ocean fog, vertical spires, stately towers, steel lacing. The twenty-minute drive calmed him, encased in light Volkswagen, lightest used Volkswagen, spinning along with a nervous thumb on the wheel and a little clatter in the motor.

There were sailboats on the bay. There were tennis players on the tennis courts. He stopped for a light. The tennis players were playing doubles. Population explosion. The sailboats were yearning toward each other in wide arcs. Small craft unwarned. (Past the Palace of Fine Arts he drove, that toothpaste-colored restored relic; past ponds and patches of eucalyptus, past army installations and Nike sites, past Pacific Heights and the glint of setting sun on picture windows—the order of these things was reversed in his mind, the times were changing . . .)

"Hiya, thank you," he muttered to the hand fetishist waiting to receive his money. The coin leapt like a trout into the hand, the red light flashed green and spelled THANK YOU correctly; he was on the bridge. The heat of the day was bringing billows of ocean fog in through the Golden Gate, heaving softly up the bare hills, causing a sudden chill. The Volkswagen shuddered and he held the wheel more tightly. High above the spinning water, he felt the thrill of achievement; he kept the car on the road, along with hundreds of thousands of other motoring Californians. He could do that well. He kept his economy car on the swaying bridge, despite his temptation to fly through the screen of supporting cables, down

through pillows of fog, into the blue and green and
sun-speckled water.

Over three hundred suicides had jumped off the
Golden Gate Bridge, but Al did not find this in his
line. For one thing, he knew what happened to the
bodies after their glamorous arching tumble through
ocean space. They were fished out by the Coast
Guard. The crabs were eating wherever there was
flesh exposed. The head and hands would be covered
with crabs; wherever the tides or anxiety had caused
disarray, the crabs busily stationed themselves. Coast
Guardsmen learned never to commit suicide by jumping off the Golden Gate Bridge into the bay. They
had seen unfleshed bodies and skeleton heads; they
had hauled up thousands of crabs mid-meal. Coast
Guardsmen expressed their final emotions more
staidly, with heads in stoves or bottles of Seconal.

Anyway, Al decided, too much life in the bay already. If you sought escape from human society, you
wouldn't want to flee to fishy society—mussel larvae
eaten by clams eaten by bristle worms eaten by bat
rays eaten by sharks. The bristle worms did a cruel
job on the clams, grinding right through their shells.
The crabs were even crueller, going straight for the
suicide's eyes. There used to be shipwrecks at this
neck of the Pacific Ocean, ships caught in fog at the
Gate or at the Farallon Islands, but now there were
only suicides. The ships had radar, but the suicides
had none. A billion times the human population of
San Francisco filled the waters, plankton, oysters,
snails on the bottom; seafood restaurants perched on
the shore. Crabs scuttled into caves on their high
heels. Wandering-eyed flatfish. Sharks, eating oars,

fish, and swimmers, and eating their own entrails if wounded. And above this society of swimmers, crawlers, seepers, and drifters, the cool fog, the stately bridge, the waw-up, waw-up of fog horns. The conquering human species cast only its rejects into the bay, which was the last stop going East toward China.

The rock station was playing spiteful Dylan: "Something is happening"—funny, funky, busy, sly—"Something is happening and you don't know what it is, do you, Mister Jones?"

Al slowed down on Bridgeway through Sausalito. The kitchen help of seaside restaurants were out blinking in the last afternoon sun; a few retired fishermen strolled among the tourists; Sausalito awaited another easy evening of airline hostesses playing the Byrds or the classics, such as "Black Orpheus," recent graduates pushing sub-recent rock, the mid-week partying of a former fishing village. The clever nostalgists had stepped into their rainbow and tracked it down here to the pot of waiting along the bay of San Francisco; the secret, unnameable hopes had been discovered, and the hopers condemned to live in the Arcadia of their dreams, still hoping and waiting. Sausalito, slow and arty, and San Francisco, gracefully, whitely rising between, and Berkeley, despite its Nobel Prize winners, were all of a piece, dreaming of comfort and ease, of living forever in the fields and seas of April while managing to do the work of the world. These were not just loafing towns. The people were busy being atomic physicists, insurance salesmen, used-car dealers, coffee merchants, fishermen, alcoholics, suicides, artists, girls, and boys.

On the far side of town, Al drove over the unused

clumps of railroad tracks leading to buildings scattered between the road and the water, the shops, junkyard, sculptors' patios, and the houseboats and barges. There was a tidal field of abandoned tires filled with water and shoots of bamboo grass and then a freshly painted totem pole with the head of the mayor of San Francisco carved at the bulbous glandular tip, a bidet at the base. The Volkswagen lurched to a stop before the ditch, unpainted walk, and steps leading to the Howes' barge. Al felt himself sneaking out, a habit ever since that troubling time when he had gone away without their knowing he was there. It was safe to visit them now. He could hear the two girls playing, singing to their dolls something like, "Flo flo flo-me-la," a song from a Nina Simone record. He stopped a moment in the late flat glint of sunlight. Warmth on his face; then he started toward the makeshift wooden bridge across the ditch. A horsefly with satiny eyes buzzed up and examined him abstractedly in the air over the ditch before carrying the news off toward the airline stewardesses moored on the adjacent barge with their martini flag up; buzz-buzz, with satiny eyes.

Al strolled up the ramp. Outside this door, beyond this bedroom window, while the two girls played on the front deck, Al had once before arrived for a surprise visit like this one and heard Ellen Howe's voice crying out, "Oh! oh! oh!" as if she were being terribly beaten, crying out in pain, and then suddenly sobbing, "Oh, darling, darling."

Al had run away through the buzzing cone of flies over the ditch. The grief and love in Ellen's voice had made him see Jarod's striving flesh in her, pinioning her. He wasn't a spy against them. Against himself. And now he was back at that door, waiting again, trying again, in the desolation of his middle-of-the-night solitude, when he felt no likeness between his limbs and those of human others, his hopes and those of living others. Low sugar in the blood, ebbtide in the soul.

He had been here many times, and left with the main thing untold. Mouth dry with talk, head spinning with wine and the noises of friendship, belly distended with food and drink, the salty kisses of little May and Sarah on his lips—what else was there? Untold. There was a secret life and Ellen crying out in love or pain. Friend or friends, yes. But he had not said it, the main thing. Jarod and Al shared something, but not enough. A sumptuous distention in the belly, but the truth unsaid. Work, talk, hiking in the Los Padres forest, and the elaborate kidding between maestro and apprentice. And it was not enough.

Well, he had no right to ask what Ellen's sobbing meant. Tonight there were no sounds of love-making or weeping. Outside the barge there were husks, rinds, splinters on the walkway, grit flying through the salt air; Al was seeing the planet from his spacecraft; oily puddles gleamed far below, continents of dust shifted in tremendous earthquakes over the abandoned Chevies and Volkswagens of the waterfront. The wind blew and it was Australia, and blew again, and Australia became lopsided California. A couple strolled by in jeans, Levis, and beads; they were laughing. Dust flew and man is made for trouble and joy. Al heard sounds from elsewhere. Filled with the hope of elsewhere, he thought, There, there, someplace on earth there is beautiful pleasure, truth, and connection!

"My favorite track," said the boy in Levis, "is the one where he gets into the sitar stuff."

"Man, that's a groovy track," said the one with the extra beads and buckskin fringe, who was a girl.

Al knocked. Ellen's footsteps down the long hall. Her face creased in smiles and she welcomed him. "Oh darling, darling!" she cried.

8 It was an afternoon swarming with the banana-belt ease of Sausalito. The door came open through welcoming routines. They checked the minute alterations in each other—another day alive. Ellen was almost breathless.

"Darling, you ought to telephone so I can—"

"I told Jarod I might get over here."

"That monster, he never tells me anything."

The voice of Jarod accompanied its master down the long wooden hall: "I jes' assume she'll know. White folks have that intuitive power—" He lumbered toward them in shorts, the heavier brown of his face sleek with sun, a line of suntan showing above the neck of his white tee shirt. "Come on out. Take off your shoes."

The children, May and Sarah, pushed and tugged like puppies. Jarod took Al's arm, led him to the refrigerator, poured lemonade for them both, poured gin in the lemonade, and they went onto the deck. There was a wet shape on the wicker chair where Jarod had soaked into it. He sighed, settling back. "Tan jes' lak a wide man, deed ah doo."

Al gave him his War Criminal or Obedient Graduate Student smile. Then Ellen laughed and Al reluctantly joined in the old joke, and the children laughed because everyone was laughing. Jarod lay back and shut his eyes into the setting sun. Slap-slap of water lapping at the barge. "Daylight savings," Jarod said. "Lazyman's time."

Jarod had earned his lazyman's time. This season was an interval of gathering strength in a riding career. His papers and book, and then his smiling, coiled presence before committees and in private sessions, had served good use. The majority decision in a crucial Supreme Court rendering had cited his analysis of the effect of segregation on the psycho-social structure of black neighborhoods in both small towns and large cities, beginning with an acute comparison of the Negro ghetto with the two-way segregation of traditional European Jewish ghettos. The history of Judaism, with a separate culture, language, scriptures, and philosophical justification, "tended"—as he put it in sociology—to support family and personal ego-structures; the Negroes—*blacks*—broke down in precisely the areas where the Jews drew renewed strength. It was a difficult analysis for a Negro (black) to offer. Jarod had struggled with misunderstanding and bore scars for it, including an irate review from the American Jewish Committee ("Jews are just as rootless as anybody") and a bruise on his forehead where he had been punched by Duwayne Upgood, a Black Panther graduate student in anthropology. This incident had occurred during a meeting at a convention in Ann Arbor where he defended his comparative study of the Warsaw Shtetl and the Oakland, as he called it, niggertown. Later Jarod hired Upgood as "personal research assistant for anthropological footnotes, and also bodyguard. I may need one. I'll get the direct action people to work for me, long as my federal money holds out."

Al Dooley had grown a little jealous of the intimacy between Upgood and Jarod. Jarod had advised him that the best way to resolve an infantile reaction, such as jealousy, is to develop friendly feelings, such as non-jealousy. Jarod's conflicts had continued, and not only with black equalizers and white liberals, Uncle Toms and white bigots. Some of his colleagues believed him a teensy bit anti-Semitic in his emphasis on Jewish ability to survive and the internal cohesiveness of Jewish institutions.

"Ah'm a Joosh schwartzer," he had told Clayton Frisch over lunch at the beginning of the fall quarter.

Clayton, Chairman of the Department, squirmed and wished for revenge. He and others were jealous that so many handicaps, color and the jitters, could be turned by Jarod into power and great success. Well, that was only a couple of handicaps. He was liked in Washington. He was intelligent and energetic.

He was effective. He did not worry about who he was, since he had no chance to be anybody else. If he was nothing, he was still his own nothing. And he was not nothing. He made a lot of whirring and grinding wherever he went. He plugged up some holes. He dug out some looseness. He made trouble. He fixed things. He had been a mulatto full professor since Jesus Christ was a temporary instructor. He used Right Guard. His wife brought the chicken and the children to him out on the deck. He was doing okay.

And now, on a weekend evening in fair Sausalito, he was tired. He shut his eyes for a moment.

"Hey, I like the mustache," Ellen said. "Letting it grow longer, aren't you?"

Al's hand flew to his lip. He had forgotten. It gave him pleasure each morning to shave around it, soft flanges of tan hair.

"The hair of a dropout," she said, "the Che Guevara phase, but on you, I hasten to add, it looks manly and boyish and sexy, Al."

"Thank you."

"I suppose I should have ignored it."

"I'll shave it off."

"Don't! You're not a surfer anymore."

"Okay, I won't," he said. "When was I a surfer? I surfed a little, but I was never a surfer. I carried a board, but I never liked the Beach Boys. I rode the waves a little, okay, but—"

Ellen patted his knee. "Don't get all tense, Al. You were one of our truly sensitive and intellectual surfers."

The wind stirred and a few chicken bones fell to the plank deck. The children began clearing the table,

taking plates one at a time, chattering and clattering.
May tripped, fell; a plate bounced. "Melmac," Ellen
said.

Jarod said, "These poor children are going through
the latency period without ever learning that crock-
ery breaks—come here!" He grabbed for the child,
who shrieked with joy. He handed her a chicken bone
and she sucked it eagerly—Daddy's chicken bone.

Jarod was in a high-riding mood; he grinned,
glistened, scrubbed his fist through his mat of hair.
"One of my nigger days," he said. He took his white
wife, his partly white daughters, his friend, and his
half-white self on a tour of the old repertory about
how he was African and a headhunter and a Southern
bastard who didn't know his father and a watermelon eater and very slow-moving at catching on but
a natural sense of rhythm, good at jiggling, shucking, and jiving. "Down, down boy," he said to Al, and
Al sat back hard. Al was thinking: They all turn me
off, Milly, Sue Cody, Jarod, even Ellen in her own
nice way, all of them; and Jarod plays nothing but
games.

High as he seemed, Jarod found Al's mood. He
may not have cared, but the techniques of intelli-
gence ground up the data in its peculiar fashion. He
did not say, You're depressed and anxious; he did not
say, You're in trouble and worried; he did not say, Rejected by the service got you where it hurts, eh? He
took his time. He buttoned up the bleached, navy-
issue officer's shirt. He lit a small cigar. Blandly he
watched the children running about on the planks,
chasing toys up to the barge railing above the black-
ish water. Reinforced chicken-wire kept them safe;

they bounced off it like punchy fighters. The girls waited to be called away to bed; Jarod waited for Ellen to call them; he said nothing. The family was set to his pitch and the note was one they knew.

"Come here," said Jarod softly. "Here, kiss Daddy goodnight."

Sarah did. Then May. She threw her arms around him as if she were saying goodbye forever, sobbing. Sarah started to cry, too.

"Oh, it's just goodnight," said Jarod, "oh, come on now."

They both clung to him. He kissed them sweetly. "Tomorrow, I'll see you tomorrow, that's only a little ways off," he said. Consoled to bear the journey toward sleep, they ran inside. Ellen was waiting at the door to take them. Jarod sighed. "I make them a little nervous sometimes," he said. "They think I'll go away. They think I've gone—they feel all alone in this happy family."

A family anyway, Al thought. Worked out their own way.

"Look, pal," Jarod said, "I'm glad you made it out. But what's the trouble?" He waited for an answer. "Tell your friend and uncle, speak now." Al was too slow. It was spinning in his head, but it only came out cherries. Jarod said, "Okay, makes no never-mind, pal" —and he began to sing one of his impromptu songs:

> "Every time of day or night
> Ah feel so good, Ah feel so right
>
> Cause somewhere, somehow, someplace,
> Black one or white race

Despite Ah'm lonely, despite Ah'm blue,
Some chick is turning twenty-two—

"Ha! ha! ha!" came his braying laughter, and he
looked down his hairy legs in sawed-off blue jeans,
his feet in untied tennis shoes, and said, "He he he.
Spittin' de seeds on de groun'." He held his gaze at
Al and said, "I got to talk with you," and then rhymed
compulsively, "*Some girl is turning twenty-two*," and
then shook his head angrily.

"Kid, you do the footnotes just fine. I could make a
little career stealing your stuff—improve my big career. We might could write a couple dozen papers together, and then I'd reward you by making you a
staffer at the N Double-A, or find you a job at Michigan or NYU, or maybe get you taken on at Health,
Education, and Welfare, if they don't turn out the
rascals, but shee-it, man. You know?"

Al did not know, but something was implied. Wittgenstein, the Cambridge analysts, the logical posi-
tivists, and all the money from the travel agency in
Santa Barbara had taught Al Dooley not to try to
answer pseudo-questions.

"Smart boy," Jarod said approvingly to Al's silence.
Al would wait for explanations. In fact, his silence
was more depressed than cunning, and Jarod knew it,
and Al knew it, but still it was clever to wait. "Uh-
huh," said Jarod.

He was full of little grunts and noises tonight; jam-
packed. He swung around and put his head in the
socket of his hands. "I'm worried about you," he said.

The confession waited in Al's mouth like a host of
bees in a hive. Everything led to confession—loneli-

ness, trust, male bragging, the history of talk between them. Al was waiting for something extraordinary— the exceptional decision; he was waiting to find this decision within himself, the act unfolding, the ripe and luscious unfolding. And yet he did not speak it out, and across Jarod's face came a disappointed frown.

He looked both amused and angry. "Boy, for a fellow who wants to confess terrible crimes, you sure don't hold up your end of the conversation."

"There's something in that Black Muslim study," Al said with effort. Ahmad Jamal, mumble-mumble . . . Moslem, Muslim, Malcolm, mumble . . . Mumble, movement, mumble . . . "If you can cut me into your federal grant—" Uh, Al heard himself actually talking. ". . . like to help." He heard himself come to the end. "Maybe."

"Thanks," Jarod said dryly. "That's the enthusiasm of the vital young folks we been talking about. Get this country moving again. Thanks a lot."

"I mean it. A little tired tonight is all."

"Okay," Jarod said. "Let me talk it up a little is all. Let's say we expand the federal problem to include a study of Muslim recruitment in the Fillmore, say— Oakland, Hunter's Point. They raise the kids to be the Fruit of Islam. Those Ivy League suits and pouting faces. Knot straight on the Adam's apple. Fruits, man, goo-od!" This was the moment to decide whether to slip into his kidding nigger-talk or remain himself, Jarod Howe, B.A. Harvard, M.A. NYU, Ph.D. Columbia, Uncle Tom Chair of Intuitive Sociology at Harvard, finally enticed to Berkeley to teach sociology, not because he was a Negro, as a demonstration, but because he was slightly erratic, more like an anthropologist than a sociologist, more like a psychologist, more like an intuitive thinker, and the most brilliant sociologist around, and also he was definitely brown. Well, he could do social anthropology if he got too erratic. And if he settled down, he could do conventional sociology with a touch of Charlie Mills wildness about it. But with less political boat-rocking because, after all, C. Wright Mills was a Texan and white and Jarod Howe would always remain, one could hope, a leetle bit . . . oh, not cautious, but *aware*. Yes, that's the word. Responsible.

Jarod was talking and Al had not followed. Jarod was saying: "The thing about San Francisco is Nobody Came First. The Jews, Japanese, the Chinese all got here almost the same time as the hairy prospectors. The Australian thugs and sailors, too—the Sidney ducks. The lice and the fleas. The Shanghai experts. Look, you walk up Fillmore and you see the traces: the Exposition of 1905, Pacific Heights, the Japanese —oh, they were relocated during the war, they still grind their teeth about it, they remember, and the blacks sure, they moved up from the South, then out of the shipyards, the ghetto at McAllister, a synagogue, corned beef, the bagel factory—all mixed up. Nobody came first, but the black man comes last. No wonder."

"I suppose I should get into this," Al said.

"Race conflict is a good thing, eh, pal? Want to take over the burden?"

"I don't mean freedom-riding—"

"Well, why *not* freedom-riding or sitting in? That was four years ago, you mean? Or lying in with a Fill-

more or Hunter's Point lady? Man, you is too *cautious*,
baby." He made his play-acting chuckle.,
    "I think I'd better go," said Al. "I meant to see you
tomorrow. Isn't this the wrong day?"
    "Have some coffee."
    "I already had dinner in town."
    "You already had dinner *here*, boy."
    True; he had eaten; he had been chased by Milly
and had come for dinner. It was still the wrong day.
    "Weltschmerz?" Jarod asked. "Up tight and out of
sight?"
    "Something, Jarod."
    Despite daylight saving, there was a limit to what
you could save of the day. The purple glow of San
Francisco through a low bank of fog, around the curve
of bay, seemed to be stretching toward them in the
evening air. The day's warmth flowed in a soft river
out of the low hills. Barefooted, in short nightgowns,
the sulky, cuddly daughters of Ellen and Jarod Howe
ran forward to say goodnight. Like Arab urchins they
looked with their greenish eyes and their long hair.
They put up their mouths to be kissed, and Al kissed
them each on the mouth, each time feeling an illicit
pang, jealousy and desire, as he did when he contem-
plated Jarod with Ellen, Jarod at the university, Jarod
playing tennis and deciding great issues at the Cal
Club with the tennis-playing Supreme Court justice
with the pacemaker implanted in his heart.
    Al loved the girls, just as he loved Jarod and Ellen
and, for all he knew, the Supreme Court justice.
    At the same time, he meant to find something ex-
traordinary. Perhaps robbing the Crocker-Anglo Bank
would be worthy of his desire, something to mark

him out in a seamless time, mark him for Milly, for
Sue Cody, for Jarod, for the daughters of Ellen and
Jarod, for all these people and other strangers, because he did not want to be just a dues-paying member of the population explosion. He couldn't know
who he was until someone else knew him. To look
into the mirror and see nothing but skin, hair, mustache, and desire gave him an insanity. It didn't help
that others saw the same madness in their mirrors.

In the failing light which now made them both almost the same color, an orange highlight on Jarod's
cheeks catching the sky glow, Jarod leaned forward
to whisper rapidly, "Got my own troubles, too, pal."

"What? What about?"

Jarod put his finger to his lips in a shushing gesture.
Ellen could not hear; she was busy with the girls. He
looked around, rolling his eyes in a minstrel mime of
consternation.

"You don't want to tell me?" Al asked.

Jarod stood up, yawning and stretching. "You don't
want to hear! It surprises you I got troubles! You
come with your own and I got mine! Naw"—stretching and yawning and dismissing him—"naw, you don't
want to hear. You got no need to come creepin' round
here in your yard shoes and hear my troubles, right?"

Jarod's charity was to heave him out into the world
with no more maestro to conduct him. Jarod had suffered the adulation of graduate students before Al
Dooley, and then sent them out into the cold world
with only the letter of recommendation to remind
them that Daddy could be counted on back home in
Berkeley. Nice Jarod. Kind Jarod.

No.

No, it wasn't like that, either.

On this creaking barge, Howe's Landing on Airline Stewardess Row, water lapping against the rotting timbers, Jarod was opening his heart in his peculiar fashion, just a crack, just partway, to let the trouble within be visible. There was trouble within. He had traveled through understanding all the way to misunderstanding. He would not come to Al's aid.

Pinned in the crowd and vainly trying to signal to his friend watching the parade across the street, Al wanted to make Jarod look at him before they were lost to each other. The friend laughed and remained engrossed in games.

Jarod sometimes described himself as the brown C. Wright Mills, but Al knew him to be more canny, therefore more influential than poor Mills had ever been. When he played tennis with the Supreme Court justice, he made his points off the court. He didn't publish what would get him in useless trouble. Mills sold more copies in paperback, but Jarod Howe was studied in Washington. What point was this cautious person making in Sausalito and Berkeley? The touch of bohemianism had counteracted the touch of Uncle Tomism; the pedantry had balanced the anger (his thesis showed how the ghetto not only degrades, it destroys, it proves the white case by making the Negro an animal, and he said it with bell graphs, tables, and surveys). But was Jarod proving something else now, or merely being the proof of something?

Al was being amiably propelled through the length of the houseboat. Jarod cutting him off, Jarod giving him nothing. And though he wanted to help Jarod in his time of trouble—giving help is a way of receiving it—Jarod cut him short there, too. "Wait, I'll get my sweater, I'll have a little walk," Jarod said at the door, and disappeared.

Ellen came up to Al in this instant. She darted forward as if she had been waiting for the chance. "Pregnant again. This one wasn't planned by our friend."

Jarod heard the whisper and parodied her, hissing. "I thought we weren't going to say till we were sure?" He was furious. He stood like a boxer, his sweater tied around his neck, his eyes squeezed half shut, his knees bent, in a rage.

Paralyzed by the anger in both of them, Al's lips made the gesture *Congratulations* without the sound being struck.

"You know what Al was telling me?" Jarod said. "Said sometimes he feels like committing a horrible crime." Al had not been telling him; he had only been thinking about telling him. He knew. But it was not a horrible crime; it was just a little expressive crime, like a burglary. "And you know what?" Jarod asked. "Some crimes are not so much like crimes, you know? Like sitting in if you're a black man, and rioting, and disobeying the men's room signs. And aborting an unwanted child."

Ellen made a toy squeaking sound. She disappeared as if whipped.

"You still looking for me to play mentor with you?" Jarod inquired pleasantly.

"No, Jarod, you still carrying that load?"

"Good touch. Nice play, Al."

"What's going on?"

"Nothing," he said softly, "nothing, plenty. I'm sorry." He untied the sweater, slipped his head into it, and pulled it down with a jerk. They descended the creaking wooden planks, they walked along the ditch, they stood a moment by Al's Volkswagen. Al got in. Jarod remained near the car and hunched down toward the window when Al started the motor. "Black days and nights," he said. "I got everything I want. The bread, the name, the love of a beautiful white woman, I suppose. I got it made, and without going into medicine or the numbers. I'm all by myself out there. Yew-neek. They even want to do a TV interview with me on the barge. And yet the black loneliness I got, Al."

"Me, too, sometimes. Right now," Al said, feeling not sadness but relief. It was coming into the open. They could regain their friendship. "That's what I wanted to tell you."

Jarod turned his smile upward to catch the light of the street lamp in a parody of the watermelon min-strel-show boy. "Got up in the morning, boy, you know? And I ate me some good greens yesterday— lettuce, celery, you know, *salad?* And had me a good crap. And stood up afterward, and you know, son, I felt young and tall. Deed Ah did, son. Young and tall and *African* black."

"Goodnight," Al said. He whirled the car about on the jumping ruts of dried mud. Jarod was shouting after him, "Got my own troubles, Al!" The car was spitting flinty lumps back at him. Through the rear-view mirror Al saw him shouting and gesticulating. "Got my own troubles, goddammit! And I'm not free, white, and twenty-two, goddamn you!"

Al was out on the road. San Francisco lay in tatters of summer fog on its hills across the bay. Reinforcements of fog boiled through the Golden Gate. It suddenly grew chilly.

Was Jarod cracking up? No, probably just life caving in on him. Yes, and a girl, Al thought angrily, ah, that's it—symptoms. Why couldn't he roll all the white girls up into one big white Ellen?

Al closed the window and turned on the heater. It would be cold for three minutes across the bridge, and then no more fog. He felt his mustache with his fingertips, as if he could tell what time it was by how much the beard had grown. In the dampness his face felt sticky. He had been sweating. Jarod was trying to tell him to do his own deeds, whatever they might be. Okay then, Jarod was saying that all his powers and works were not enough. Okay. Even Supreme Court justices had to go looking for adventure. Even the subjects of teevee specials. Cold will shuddered through him.

The Farallon Islands lay athwart the shore, many leagues out, invisibly a menace to mariners. Sometimes, on a clear winter day, Al had seen them, low lumps of rock in hiding at the horizon.

There was a Special Delivery letter in his mailbox. The box was a couple of shingles made into a birdhouse by the previous tenant. The birds had gone elsewhere and Al had swept it out and made it into a mailbox so the mail wouldn't get rained on or blown in the wind at his door. Sometimes he went for several days without looking for his mail.

Stranger
Strange Land
2 Aquarius 4

Gemini's true function is often to make life
more beautiful for others. I didn't really
mean that about you work too hard. You do
good work.

S. Cody.

The postmark was Los Angeles, but there was no return address, of course.

And his deed would have to be good work and a hard one.

9 ". . . And would you please pick up Pat for me?"

Being dutiful, Al put the requests of his friend before his own judgment. Al was often obedient. If he had been planning suicide, he might have waited until he finished auditing Jarod's course, and so he agreed to come out to Sausalito for the television team which wanted to record him for a program on Negro Affluence. *What?* "You heard me," said Jarod, "a special. The Black Influential. Well, I'm supposed to have some friends and colleagues. That's you."

"Thanks."

"My man, it is an experience."

Unwilling to say No to experience, he agreed to play
the role for television film which he played in real
life. Jarod's secretary would take dictation and beam
in the sun and show herself, a white girl, one of that
corps of women who never leave the university, part
of the entourage of the distinguished sociologist and
black man, Jarod Howe.

"Christ."

"That means okay, Al?"

Pat Livard was drunk when he arrived. She did not
know how to prepare for television, what colors to
wear; she had decided to wear drunk. She seemed
to have rehearsed her life's story to get a higher Niel-
son rating.

"I want to tell you," she said, "why I like working
for Dr. Howe so much. Jarod, I mean. Just love it, I
mean." She was a woman of about forty, and had been
forty for much of her life; she had a nasal, long-nosed
voice, blue-rinsed hair, and a husband who now lived
in Caracas because he wanted to learn Spanish. They
were separated, but had decided not to get divorced
because they were working out their problems together, he in Caracas and she in San Francisco. She
had learned a great deal from her husband, but even
more from Dr. Howe; for example, that you have to
really get into a book before you can enjoy it to the
utmost. Most of all, right now she wanted to be a
good, worthwhile person and do well for Dr. Howe on
this, her first appearance on television, and she needed
to oil up the gears of reminiscence. And so, blue-
haired, nasal, and rather formal about it, she told Al
Dooley how she had been tampered with by nine
boys one memorable night long ago, and thus had lost

her virginity, and how, passing strange it was, this had led her to Dr. Howe.

"Well, it wasn't nine, it was only five. Well, I rilly hate to talk about it, because it was the moment of truth, I can tell you that for openers. It's a time when you rilly find out the metal you're made of, the seamy side populationwise, the whole bit, gut-level and up-front. Well, these boys picked me up in their car and said, You wanna ride home? And I thought they knew me because they used my nickname, Sunny, you know? The whole bit. So they drove me out in the country and said they were going to gang-rape me. Actually, the word they used was 'fuck,' but I don't like to use that word myself because it doesn't express any of the real spiritual communication there can be in an experience of that nature. Maybe you can say it on the non-profit channel, but that's about all. I just looked at them and thought to myself: "Well, Sunny —I was called Sunny in those days cause I was always smiling—well, Sunny, how you going to get out of this one? Well, it turned out I wasn't. When we got out into the country, I remember that evening so well, the stars and crickets and all like that, I said I had to answer a call of nature. That was quick thinking on my part because I thought maybe I could think of something. Well, they let me, but one of them went with me. He was the nicest. They thought quick, too. I was rilly embarrassed. I used leaves. It was an *imperative* call of nature. Then I thought to myself: Now keep cool, Sunny, and don't give them the satisfaction. I rilly knew that country, hiking you know, and I could run real fast for a girl—you know, track, standing broad jump, hurdles, the whole bit. But the cattle fences. I was sure they'd catch me on a fence and then I'd rilly be stuck. So I just decided: This is going to happen to you, Sunny. And right after that it did. Twice. I mean five of them, twice. The whole sex-horror trip. But I didn't say anything to get them excited. I didn't lose my head. I thought it all through. I just kept thinking: Sunny, is this happening to you? It was like in a paperback, though that was before they had so many paperbacks. I tried to look at it philosophically, like Martin Buber and, uh, Confucius. But Sunny, this was happening to me.

"Well, afterward, they were just dumb farm kids and when they got stuck in a ditch—that was afterward—I said I'd go wake up a farmer and get him to pull them out with his tractor. They were too weak to do it themselves, I guess. I forgot to say we were back in their car, a big old Hudson with a weak motor. But I didn't wake up any farmer, I wasn't going to be nice to them after what they did, I just hitchhiked home and as far as I know, they're still in that ditch. That was more than twenty years ago. But you know, there's a funny side about the human mind. You get funny ideas about people when you lose all trust. I mean, the thing that rilly worried me as I hitchhiked home was I'd get rape-fucked by the person who picked me up hitchhiking. I mean it must have looked funny, me out on the road, a girl, at four in the morning like that. I haven't been the same kind of humanitarian since. I mean I believe in the causes and all, but there are things in human nature you never dream of in your idealistic side. Anybody got to admit that, even if you never been gang-rape-fucked like I was by five youths. It's sort of funny how a thing like being rape-fucked by five crazy neurotic kids will change the whole way you look at things."

"I see that now," Al said.

"Say, Al, can you use fuck on network television?"

"What'd your parents do?"

"I never told my parents. But I checked with a doctor and he said I was okay, no rips or pregnancy or jazz like that. He thought I was pretty lucky. He said some girls would get hurt and I was pretty smart to keep calm and not a rip. And now I got a healthy fourteen-year-old by my first husband, the social worker, and she hasn't been spoiled, either. I taught her to have trust, but a little suspicious of five farm clunks in a car. You don't accept rides from strangers even if they know your nickname cause you smile a lot."

"But," said Al.

"And that's how it happened," Pat said. "I guess it's most important to get my basic message across and so I'll use other words. Assault. Violated."

"But how does he come into this—Jarod?"

"Well, I had counseling afterward, in college, you know. Attacked. Tampered."

"Was Jarod counseling?"

"No, but the counselor said, you know, he asked me: Were any of the boys dark-skinned? And I said, no, no, not as I can recall. Seduced with force? No, horribly mistreated. But then it came to me, blooey! Then it came to me! I wished that one of those boys could have been dark. I mean—it was hysterical how he knew! I mean, I had a dream once in which it was like one of those war movies, *A Walk in the Sun*, you know, an Irishman, an eye-talian, a nice young

boy of the Jewish persuasion, a hillbilly from the
mountains, a boy of the colored persuasion, an elegant
Easterner—"

"Of the Harvard persuasion?"

"Yeah! You know, a rilly American group, instead
of just those nowhere, nothing Iowa farm kids from the
great American breadbasket. And so I thought I'd
make it up to myself, you know? I started making
friends with all kinds of groups. My husband, for example, you know, he loves languages? Well, that's because he's part Mexican. He was a Latin American
specialist in college, was how I met him. And then I
met Jarod and I just got kind of like stuck. But if
only all American girls could have my experience
there wouldn't be so much prejudice abroad in the
world today. Synanon helps, too. But it's hard if you
can't tell it like it is on the networks."

And she closed her mouth as if he couldn't pry another word out of her.

Amen, thought Al. They'll put a beep through the
whole segment.

There was a freighter with Japanese markings visible in the bay, plowing through choppy seas at the
Golden Gate. Another load of transistors. Some of
us have keys in our backs, like this lady Pat, and
some have transistors, and all of us cross the Golden
Gate Bridge to get from San Francisco to Sausalito.
If you robbed a bank in San Francisco and wanted
to spend the money on leather pants and jewelry in
Sausalito, you'd still need a quarter for the toll booth.

The narrow dirt road leading to the houseboat was
crowded. A generator throbbed on a network van; another truck had disgorged coils of cables, sun-reflec-

tors, ladders, scaffoldings, what looked like a marriage between an advanced fire department and a mobile radar installation. A crew was already aboard. Helpers smoked and loitered. The producer would be getting acquainted with Jarod's family.

Before they jumped out of the car, Pat Livard recalled something she had been taught: "Now you must tell me all about yourself, Al. Now it's your turn."

"Thank you, later," Al said.

They climbed up the dusty path to the barge.

"That's hysterical," she complained. "Sometimes I think I'm just a little old blabbermouth. Do I talk too much, Al? It's just I want to analyze everything—rilly understand it."

"No," Al said.

"Well, so long as you don't think I talk too much. Some men don't like your intellectual-type woman. I've found that to be true in the Synanon game. Some men are rilly aggressive—I never knew that before."

On board the barge, which Marvin, the producer of the series, kept calling a houseboat, each good soldier marched in his place, following orders, in individual combat deployment. Marvin had a short dark beard and a commanding illiterate presence. He had been commissioned in the field. "I'm Marvin . . ." he said several times, and Al kept hearing dots after his first name. He wanted to be called Marvin, but he was in command. The campaign had the working title of "The Affluent Life," but everyone knew it was really The Influential Negro. The enlisted affluent personnel were a group, but isolated. Pat and Al looked for their places.

"Yes, sir, I'll wait over here," Al said.

"Caw me Marvin," Marvin said.

"You want me to put on lipstick?" Pat asked. "Hey, Marv, you want me to look more formal, or just Berkeley it up a little?"

"That'll be fine, honey," Marvin said. "I'll let you know when we need you. Just cool it down a beat, okay?"

Barefoot Jarod, in khaki pants and white Brooks Brothers shirt, sleeves rolled up, padded gracefully about, patting his daughters' heads, smiling at his wife, conversing affably with Marvin, the director, and the writer. He handed his wallet to Ellen because it bulged out his hips. Jarod was well equipped in leather goods—blotters, leather key-holders, leather wallet and non-plastic leather bucket seats. His own hide was tough, but his billfold bent in tender pigskin over all those credit cards. He greeted Al with a warm clap on the shoulders. He introduced Pat as his office wife—the girl who kept him going. He winked. A moment later he was speaking with the writer, a pipe-smoking and sullen young man who seemed to be mostly a witness and a handler. If Marvin had been a boxer, the young man would have worn a sweatshirt stenciled with the word MARVIN. Jarod was telling him: "There is nothing to do about death but to contemplate the nothing. However, the something of life is often not very much more—unless there is struggle. That's why we blacks are fortunate. We have a something which is more." He paused a moment to make sure the man was taking notes. Then he remembered the tape recorder silently spinning. The writer would edit and cut and make it fit; that's why he was a writer.

Jarod said, "If you knew you were to die, I suppose you'd have to contemplate the nothing anyway. It seems like that. But we all know it, and we don't. Not very often, anyway. We keep busy with the something."

The writer cleared his throat, glanced sideways at the tape machine with a lover's look of reproach (why was it not recording him?), and said, "Does being a leader in the Movement touch you more as a political figure than as a scholar? Are your children in private school? What is your opinion of the fragmentation of the two major political parties?"

"Answer Yes or No," said Jarod, "on a scale of one to ten."

"Pardon?"

"I was kidding."

"Oh, yes. Ha ha. Well, I just throw up these questions to get us started. Actually, we want the personal stuff first. Our commentary will get the think stuff."

"What did you say your name was?"

The writer answered.

"Is," said Jarod. "Sorry."

"You went to Harvard, the bio says."

"The bio is right."

"I went to Colgate. Harvard was my first pick, but I couldn't get in."

"You mean, if you were black or brown or red you could have gotten in?"

"I'm only speaking from my experience," said the boy from Colgate.

"Well," said Jarod, "I'm a little older than you are. They didn't give so much credit for color when I went to school. And in fact, you know what? I had

nothing to do with my color, except to darken it a
little in this sun. Who I am though, and what I do
with my color—that I ask some credit for."

The Colgate man flushed. "I know, sir. I respect
that."

"You were well brought up," Jarod said. "I just
wanted to show I can be as sincere as the next fella
if I have to be."

"You'll find us pretty straight, too," said Colgate.
"Have to be in our business—the business of people."

"And I'm grateful for that," Jarod said.

Thinking about the words Jarod had cast out—
death, life, nothing, something—Al went to talk with
Ellen. She was patiently answering questions put by
an assistant producer: where she was born; where the
electrical outlets could be found on a houseboat
(barge); where she first met Jarod; how it was to be
married to an, ah, celebrity—"he's a black man, too,"
she said to be helpful; whether she helped him in the
Struggle; whether she did all her own cooking;
whether she had both cleaning help and baby-sitters
("Non-Caucasians," she said, "Japanese").

At Ellen's side Al smelled something peculiar, the
assistant producer's breath, an exhalation of meat; it
was mixed with Ellen's light perfume; and the heavy
and light smells made an impression on him; not, he
decided, very pleasant. For some reason it made him
think of jealousy and desire, or perhaps in the other
order, desire and jealousy. And yet it was only a fraz-
zled, skinny man with bad breath—older than the producer, an eternal second—asking questions of a
stranger, a gracious and intelligent lady who somehow

managed to answer these questions. Do people ever make trouble? Did your family get upset or commit suicide a lot? What about the children—they nice well-adjusted mongrel kids?

Al thought, He wants to ask if the organ of a Negro professor—well, take your average mulatto—is larger than that of shriveled, red-haired, bad-breathed assistant producer of a television spectacular. Bigger, longer, heavier, stronger, or—"Is there a church of your choice in the neighborhood?"

"Would you excuse me, please? A slight . . ."

She didn't say a slight what. Al walked with Ellen toward her bedroom. His feet sensed water, a sway of water beneath a barge moored on mud flats with the tide out; the feet and the ears knew water below. Ellen kept her head down, like a speaker avoiding the audience. She said, "I don't know that Jarod has the right to put the children through this, but."

"But what?"

"But I married him partly for a demonstration, I suppose. I think I would have married him anyway, but I'll never be sure. So now he is demonstrating."

"Yes," said Al.

"Also I married him because I loved him."

"Why are you making these judgments, Ellen?"

"Whatever that was," she said. "Will you excuse me? I'm going to close the door and lie down and hope these creeps don't come pushing their cameras in here." She touched Al's hand. "What chance do you think I have?" She closed the door.

Pat Livard had cornered May and Sarah on the back deck, her arms around them, her eyes rolling. "Nice, nice kids. Poor poor poor nice nice little kids."

May was concentrated in furious struggle. Sarah was fighting in an opposite direction. Together they might have broken Pat's embrace, but in their rage and innocence, they didn't pull in the same direction.

Pat was in a fury of love and hope that the cameras would dolly toward her, if that was the word. She would grip these kids until the director spotted her if it killed them, she loved them so, um, um, yummy, it was a natural. May struggled, but Sarah suddenly relaxed. She watched Pat out of round, innocent, childish eyes. Pat was busy with May. Sarah took aim. Sarah sharpened the points of her patent-leather shoes with her magic will. Nice, nice shoes. Sarah delivered a boot to the shin that made Pat forget immortality with mulattos on prime time.

The children skidded off while Pat sobbed for unrequited television and rubbed the welt forming on her leg.

Al went up to Jarod, who was smiling into the empty air, no, who was smiling at the salt flies in the empty bayside air, and said, "Why did you need me?"

"My staff."

"Jarod, you're playing."

"I'm sincere about using people," he said. "Look" —and he pointed with a sweep of closed hand out to the bay, the water, the fog, the sun glinting through fog and on water, the reactivated destroyer, the redwood ark built to the greater glory of Zen and LSD, the seaside houses across the bay, Angel Island, the horizon. Why didn't he open one finger if he was pointing to something? "Look, the flies," he said. He was pointing to the flies spinning up an invisible chimney of air, never alighting, never buzzing, just

silently surfing in air. They were not houseflies or barn-
flies or horseflies or fleas. They were San Francisco Bay
flies, air flies, subsisting on pure delight, it seemed,
eating no meat.

Jarod grinned. "I think I'm very sincere about the
Problem. Automation, massive expansion of the quantity and quality of education, the relation of the
federal government to cultural matters, urban de-
terioration, disarmament, making the United Nations
viable and useful, the world population explosion,
distribution of goods—hell, I can bring everything to
boil. It ain't all color. I can use those other things,
too."

Something's gone out of it, Al thought.

"Tell you what. You haven't stylized yourself yet,
Al, but life is easier that way. If you're empty and
know you're empty, then you're not really empty,
right?"

Jarod looked around with boyish eyes. They
strolled back out onto the deck and into the sunlight, Jarod very graceful in his bare feet with the
grayish, stubby toes. The airline hostesses in the barge
down the way had their martini flag hoisted. From
their cabin with its Howard Johnson surplus curtains
came the sound of music—saxophone—no, trumpet—
the Tijuana Brass. The sadness of music over water;
the sadness of the unattainable; the airline hostesses
were entertaining a pilot who was explaining what
he had learned on a recent trip: "We're entering the
Aquarian Age, Aquarius. Oh, beautiful. The Second
House of Atreus is ascended. I dunno, beautiful.
We're all going to slide down into the San Andreas
Fault anyway, I felt it this morning—beautiful!"

"Groovy," said a hostess. "Wow."

The hippie pilot, preaching the apocalypse, preened himself. For sure he would have her tonight.

Jarod listened across the water. "I don't like myself. Or maybe it's the other way around." Al tried not smiling to see what difference that would make. Jarod's hands were grayish; his face was gray beneath the color. A jolt of amphetamine for courage today?

"I don't think of myself as a man of feeling," Jarod was saying. "I used to be. I was the world's runner-up egomaniac. I had delusions of melancholia. What it really was, well—traveling first class and having the ear of a Supreme Court justice from Tennessee and getting into the pants of little tricks with red MG's. That's not necessarily feeling, pal." He looked out at the weather of the bay, salt smells and flower scents, California ease and loafing, and he grasped the storm for himself (what storm?); he hated, he grasped hatred like wings, he soared toward the sun on wings of hatred and scorn. Oh, an internal storm. Once he had seen a black man kicking a black dog to death in Oakland. Black dog, black dog, *black* dog! A mutt with entrails sticking to shoes, and the man blown by his storm and people just moving around him because that dog might be related to him and he had a right.

"That's not necessarily feeling."

"Aw right, man," said the director, "you like to chin yourself on that bar? Keep yourself in great condition, do you?"

There was a chinning bar in a doorway.

"Yes, for what comes," said Jarod, "man. You know what's inside this door?"

"What's inside this door, Dr. Howe, man?"

Jarod opened a door into the Fire Hazard Room of his houseboat. It was a room in which, as an experiment, he put all the paper which came into his house —bills, letters, coupons, newspapers, notes, requests, converted forests of city silt and drift. He explained that he had thought to see what a year's paper would amount to. But the room filled up in less than six months, and then he spent a day destroying it, and then, like the eternal return, it filled again. "It helps me know who I am," he said. "I'm not Buckminster Fuller or Marshall McLuhan. I'm not What's-'is-name. I'm the smart brown man with lots of paper."

"Oh, that's cute," said the director. "Oh, we got to get that." He made a note on his clipboard. "Oh, we got to set that one up."

Marvin was in his reverie, his Prime Time Special Reverie. That's how Marvin got to be a legend in the television industry of our time.

Jarod turned to Al, continuing where he always left off.

"All this is too much for a black nigger or an Uncle Tom or a Snick protestor or a watermelon-eater from way back. It's not happening to me. I can't believe it's happening. I'm just an upward-striving ofay in my black skin, all by myself. No wonder I'm tired sometimes."

Al said, "Why not settle for California?"

"You mean good wine, weather, and sex, and fun, kids, cars, sports cars—why want the rare experience, too? Why want the piece of strange just because we're still alive?"

"Aw right," said a voice behind them. "That's great

stuff. But you didn't warn me, boys. How about you
take it again from 'a piece of strange,' Dr. Howe, sir?
—man?"

Colgate, the writer, was the hovercraft behind
them with a whirring tape recorder. Marvin had one
hand on his forehead—reverie plus Athena plus the
muse of public service. He was struggling to get it
all into the can. "I'll do a voice over scene, maybe at
the beginning like that, you two looking out over the
horizon, see, you're thinking the white man and the
black man, looking out over the horizon, see, you're
thinking, the white man and the black man, looking
out there. Okay, Doctor, now you begin with 'a piece
of strange.' Just see if you can find those good semantics again."

"Because we're still alive," Jarod said in the reso-
nant baritone which was one of his voices.

"Hey, just a sec," said the producer. "Listen, before we go on—and by the way, that's a good bit in
there. Hold it. Life, basic values, that whole scene.
We'll want to pick that up. Listen, you always comb
your hair like that?"

Al was thinking of Ellen behind her closed door and
unwell.

"If you want to ask," Jarod said, "do I wear a hair
net, the answer is No, I don't wear a hair net. Nor do
I conk the hair—that's lye and soap and potatoes and
it straightens the hair out nice and white. No, I don't."
He scrubbed his palm across the curly scalp. "I like it
nice and dry like it is, short, not too Afro."

"That's fine, great, you tell it like it is. Sock it to
us, Professor."

"Will there be a little group behind us on the soundtrack? The Budapest Combo?"

"Don't be short with me, Dr. Howe," said Marvin, who was a small man. "I'll answer your question, however. Natural sounds. Just a little . . . uh, under the credits . . ." He looked to the assistant director.

"Bongos," said the assistant director.

"Just under the credits, you know, my name, his name."

"I get it. A steel band, calypso, Marine Corps whistle, bamboo pipes—"

"No—bongos. Rhythm stuff, you got it, for mood."

"Right! Okay, you want me to take it from Tolstoy and we're still alive?"

"Oh I love those semantics, Professor Howe."

"Because," said Jarod, "what bars our way on life's road only makes us want to travel along it. That isn't what I said before, I realize. That's Camus."

"He's got some great semantics, too."

"I'll sock 'em to you."

"Come-ear, come-ear!" Marvin turned to Al. He smiled ingratiatingly and nodded encouragingly and beckoned him closer.

"As Dr. Howe's, Jarod's, special student friend among the young generation, the new involved committed flower-child love generation, I want to ask you one question, Al, okay?"

"What is it?"

"Do you use drugs?"

"Thank you for that question," Al said.

"And if so, do you think they are habit-forming, destructive to the germ plasm, and expand your mind to new perceptions of this day-to-day reality we live in?"

"You're an asshole," Al said.

"I appreciate your frankness. We'll catch that on tape with a beep. And one more question, sir: Would you call yourself a part of the NOW generation? And why aren't you in Viet Nam?"

"That's two questions," said Al.

The director bent to his clipboard-bearer, a tiny girl with a mane of fall, finely bleached Korean or Sicilian hair. "I think we might try a few bars under, you know, I Came to San Francisco with Flowers in My Hair . . . Anyway, put it down as a possible."

A zoom camera had moved close in on Al's face during this little chat and the tape was whirling. They could use face and voice or voice without face or face without voice; they could use whatever piece of him that fitted in; or they might use none at all if it happened that he didn't do.

Al hurried back to Ellen's room. He believed she was very ill.

Pat Livard was sleeping on a glider in a corner of the open deck. Her mouth was open and flies were hanging above, fastidiously warming themselves in the invisible column of hot air that rose and fell with her breathing.

The producer was laughing at something Jarod was saying. Jarod was modulating his words to make the producer laugh respectfully. Marvin felt that the black people had made a great contribution to entertainment in this country, but not many people know they are great scientists, too.

May and Sarah were throwing television equipment into the bay. The pilot and the stewardess in the barge across the mud were smiling and waving at the children and whispering, "Jump! Jump!" On shore, the sculptor Jean Varda was replacing the bidet at the base of his monument to the Divinity of Cuckoldry. Some of the network technicians were trying to break the pliafilm wrapping on their sandwiches, but blunt, nail-bitten fingers were driving the plastic through white bread into tunafish. An awl would do it fine, but May was just now clapping her hands as the awl sank into salt marsh. Police were keeping the gawkers from pushing up toward the barge. A tiki salesman who had left his tiki with Ellen Howe said, "But that's my tiki." A cop said, "What the hell's a tiki and I got my orders." The tiki salesman sought time to explain briefly ("Polynesian driveway fixture, only religious! Like a totem pole sort of!"), but the cop shoved him back with a gentle urging to his Adam's apple and went to ask Varda what that was he was loading in a pickup and how the hell he expected to drive through this crowd. May and Sarah were feeling sorry for themselves because they were just children and the only equipment they could throw into the bay was small tools and clipboards and portable tape recorders. A union grip said, "Come on, kids, not that it's my job, but we don't do this to *your* toys, do we?" Sarah picked up her horsy and dropped it overboard. She looked at the grip as if to say, Okay, try some more logic on me. May glanced at her boots and remembered Pat Livard's shins with satisfaction. The grip returned to trying to penetrate another pliafilm wrapping. He had tunafish under his thumbnail. The pilot and the stewardess went indoors. They de-

cided not to wait until evening, just in case the San
Andreas Fault opened up this afternoon.

Al understood how they felt. As for him, he was
still doing things which other people made him do.
That didn't make it right, he thought.

Drop City, Colorado
3 Aquarius 4

Did you find my sigh which I left behind? If so,
keep for future use. Must say Om from
tummy.

Suki Cee.

10   Like Sue Cody Jarod Howe seemed
           to consider himself bound over to
continue the education of Al Dooley. In flowered Berkeley one morning his topic was a study of the social
structure of schizophrenics. They sat in Jarod's office
—the campanile in view, eucalyptus and lawn, UCB
issue hippies with guitars—and he explained that
catatonic behavior is really a variety of communication; passive, true; aggressive, true; hostile, true;
afraid, true; but it transmits all these states of spirit

and more—the desire to communicate a desire not to communicate. There is even a pecking order for picking up cigarette butts. The most retreated psychotic is often socialized to this extent: knows when he has the right to grab a smoke off the cement floor . . . Jarod's secretary, Pat Livard, put her small stalk of a head through the door and said, "Dr. Howe. Telephone."

"Take word."

"It's long distance. Washington."

"Take the number. I'm out."

"It's the Peace Corps."

He shook his head smilingly and she backed away. The official caller would see on his CIA closed-circuit screen that she was telling a lie in the interests of social science. "Professor?" she asked, not yet out of range.

"She answers when I don't call her. When I call her, she's drinking coffee. Girls like that one, they drink coffee their husbands through graduate school. Later on, when he gets a job, he's making out okay, he likes a graduate student and wants to divorce her, they whine, But I drank coffee you through school. I drank coffee my fingers to the bone."

"She'll hear you," Al said.

"I tell her all the time." He turned reddened eyes on Al, capillaries flooded and leaking. Someday when he was very old, if he lived that long, Jarod would have eyes that come unhung, showing the eroded banks of veins. There was a look of membrane, fatigue, forced energy making tracks on the lean skull.

"You're right," he said, "something on my mind. Since I only teach one lecture course, I do research

and public service the rest of the time. And now that
the Supreme Court has acted and it's in the hands of
the lawyers again, the good hands of the FBI and the
liberals down South and the rioters up North, and I'm
just a-sitting in up here in Berkeley and there ain't
too much to do, well, I want to save not just the
races in general but this over-privileged kid in particular."

Al felt no generosity in the declaration.

"I embarrass you? Too warm in here?"

"Jarod, we've been through this lately. What am I
supposed to make of it?"

"Think of yourself as a pilot project. An example.
Or I need some personalization—want to think of it
that way?" Cigarette butt out.

Another invitation to be his witness. His trouble required a disciple. And what more disciplish thing is
there than witnessing?

"I got this metabolism. I got to be doing. You coming with me?"

"Okay," said Al. "I got this metabolism that likes to
watch people doing."

Jarod grinned. "Aw, come on, pal. Don't you get
tired of screwing and dreaming, digging for the
stump and making plans? Sometimes I think I can't
make it with another white chick, I don't wanna.
Okay, so then I think—maybe I'll kill myself tomorrow.
Or get killed in a good old Oakland riot. So this is my
last screw. Right away I'm strong. I'm Mister Up
Tight and Tight Up, Right Up . . . But I never do
kill myself tomorrow."

"I've noticed."

"You're different from me. Try to learn from an

older chap. Panic doesn't justify being disturbed. Hysteria shouldn't get in the way of calm."

"Thank you for that tempered advice."

"Al, I know you got plans for killing."

"No."

"For stealing?"

Al shook his head stubbornly.

"Don't tell me. I prefer to think my way through. Take myself, for example. Some psychopaths burn themselves out at age forty. Junkies, prick worshipers, maniacs like that. Harmless. Or good for nothing. Or maybe they become decent souls." He added, "I know this from reading and looking in the mirror. You're going through the crazy time. Well, it's a crazy time outside, too. You're thinking: All by myself, buzzing around in California, eating and fucking—what am I doing in this world?"

"Something like that. Not exactly."

"I didn't say exactly. You'd like to be yourself, a special sort, not just another fun-lover in the nimble quick. Come on, fess up. Tell me."

Al shook his head. Let him guess.

Jarod waited. No answer.

"Okay, then you want to come with me—"

"Yes," Al said.

"—cause I got this funny metabolism?"

He followed where Jarod led. They climbed into his green Morgan with the leather belly-strap over its hood and shot through Berkeley toward the Bay Bridge. Along the highway, choppy salt blue and acid smell of garbage, there was an abrupt population of sculpture on the Emery flats—giant bent-tin Vikings with radiator spears, war sloops with Pet

milk masts, a crusade of manic junk between the highway and the sea. Jarod triangulated a smile at Al. He
turned the rear-view mirror so Al could see the smile
along the hypotenuse, Jarod to mirror to Al. He took a
quarter from the ashtray; he flipped it into the waiting
hand at the toll gate; the man smiled as if he had
really caught it—the quarter was flipped into his hand.
"Perfect coordination," Jarod said.

"Thank you, sir."

"Mine," he said.

And Al wondered what losses he was taking that
he had to signify himself so constantly now, with such
intent self-flattery.

The blood-red sun descending made Jarod squint
and curse. They came off the bridge and headed out
through the city. At an intersection the cyclops eye
of a squad car roamed in its head; semaphore arms,
tangle of fire engines, snaking hoses, gutters awash.
Jarod whirled around the blocked traffic and up Nob
Hill, and then eastward and toward the ocean. "To
the Moh," he said.

"What moh?"

"The Fill-moh." The Fillmore district is San Francisco's Harlem. "First we eat no pork, then we go to a
lecture where I do no listening."

"That's clear," said Al. "What you mean, we're
going to a restaurant first. Then a lecture you happen
to be giving."

"I *thought* it would be clear," said Jarod.

Confucius say, Al thought.

The sign read SHABAZZ SEMI-DELUXE COOKING RES-
TAURANT, Sister Rocquefort, Prop., in gleaming royal
teardrops of hasty paint. A dark woman in white robes

emitted an effect of ritual greeting—lowered eyes, inclined head. Her restaurant had known a previous incarnation as a burger palace, tiled walls, tiled floor, and long mirrors bolted into the walls for lonely eaters to study their eating. Now the mirrors were covered with bamboo curtains to guard against the ancient ghosts of Fillmore pork fanatics. A complex lack of smell radiated from the kitchen—the smell of no pork, the smell of no frying.

They took seats at a dark table covered with a weathered linoleum-like strip. Sister Rocquefort came stately toward them, wiped the table, which was already very clean, and said, "Salaam Alaikum, Professor."

"Alaikum Salaam, Rocky." He winked at Al. "Just call me Jarod X."

"Why," she said calmly, "did you choose to bring a blue-eyed devil in these premises?"

"This blue-eyed devil has brown eyes, Rocky."

"Is he a pig, Professor?"

Jarod stood up. He patted her lightly on the shoulder. "I know you can't kid around, Rocky. But no fascist pig cop gets to be a friend of mine." He added, "Broil the meats, Sister."

It was early for dinner. The men in their forty-dollar Ivy League suits and narrow ties studied Jarod and Al and spoke to each other in hushed voices, with solemn spacing between sentence and reply. Al believed it a performance for his sake. They cut their meat in a way which indicated they were thinking of him. They chewed, thinking of the white devil. "Are these the Fruit of Islam?" Al asked Jarod.

"These am the Fruits," Jarod said. "But hush mah

baby, you can get yourself a knife between Adam's
rib and the next one, which must be Mohammad's, I
suppose. Cause it wasn't removed for no white lady."

The black mainstreet was separated only by plate
glass from this meeting place. One of the young men
in Ivy covert cloth was lip-reading the headline in his
newspaper: CLEAVER RAPS HONKIE PIG SHIT. It was a
language Al nearly understood. The strollers outside
peered through the window; someone pointed at Al;
they were unused to seeing a white man here. A very
fat woman moved like a ship, swollen and distorted,
across the ripples of glass. Jarod was saying: "Sometimes you look so tense, my friend. If you were older,
I'd say rest, lemon juice in hot water, cut down on
coffee and pork. But at your age—spend it! Take action, take arms against the sea of blandness. Now consider The Affluent Negro—we should have blown it
up. I played their games. What profit in it? More
foolishness spilling out."

"It's overflowed in you this season."

"The situation is overflowing, boy."

"It's self-destructive."

"So is jewelry store bank-robbing, boy."

Al shook his head. "I'm just having dreams."

"In that case," Jarod said, chuckling nicely, "oh, in
that case it don't mean nothing, do it? How about a
steak, but no pork? We gave up that pork and piffle,
just like the Jews. We talkin' good English now and
stickin' with our ideals, to wit: Firebomb the Man.
And then we'll see."

"The white man'll wipe you out, Jarod."

"The blond blue-eyed devil got no guts. He just
dream about soul food and bank robbing. You want

some semi-deluxe cooking, pal? Sister makes whatever I need and don't get it from Ellen. We can destroy America and they can make the smog someplace else. Burn this country down and ship Charlie back to the Union of South Africa. If I'd have said that to the viewers of The Affluent *Nee*-grow—"

"They'd have cut you off."

"No, friend, you haven't learned. They'd have invited me back next week. They'd have turned me into a series."

The broiled veal steaks came with crisscrossing welts of char. Jarod bent to it, cutting deftly, and popped a morsel of meat into his mouth. He chewed and considered. "Doesn't know how to season," he said, "too many ideas. She's a born leader—don't make good chefs. Some people make soup with the boiling water and others spill it on the people. If you'll just listen, I'll tell you what's on my mind. Also what I'm going to do."

"What are you going to do next?"

"Next I'm going to take you to a meeting and I want you to promise to keep it to yourself."

Al nodded.

"Cross your heart and hope to die? Trace a slanted moon on your heart and hope for blood and terror?"

"Okay, Jarod, okay."

"I'm kind of like speaking at a little old Black Muslim meeting and it helps me to have somebody with his mind on finer things which is why I want you there." He showed teeth and veal in a wide sudden grin. "I have been appointed Chief of Spies, which means I have authority to spy everywhere. That limit doesn't disturb me."

Al was thinking: Why so silly, Jarod?

"What's there to be serious about?"

Al jumped. His thoughts were being read. The clouds in his sinus were being read.

"Why should I aim to be better than the other apes? Number One Ape, sure. But why more? Every religion, every ideal, every mystic or rational belief has led to disaster and murder. Deep feelings delude, they make misery and pain. They're an exercise in capacity beyond human capacity. Listen, the brain is modified sinus." He chewed his meat. "Why are you so pale, Al? Not just ordinary pink, but pale. Oh yes, you didn't hear yourself whispering Not Very Profound. You often talk to yourself like that?"

"Thinking."

"Some men touch their balls when they think. Nice white devil! Man talk sense to himself, he's crazy. Man talk craziness to convince a crowd, he's a leader. Got to get me in the mood for talking to other people, you dig? Up now!" Jarod did not pay Mrs. Shabazz (was that her name?). He waited for Al to stand. He nodded to the lady and marched Al out like infantry.

The smoky dusk of the ghetto radiated its deepfry smells into the yellow-gray evening sky. There was a hurrying crowd down the middle of the sidewalk. On the edges of the walk, at the curbs and storefronts, those who had no jobs, the strollers, the con experts, the welfare artists, the numbers runners, the gimmickers and reliefers, stood, loafed, watched, waited. In front of the shops white owners warily surveyed the street for customers or trouble.

Jarod shoved Al through, thinking about the work

ahead. A hardware shop window displayed the Magic Hour 4-Piece Cocktail Set in Pink, and The Home Bartender (8 pieces), and a Waste Basket with Brass Eagle, $4.95; then there was the Small Fine Zion Baptist Establishment Church, a white storefront ("Death Is Awaited Hour of Triumph Not a Grief"); Hiraki Japanese Store & Restaurant; Kozy Kottage Byew-Tee Salon, Mrs. José deBing, Prop.; Ivory Coffee Shop— "White devil soul food," Jarod said. "The pawnbrokers go there for spareribs, rest up from their kosher wives." Money Loaned, Money Loaned, Money Loaned. A girl in a flannel skirt down to her ankles was staring in the window of a shoe repair shop. A shoe repair, watch repair, head repair, shave or shampoo. American Market—"No Jews, they mean," said Jarod. There was the girl in a long flannel gown, strolling and dawdling. "Not a Muslim," said Jarod, "a nut. They go out of their heads. Brain damage at birth, no prenatal care, lousy interns. Brain damage all their lives. They're not upward bound." There were businessmen from the junk shops, the markets, the cleaners, locking up the iron gratings or sitting and staring out into the street or selling the liquor or wine in the Gallo Gift Wrap, a paper bag. An awning said Club Flamingo, but the sign on the door said Congo Club and an older, faded inscription in the glass said Hickory Bar B Q. A poster showed a grinning rancher in Palm Beach suit, many teeth: FOLLOW THE MAN IN THE WHITE STETSON HAT THE TEXAS PLAYBOY FOR FUN & FROLIC.

The girl in the long flannel gown stopped them in front of Junior Executive Clothing for Debonair Young

Men. She took Al's arm. "Awful bright out here without my shades," she said. "You mens wanna come in up the street where I got my shades?"

Jarod scowled ferociously at her. "Gal," he said, puckering and booming, "you is a *dis*-grace to de hol color race. Now you jes run home and say de Kingfish tole you. And stop yoh disgracin' roun' lak dat."

She peered into Jarod's face and her insanity seemed to fold away, opening up to a delighted child. It had been something resting on the color of the skin; it just rolled off. She slapped him on the chest. "Ah comin' to hear you holler tonight," she said, "but ah sure hates to sit with the womens." She walked rapidly away, giggling and shaking her head and congratulating herself on having so much pleasure.

Junior Executive Clothing for Debonair Young Men featured the lack of lapels—no lapel jackets, no-cuff pants—but lots of pleats on shirts. "Zoot," said Jarod. "You wouldn't remember. They used to have syphilis. They used to wear wide jackets, long jackets, wide pants."

"Oh, I remember—*zoot suit.*"

"Yeah, tie your shoe. You're good at history. Your shoe's untied."

Al lifted his foot onto the bumper of a Cadillac. Jarod studied him. "You know, I was your age, I used to tie my shoe in the air for discipline. Muscular control and good training—tying up my shoes in the air, man. Now you postwar kids just go and lean on a Cadillac."

Al straightened up. The Cadillac had a cracked window. There were potato chips scattered on the dashboard. *Jarod, maybe it's not that deep feelings delude. It's they're not deep enough.* "Jarod," he began.

"Shush. Enough jabber. Now you're all nice and organized, nice and clean, let us proceed on our way with little more ado." There was a bright new storefront with a sign in orange, white, and black letters: MUHAMMAD'S MOSQUE NO. 28. "This is the Place," said Jarod. "Now you are intuitive, fella, you watch and see."

Young men stood in rows at the entrance, wearing their Junior Executive Suits and their looks of solemn anger. Women in robes passed through a separate door. The street smell of spice and grit vanished; the air was purified by rage. Jarod whispered with the leader of the Fruit of Islam guarding the door, a tall man whose height was exaggerated by a turban over his charcoal black suit and narrow black knit tie. Then Jarod disappeared inside.

The turbaned captain approached Al. "I can offer you a safe place to sit. Maybe with the womens. Jarod X says you can sit if you don't make no fuss and I guess you won't."

Wilbur X looked at him as if he were a stranger and there was a bridge with room for only one to pass. Obediently, Al entered under his guard. He guessed he shouldn't mention about seeing him on campus and at the Mediterraneum and the Forum on Telegraph Avenue. If the man was blind to him, he could be blind right back.

11 It looked like a school gymnasium out-fitted for Muhammad instead of basket-ball. There were crescent moons, satin flags, folding chairs, and a rostrum. Muhammad did not require polished hardwood floors: scrapings of feet and chairs, splinters of use. The all-stars glowered in a row near the speaker's stand, impassive, content with their lot, wearing dark suits and narrow ties from the Young Executive shop. These were the Fruit of Islam, the security guards. Amid the glittering satin banners, the ALLAH IS THE GREATEST banner, the THERE IS NO GOD BUT ALLAH banner, the MUHAMMAD IS HIS ARM banner, the HAVE A HOME ON THIS EARTH banner, the WE DE-MAND OUR LAND banner, and the mahogany and cloth symbols, stars, crescents, and Eastern signs, a very modern, small, transistorized microphone shone like the Jewel of Araby. It was a singer's microphone. It rested on a pole, but it could be detached as the per-former went rocking and wailing across the centuries from the Prophet W. D. Fard to Alphonso, the Jet Black Man of the Tribe of Shabazz.

Wilbur X in thick horn-rimmed glasses and Ivy suit moved in front of Al, closer than was friendly, ooze on flanges of nose, but very cool, and said, "Stand up, please."

"Why?" Al obeyed.

"Your name, address, city or town of birth, please."

"What do you need that for?"

"*Please.*"

Jarod was sitting in a chair at the head of the auditorium. He stared straight ahead at Al without any sign of seeing. Al gave the information.

"Excuse me," said Wilbur X. "May I touch you?"

But before Al could answer, he had lightly touched his pockets, his breast, the space under his arm. "Let me see that," he said. It was a ball-point pen. He pointed it close at Al's eyes and pressed the top. Nothing but ink cartridge. The man smiled slightly. Since Al knew it was nothing, why did he flinch? Wilbur X snapped off the top, looked inside, replaced it, and returned it to Al.

Al remained standing.

He suddenly darted close and sniffed at Al's mouth. He wore an expressionless face, just doing his job. Al drew back. He said, "We ask the same standards of our visitors as we demand for our people. You are a guest in the House of Allah. We want no winos, black or white. Do you allow drunks in your synagogue?"

Al started to answer that he was not a Jew—

"As-Salaam-Alaikum," said Wilbur X.

"Aleichem Sholem," said Al.

He sat down as Wilbur X glided off. He was wearing navy officer's shoes. Past him, on the wall, Al found another banner: WHICH ONE WILL SURVIVE THE WAR OF ARMAGEDDON? CHRISTIANITY OR ISLAM? A shimmering question mark hung separately beneath the banner.

The row of guards on either side of the speaker's stand stood at attention. The men at the far ends

saluted each other. The minister stood up, saying, "As-
Salaam-Alaikum." Peace be unto you.

Al had barely noticed the crowd. It was very quiet,
docile, thoughtful, and tense. It uttered the response,
"Wa-el-Alaikum-Salaam."

"We are facing the East," said the minister. The
worshipers raised their hands with their palms up.
Pink palms, thought Al. Eyes were closed, heads
bowed. Al squinted through his eyes, which were pretend closed. He remembered his parents looking to
see if he were asleep when he was not asleep. It was
like being a child again, but the chanting words were
strange ones:

"In the name of Allah, the Beneficent, the Merciful.
All praise is due to Allah, the Lord of the Worlds,
Master of the Day of Judgment . . . Here in the
wilderness of North America, here in the wilderness
of North America, as thou didst make Abraham successful, and the followers of Abraham, bless the followers of Muhammad too, as thou didst bless the
followers of Abraham, O Allah!"

There was a rustling of sitting down after the
prayer. The minister murmured traditional words: "I
am pleased, my dear brothers and sisters . . . It is
the purest and the most beautiful, my brothers . . . I
say to you it is the best, it *is* the best, As-Salaam-
Alaikum."

"You too, Brother!" cried out one white-shawled
woman in the women's section. Quickly a Fruit of
Islam moved down the aisle. Silence! The response
was in excess; it was a Christian response; she needed
to learn a Muslim dignity and not to be a slave.

"Now hear this, O Brothers," said the minister. "Be-

fore we hear from our dear Brother Jarod X, let me
speak these few words unto you. For I know that you
have come unto the Temple of Islam Number 28, and
our numbers are growing monthly, they are growing
faster than the Playboy clubs, you have come unto me
to hear the word of Allah and the word of Jarod X,
the commentary, the medicine and the prescription,
but before I do give you the esteemed intellectual and
intelligent Brother Jarod X, there are these few words
of counsel I must impart unto thee. First, let it be
known if you do not know it, that the Heavens have a
soul equal to the soul of men. Second, that the Heavens do not care about the souls of Christian men, yea,
or even Muslim men. Third and fourth, that we must
not complain at the lot of our own selves nor at the
destruction to be imparted to the blue-eyed devils
who have cast us into outer darkness." ("Yes, yes!"
came the shouts from the crowd.) "For they shall
bubble in the pits of tar. For they shall be torn limb
from limb in the butchery shops of Allah. For the pig
fascist cops shall be rent ten times ten, a hundred times
one hundred, a thousand times one thousand for the
sufferings they have inflicted upon the children of
Allah—"

"A million times one million!" came a shout from
the crowd.

"And so if we must destroy them and hate them—"

"Yes!"

"We must destroy and hate the racist pig fascists
without vindictiveness in our hearts—"

"Ow, wow!"

"We must destroy and hate them without miserable
white pettiness in our souls!"

"Oh, ooh, ow!"

"We must destroy them and hate them without demeaning our own beautiful hearts which are filled with charity for all!"

"Ah ah ah!"

The minister raised his hands. "Thank you very much in the name of Allah the Beneficent the Merciful. I know you love to hear the word, and I could continue, children, but today we have the presence among us of our grandest friend in this whole Bay Ay-rea, our true ally in Allah, our smart and affluent and powerful friend—we also have the World's Champion in Boxing, no matter what they try to do to him, however they may try to delude him or us, only he is not among us this evening—and we also have a man who can rise in their white devil world on his sheer brain power, his sheer brain force, his so beautiful and very fine mind—Jarod X-But-You-Know-His-White-Devil-Name!"

There were screams and laughter. "Beautiful! Beautiful! Beautiful!"

"But we do not speak his slave name aloud! It is better that way! And if you don't know, don't tell!"

Jarod stood up smiling, and still smiling, with an odd bluish light glittering on the khaki skin of his face, pronounced the greeting, "Es-Salaam-Alaikum." Then he held up his arms until the reply had finished sounding in the hall. Then he waited. There was the silence of the practiced orator—the man who knows how to let a moment of expectant emptiness insulate him from the world, his world from the world of those others; he put the crowd in his pocket and tucked them in, he cocked his head to admire the surprises he had in store for them. He sang softly:

"Got one mind for white folks to see,
Another for what I know is me."

Then he said, "You know how scared we are when it's dark outside and we're out moving the feet in Pacific Heights and we see a-walking down the street toward us four or five big buck ofays?" The crowd relaxed and lay back in its laughter. They put off the robes of sobriety; they were given permission. Wilbur X stood there with his arms crossed, watching the flock, a happy shepherd's smile on his face. "Now Malcolm called them the blue-eyed white devil, he called them the white, filthy, hog-loving beast, but you know, brothers, I think that boy was scared. Me personally, I just don't believe in them enough to call them a devil or hog-loving. I just don't think they love anything, they ain't got enough juice in them to love hogs, no, not even filthy hogs, who never look at the sky and eat their own young and their own shit. The conjunction of Jupiter with the moon has come; the anti-Christ is here, and we are ready to act.

"Now this is serious, brothers under Allah. The Christian devil says: *Hate thy neighbor.* And the Jew devil says: *Honor thy son and thy daughter.* They all pretend to say other things, but that is what they do say. And what we say we say with the truth, though we cover our mouths sometimes so the devils can't hear us." (There was laughter.) "We say they have brought nothing but death and destruction into the world. Oh, I know the fashion is to holler and

scream about these things. I will not do that, brothers.
Let me just ask you a little old question: Why are
there no white Anglo-Saxon Protestant folk dances,
brothers? Because they are dead people, they eat pork
but they don't chew good, they sexual intercourse
their wives and the wives of their friends—" He
paused for the laughter. The laughter came. "But
they can't sleep good afterward. Nobody is chasing
them. They got the nice soft beds, all the nice soft
beds a body can rest good in. Why can't they sleep,
brothers? Because there is—as the saying goes—there
is one hillbilly in the woodpile. There is how the devil
is sick and will die and will burn. There is how the
devil with his blue eyes and gray skin, he—

"Well, lemme tell you 'bout the town of Berkeley
for a little for-instance. Well, lemme tell you I work
over there in the town of Berkeley. Well, lemme tell
you I go into them bathrooms over there, them la-
trines, and I open the medicine cabinet and I see
tranquilizers! dexies! benzies! meth—"

"Hoo-ee!" someone shouted gaily.

"I see dope over there in the pretty city of Berkeley.
I see uppies and downies and sideways dope. I see
LSD dope. I see every kind of dope they is, but I
won't tell you where and who, but I'll tell you why.
And lemme tell you why. They is out of touch with
the soul and the flesh. They is dead . . . Lemme tell
you now about white girls!"

"Yeah! Tell!"

"Wide girls." Jarod's voice abruptly lowered. He
was whispering in confidence. "Well, them wide girls.
Them young white girls like to fuck, they just don't
know how."

Applause. Guffaws. Clapping and stomping.

"So I try to teach them! Mah teach-in, I calls it. But you know what? For mah-sef, I have to go off sometimes and fuck fine old gals, too."

They were leaping and stomping and laughing. Jarod put up his arm.

"Now I know this isn't a subject to broach in the temple of Muhammad. Now I know this is the wrong subject for a healthy, clean-living Moslem to talk about in the temple of God. Now I *know*, brothers, but a fack is a *fack*. Let's deal in facks!"

"*Fax, fax, fax!*" came the roar of the crowd.

"We got to fuck America!"

"Yeah!"

"And this black ass is doing it!"

There was a roar of echoing enthusiasm. Jarod raised his hand. Silence. And then a voice shouted, "*Brown!*"

Jarod turned to that direction in the hall. "Brown am I?" he asked. "Okay, I'm brown. But I'm black anyway, brothers. A cat can have kittens in an oven, but that don't make them biscuits. I was born in Oklahoma, but I mee-ow like an African. I'm not American! I'm African! I come from Great Africa!"

There was a diverse and swelling roar of pleasure. When had Jarod removed the microphone from the stand? He was pacing up and down and breathing into it. He stopped, he changed accents, he slipped and slid over, he continued. He loved the game. "Great Africa!" he shouted to rouse them again.

Al remembered Jarod's telling him that the lack of salt crippled African civilization. It made the development of great cities impossible. Instead, there were wandering nomads, bent on salt links, pursuing the rumor of salt; there was starvation and craving. Like the salt-starved Africans, Jarod now had no time to think of himself, and yet was busy playing, making himself real, salt-starved, demanding the sweat of a mob. Noise, dust, greed, and egotism served under this sky as under others. Jarod was striving to found a community by thinking of himself, his true self; and in a community, he could discover a true self, an action, a need in the world, a soul.

San Francisco was an oasis of comfort, a mirage. The desert licked all about it.

"From Great Africa I came, but now I am here!"

There were howls of joy like pain. Jarod's arms stretched out and he reached toward the crowd with love and domination, and his smile told Al that Jarod was someplace watching Jarod, tickled by what he could do with a movable microphone.

The eye fell upon Al. He paused and his gaze explored Al's face.

He was talking to Al, not the Muslims. He was telling Al there was nothing but his own will between himself and the will of the mob. That he was frozen until he was unthawed. That he was in bondage until he broke free.

Sometimes Al had suspected what it would be to be himself, really himself, undimmed and in focus, a unique soul on the unique earth. Once on a summer day something had snapped and he became a person —swimming, the cool water sweeping over his skin, diving, feeling body, body, body, his own. He was thirteen, Al Dooley, no one else; he had a soul, he was unique, he existed. That was the moment when he became a person; that was the person, whatever it was, which he was—the one who felt the sweep of water on skin. And then in a fight with his father when he screamed, "Stupid, stupid, stupid!" The old man had looked through his goggle eyes, his travel agent's goggle eyes, goggled from collecting a percentage of transportation to Acapulco and hotel rates in Hawaii. A tear had formed behind the over-curved lenses, and seeing it, Al had remembered once more: *I am I. I am I.* Once or twice he had a clue to it again when making love, but no, that was strong pleasure, that was riding with the body, it lacked the strict privacy of discovery. Oh yes, the time when that girl— what's her name—did that thing, what-do-you-call-it, to him. That was private, yes. Sue Cody. Yes, it was a fine swimming feeling. And if he would take that little bank, yes. And now.

"A philosopher said the unexamined life is not worth living. Socrates, I think he was a black man, I do think so—a dark man, a Greek. What he meant is the uncontested life. He means we have to fight now, think later. And if he didn't mean that, *I* mean that . . ."

A crowd's joy. A smell of excrement.

Yes for now. Jarod ransacking his face in this crowd. Spitting out rage and laughter, delighting in his disgust and fury, yes for that. Al was sharing with him. Life and alone and alive. Swimming—yes to this.

There was a strong smell of nerve in the air. It came from everyone.

"White folks, pardon, the gray devils are not really inferior, brothers. You mustn't think that. Why, give 'em a chance and they can do lots of things. Why, if

you go back in civilization, you find white blood—
pardon—gray blood in many acknowledged geniuses
—Alexander Dumas, Pushkin, they were all part
white. Give a white man an education, the right kind
of education, and hell, he's as good as the next man.
Course he can't run so fast or screw so tight."

"Yeah," came a voice, "but they dance pretty good."

"No," called Jarod, "I mean serious things. Science.
Engineering. Sociology, whatever that may be.
They're not really lazy, they just discouraged. Look
through history. There is reason to believe Shake-
speare was a gray man. Well, that's a bad example.
We don't really know much about him—"

A man with a shaven head, a muscle addict with the
bulging clothes of the beach freak, a tumbler and
weight nut, nodded furiously, solemnly, as if Jarod
were not just doing another of his vaudeville routines. A vein quivered in the bald man's forehead. The
vein ran across his scalp like a scar.

"Homer?" Jarod asked. "Maybe. Albert Einstein
was a gray Jewish devil, but Mai Britt? Lyndon Bee
Johnson? Stan Kenton? Marlon Brando? They are all
gray folks. So we have to learn to respeck the grays,
give 'em their dues."

The crowd was enjoying Jarod's fun. He was not
merely screaming out anger, he was funning his time
on this earth of pork and decay. They allowed themselves to be delighted. They may not have laughed,
but they enjoyed Laughter X, Sharing X, Pleasure X.
Al felt Jarod's attention on him. He was busy with the
crowd, but he was thinking about attending to Al
Dooley.

"Mister Charlie got dead guts inside, he don't take

a good crap, he need a shit enema to make it grow
again!" Jarod cried. "Now I know about these things
and it's true. If your guts is rotten from taking the
wrong kind of cillin or mycin, if your natural bacteria
is rotten and you got the fungus, the like mushrooms
growing, you itch and scratch and bleed and it's awful, brothers. And you know what St. Joseph brought
the white man? He brought him aspirin. And you
know what aspirin is? To make you bleed a little inside is what it is. So's you don't notice. Well, you
know what they is prescribing now for the dead guts?
The doctors is prescribing? Yeah! A shit enema to
make it grow good shit again! Let me lay this concept
on you." Pause. Pause. "No, I won't repeat it, because
you know it good already, you are smart. We know all
this about the gray folks, don't we, brothers? Because
some of them is us." Jarod pointed to his face. "I got
gray in me, look. Yes, I admit it. The brother reminded me and it's true. It gives me a bit of the devil
inside. I may even be more than half gray. Some of
them is me, let us confess and absolve ourselves,
brothers. But I got enough good black stuff, too, so's I
don't need no shit enema! I is in balance, brothers!"

"Lay that concept on us!" someone shouted. And
"Yes, Yes, Yes!" came the swelling assent. And "We is
they!" someone screamed.

Jarod's gaze crossed Al's face as he swept the crowd
quiet again. It was like a desert wind over his eyes.

"There is this time change as you travel, Western,
Mountain, Central, Eastern, and the same with the
blood," he said. "When there is Daylight Savings,
their boys crept over the tracks in the fading dusk
and stuck it in our mothers, so there is also this blood

change like there is this time change. But we will daylight savings it right back to them now, won't we,
brothers? We will give them the shit enema right
back. They gave it to our wives and sisters, they made
us in our mothers, we know all about it, because listen: *Some of Them is Us.* That's the concept I got to
lay on you. And now I want to tell you something personal, brothers. I brought—"

Al knew it was coming. Jarod was looking at him,
telling him he was in danger. Jarod was preparing
him for sport. And instead of fear, Al was feeling
philosophy. Ah well, there was nothing to fear, but the
truth is always with us, along with the falsity. Al was
thinking: I want something, I want it, and what am I
getting? I am getting this tour of my friend's disaster,
is what I am getting. Contempt breeds familiarity. Oh
Jarod old teacher you leave me so lonely.

Jarod sang his song to lonely Al Dooley:

"I wanted to let my pal Mister Charlie there hear
the truth about me and us. I brought him on purpose,
expresso. There he is. Look at young Mister Charlie.
He could be here, like he is, instead of home jumping
on my wife. But who is jumping on her while I talk to
you here? Who knows what goes in this white devil
world in which we wait our turn? What has gray
young Mister Charlie got on that gray young white
devil mind of his?"

Al Dooley was the center of attention. A silent
lynching. Hatred, isolation, and contempt were the
rope. He had a sensation of dullness despite this focus
upon him; unawakened murder made him move as if
turning in his sleep. He noticed a neon crescent,
though it was daylight, a neon crescent blinking at

him. The mustache of a man in an Ivy suit, with a thin black tie. Shined shoes. Sidewalk.

He was on his way someplace.

On the street, sunlight. A silent door behind him. He knew that with his leaving, Jarod was finished. The speech was for a mob, was for one man only. The friend's disaster.

He was on his way to Ellen. She must be in bad trouble.

He was on his way to his deed in the bank. He was in bad trouble.

The city lay white on its hills, a town like a Mediterranean port, blazing white, low, a jewel of pleasure on its little finger of America stuck out into the sea.

The uncanny city of San Francisco, which has a history, though it begins later than most, little more than a hundred years ago, the yerba buena cleared off the shifting sand dunes; and the raucous, gold-mad miners came and stripped the ships for their timbers, building, cleared by fire, building again, cleared by fire and earthquake; and finally the rich widows and the amnesiac sons of miners settled, squatting on their shit enemas (plus culture, charm, and taste) and sought to forget the whores, madmen, suicides, murders, vigilantes, the naked greed of only a few years ago, of yesterday, in fact, of today.

Ellen.

A bank or two.

Wa-Alaikum-Salaam. And unto you peace also.

12 Al drove along the shore near the barge—bayside silences, crunch of tires. The children would be asleep by now. Ellen would be reading, or lying barefoot on the floor, listening to music, or writing a letter to one of those college classmates she liked to keep in touch with. She had been secretary of her class at Barnard. And now she liked—said Jarod—being Alumna Class Secretary and honey-fuggling with her spade husband.

He was still thinking that word as he balanced himself across the wooden walk on the mud flat. Because honey-fuggling is something you can hardly do with the wife of a friend. For one thing, you can never take the time.

And the big thing, wasn't it, was being here with some thought of rescuing Ellen from her shipwreck. There was her husband, raving and cunning on Fillmore, preaching desolation. And there was his friend and student, Al Dooley, visiting his wife and, well, knocking at the door. No answer. Knocking louder.

A large blue eye appeared at the peekhole. "Al!" Eye crinkled with pleasure. Then eye clouded. "Al, go away, I don't feel well."

"Let me in, Ellen."

"No, go away. I'm sick."

"I came to see you. What's the matter? Let me take care of you."

A click and the peekhole was shut. A moment of deliberation. And then the double-locked door opening. She was standing there, swaying slightly, like the strolling girls of the Fillmore. "If you don't go away," she said, her voice slurred, "you might be glad. Come on in, Al."

"What's the matter?"

"First in," she said, pulling his arm, "then what's the matter."

"What is it?"

"You're in," she said slyly, "I guess I owe it to you." She took him by the hand and led him down the hall.

"Where are the children?"

"Asleep. Nervous, so I gave them a little phenobarb. It's better than turning on the gas."

"Ellen!"

"Can't you tell I'm kidding? Asleep."

She sat him down. She sat across from him. There was a hazy look of inconsequence on her face as she said: "I'm sick. I'm bleeding."

"Have you seen a doctor?"

"My husband's a doctor. A pee-aitch-dee doctor of sociology. And while he confers at the White House with the President, or just before, he gave me a cancer of the . . . Well, I don't want to be dirty. He does it so hard."

"What did the doctor say?"

"I did."

"What did he say?"

"He said it's nothing. I should take these pills. I suppose if they don't work, he'll give me Thorazine, and if the Thorazine don't take, he'll give me shock."

"Ellen."

"It's no fun getting crazy from catching the cancer from your black loved one. Brown."

"Ellen, you need help."

"Deed I do. I bleed once a month for three, four, five days. I'm dying; I'm staining the world. The rest of the month I bleed from my heart. I want to know if there's an after-bleeding in the afterlife. I'm going to call the Question Man at the Chronicle."

She started for the telephone, groping in the light as if she couldn't see. He seized her hand.

"Ellen!"

"Al."

"Ellen!"

"Oo-ee. You say Ellen, I say Al. You say I need help. Well, you need help, too."

"I suppose."

"Let me help you. It'll stop up the bleeding. The pills don't help. I lied about the way I caught the cancer from him. He didn't do it enough. That's what's so hard—marrying a man because you love it and he loves it and then it turns out he doesn't any-more. My brown black monster man is so delicate now. I suppose it's because he's got himself another pink gal with pink toes and pink nose and nice pink all over."

"No."

"Yes." And she was reaching toward him, not to-ward his arm, not toward his hand, not toward his shoulder; toward him directly. "Honey," she said. "I just said half a word." And she would have laughed, but she was too cunning. She wanted him to ride with the game, not to laugh.

Why? he was thinking, exhausted. And: *Why not?* No reason why and no reason why not.

"This is very foolish."

"Very foolish."

Her hand on him.

He touched her hand to pull it away.

"Oh let me, Al. Let me! Let a crazy woman try to heal herself. I know, I *know* what I'm doing."

Al thought he was trying to remember something. Evasion.

"You see? Just let yourself. That's what *he* says. Let, let, let."

A sudden swelling flood of silk of legs, crease of smile and eyes, flash of clothes, resonance of love— the whole tidal array of love rolling over him: and he thought, egotism, egotism, just busy with myself again. I'm an old child, I'm thinking only of myself. And he coveted her.

"I want to! Oh Al, let me, I want to!"

His vision dimmed. There were little bubbles at the ends of her fingertips as she undid him. Bubbly fingertips. If she let herself go, she would be fat. But she was slim. She was laughing like a delighted child. "Oh gee!" she said.

"What?"

"It. You just sit there. Don't move. Don't move."

"I feel silly."

"Shush. Just sit there."

His pants slipped down around his hips. Propped like a doll there on the leather sofa. Cold leather against his buttocks. He tensed his legs and braced his back and lifted up so that she could pull the pants further down.

"Oh, look, an eye, it's blinking at me. It's smiling."

"I never noticed that."

"No, not an eye. Oh, let me touch the rim. A smile winking at me."

Ignore that. Let it go.

"Mmm," she said, sliding to her knees before him. "Let me."

A clamor within of heat, honey, and salt; licking hot honey and salt; Ellen laughing, "Oo-ah ditty . . . That's what the black girls say. Oo-ah ditty, Al."

The room was close. Laughter. Cresting.

"Mm, oh good, let me."

Al was thinking, She said Mmm. And then she just kept sliding and finding.

His back hurt. Contracted ache, not ease. Ellen said, "Do you like Chinese food?"

"What?"

"I hear the girls say that nowadays. Afterward."

Al straightened and stretched himself together, his skeleton clicking. "Ellen, shush."

"Is there a life after life? That's what we used to say. I'll call the Question Man and ask him that one."

"Ellen."

"Did you know Jarod has three of them?"

"Ellen, please."

"Yes." And she put her hand on him. It felt warm again. Not seizing and pulling; she was just warming him. "Not two, but three."

"That must make for an unusual man."

"You'd think it makes a more virile man. No. It makes one ordinary man plus one weak man, and you never know which one you're getting. Would you like some Kool-Aid? I keep it for the kids because . . ."

There were tears running down her cheeks. The wildness sprang like spiders up and down her veins. Invisible detonations made her tremble.

"Don't have cancer," she said. "Just talking away, crazy like that. I'm going to have a child. A quick one before his last trip to Washington. In the morning. Because he was too sleepy to get up. He kept the President waiting, you know, because he did that quick one on me. So Al. So Al. So Al."

"No," he said.

"So Al child, we didn't have to do it that way, even without any . . . we could have . . ."

"Ellen, shush."

"I won't tell him. But he knows."

"Ellen, please."

"He's a friend you can count on in emergencies, Al. Only if you need him. If you don't need him, he isn't there. But he'll hate you for making out all right. Not this. Not what we did. He doesn't care about what we do—"

"You're not going to tell him!"

"Child," she said.

"Do you know about the Muslims, Ellen?"

"The whats?"

Ah, there was something the child knew ahead of her. "The Muslims."

"Oh he plays games, Al. Like you all play games,

white and brown. You all need to play games because
you can't get your own cancer all by yourself. Of the
cervix."

"Ellen, I don't suppose this is important. It happened was all."

"You were upset about Jarod. How he abuses me,
right?"

"You're saying it all wrong."

"But we did it all right, yes? Look. Go. Go away
now. This is never again. This never happened. Never
speak of, never do."

"I understand that."

"It stops the bleeding. There's a contraction inside,
you can't see it, oh you don't understand anything
about women. I love him anyway."

"I know you do."

"Goodbye. Don't think you did it to me. I did it to
you. He did it to you."

"Goodbye, Ellen."

It was night and the lapping of water. The tide rustled against the remains of a pier. Al made his way
across the tricky path of planks to high land. There
was a parked Morgan with the headlights dark. He
could see nobody looking at him inside. Jarod would
know that Al saw him. Al knew that Jarod knew that
Al had not seen him and seen him. He remained still,
a clever quarry invisibly stalked, and knew all he
needed to know.

Nobody did it to me. I'm doing it to myself.

From *Al Dooley's notebook:*

If I discovered I am to die tomorrow, what wisdom would I gain as a dying man? None. What would I have to do to put my life in order? Nothing. Where would I go? Nowhere. Whom would I tell? No one. What has my life meant? Whom have I justified myself to? Not God. Not love, not a loved one. Why have I lived if I die so alone? For no reason at all.

And is this the worst of it? No. The worst is that I am like so many others, and like more and more others, and perhaps I am a sort of prophet for the future. And someday, if we extend me out to eternity, everyone will be me.

But maybe I can start another way by feeling my own strength. Why not try this? Since I have the dream so clearly, why not try it?

This time I'll go all the way. Do it.

13 Al passed the day in thought. There was a little branch bank down near Market Street. It would be busy during lunch hour, and there would be a crowd on the street into which a fine young man might slide and melt. Al made a few

purchases: GI suntans in the army-navy store, dark
glasses, a pair of rubber gloves in the Surplus, a
toy pistol in the Woolworth's. The clothes were
to be thrown away later; the rubber gloves would
beat the fingerprint problem. He had to dump one
glove, since they were having a three for two offer on
rubber gloves (for housewives with a surplus hand?).
He rented a coin typewriter in the public library for
a half hour in order to write a brief message to whom
it might concern:

> FILL THIS BAG WITH BILLS OF MEDIUM
> DENOMINATION. NO FUSS. THE PISTOL
> IS LOADED. I AM NERVOUS.

A librarian smiled at him and touched her lips. He
had been whispering his composition to himself. New-
style smiling librarian with Twiggy cut and manicured
silence-finger—a winner.

That was a morning's work. It's not so hard to be a
lonely bank robber, but you have to lay in your sup-
plies. He was lying a little; there was no water in the
pistol.

Then he went back to check the territory. He would
make a map in his head of intersections and traffic
patterns, nothing on paper. Keep it simple; apply
Occam's Razor, the principle of parsimony, avoid unnecessary complication (William of Occam, died circa
1349). A clear thrust; a moratorium on fret. A television crew was doing the crowd on Market Street near
the bank. Al stopped a few moments to watch (remember about that one-way street) and then he saw a
familiar face. The face wore a checked cap; the body

wore a flowered Hawaiian shirt; the pants were of a soft maroon silky stuff, velour probably.

"Establishing shots for 'Affluent,' " Marvin said.

"Wha?"

"The Affluent Negro—second unit stuff. Pulse and beat of city, you know that jazz?"

"I dig," said Al.

"Cable cars, gulls, Fisherman's Wharf, Golden Gate Bridge, blah, blah, blah, for them is the semantics of it. Normally wouldn't do it myself, not on your union card, get a second unit man. But this is a *special* special, you know? A history-making groundbreaker, not to speak of ball-breaker, and first run all across the country. I even get a first supervision at the ads in the trades and *The New York Times*, you know about that?"

"It must be your big chance."

"Heck man, I get lots of big chances. I pick 'em up and I throw 'em away. This is America, you know?"

"I know."

"Say, you want to have dinny-poo tonight? Drinky-poo before? No, I suppose you're busy."

"Busy," said Al.

"I dig," Marvin said. "Don't like me personally, my type, here today and gone tomorrow on the wings of the semantics of it all. I understand. But this isn't just syndication—this is wide-world time, Prime City."

"I'm really sorry—"

"Say no more. They took me in off the streets when I was a well man, gave me this job, and made a sickie of me. Oh-ho, you're not laughing."

"You're a terrific stand-up comic," Al said.

"Thanks, I'll always remember you for that. And now farewell."

Al drove back across the Bay Bridge to Berkeley, feeling queasy, heading home. He hadn't lied when he wrote on the coin-operated typewriter about how he was nervous. The part about the gun was a fib, but the part about his nervousness was all true. He also bought a little bottle of surplus One-a-Day Vitamin Tablets. They were dated and the date had expired but Al was sure that many of the little vitamins were still alive. He took one for today, then two more—one for yesterday and one for tomorrow. When the plastic top popped, Al's heart leapt. He took another vitamin pill—discretion. He hoped it would prevent beriberi and scurvy and afterthoughts. He looked at his "Light My Fire" poster and forgot which Beatle it was. He lay on the floor of his apartment to quiet his pounding heart. He flung himself down and just rested there in the cool dark, staring at the ceiling, with the shopping bag containing his recent purchases on the floor beside him.

Excitement, under pressure, put spots of blood in his handkerchief. Like a woman. His nose began to bleed.

His nose spurting blood.

He felt like a bat swimming in the dark, its radar broken. He was home, but couldn't find his way home. He was not home, but did not care to go home. He was lost. He kept hearing the word "homey-poo." He thought of getting some tranquilizers, but decided this would be cheating. The moral decision, making rules, made him smile. It tranquilized him. He needed his reflexes. He would make a virtue of being lost. He would take another day to get ready. The next morning he would spend hanging around the neighborhood of the bank, getting the feel of street patterns and crowd thickness. He would try not to make a big scientific thing of it. He would be an intelligent, hunchy, old-fashioned entrepreneur. He knew from the American air all about how the clever and scientific criminals always make one fatal mistake. The story is always clear about that. Some murky miscalculation—a human factor. Well, he would avoid that pitfall. No human factors in his life. He would make a lot of mistakes, perhaps, but enjoy good luck and happy inspiration. Which Beatle it was would just come to him. He would improvise, like a jazz musician. He would swing and ride in easy San Francisco.

There was a good chance to be caught. There was a good chance to get away. He would try his best chance.

He thought of telephoning Ellen, but what was there to say? She was in trouble. He was in trouble. There were no connections. Avoid human factors. He let the telephone alone and it let him alone. Two people in trouble in different ways, with different causes and different ends—no way to help. The weak do nothing for the meek. Poor Ellen.

At this stricken private moment of his life, he did not know himself even at second-hand, he had ceased to know Ellen, he had never known Jarod, he knew clearly neither deed nor intention about himself. Therefore he needed deed and intention. In his deep yearning, Al Dooley lay becalmed and watching. He lay abed, staring at the spots on his eyeballs, pressure become light, the pseudo-vision of tension. Bad as this time was—he heard the dust in the air, he smelled the time of his age, his blood chopped like a bad squall in his inner ear—it seemed to refresh him, this bad time, for his angry swipe at the world. Nasty world, he thought—like a fly buzzing—must be squashed.

If we want to know everything, we find only lies. If we seek love and friendship, we wade in lies. If we use our own hearts and eyes we may find everything, or enough, or something. *Or nothing,* he decided.

Tranquil now. He had thought it through just far enough to take the next step.

John Lennon, that's the Beatle it was. Or Jimi Hendrix. Or some other Beatle.

Before he left the next morning, the telephone rang and it was not Ellen. It was Milly Peck. Her low sweet voice was whispering little apologies for what she called "the unpleasantries" of the other evening. She didn't know what got into her sometimes. Like that time. Often. Especially that last evening together. She realized how Al just wanted to protect her from that awful Poopie. (Her voice rustled sweetly. Her sighs blew electronic regret at him.) She had behaved foolishly—ungratefully. She was coming back to herself, she promised him. She was on the way. Pretty soon. This was a phase of rebellion. You know, youth finding herself. Youth is in the sidesaddle and will ride mankind—y'know? The poem? But Poopie had gone too far now. She would not put up with it. There were teeth marks on her cheek. The shoulder isn't so bad, but the cheeks! It can scar a girl visibly. Poopie was mean.

Al murmured that he certainly wished her well in

all things, and also that she would get bit a lot less where it showed.

Milly murmured that it was sure nice of Al to have her interests so to heart. "You know?" she said. "I like you a little better for having said that."

"Thanks."

"But Al? Al?"

"Yes."

She worked hard to express herself. Self-expression is an important part of vital living. It's really heavy. She was really into self-expression. And so, Al, now she had this little complaint. He should work a little to express himself to her, too. And so. And so. He seemed somehow, over the telephone, abstracted, you know? "Abb-stracted," she repeated, bemused, as if he weren't truly interested in her and Poopie.

"I am," said Al. "I already told you how you're rebelling and all. Your father, it's a problem of creative individuation, yukh."

Yukh was a word Al Dooley used when he hated to listen to himself. When he heard himself talking in strange and boring tongues, he judged himself harshly —*yukh*.

"Oh, I don't think of Poopie as my father figure!" Milly replied. "Nor as a rebellion, you know? How many times do I have to tell you and repeat myself? I really just want him to like Poopie—my father, I mean. I mean I want my father to like Poopie."

"I know," said Al.

"But he doesn't. Resists and *doesn't*. Smiles, but inside he's grumpy. Says a man who beats me up, uses bad grammar, has no education, married with kids, a

part-time pimp—*part*-time, Al—is not for me. Fortunately I'm going on twenty-one and I think for myself.
I tell him Poopie plans to straighten out, a job as a
musician, only he can't read music or play an instrument too well. Too good, like he says. It's natural *chez*
him. But he has ambitions, just like everyone, only he
hasn't had the advantages of a university master's de-
gree. Al? Al? Are you still listening? Are you there?"

"Yes, Milly. What did you just take?"

"Listening and listening, there's two kinds. You listen kind of abstracted, you know? I don't *feel* you
listening. Say, did you find your shoe? I threw it out
after you, didn't you find it? Al? Will you come see me
real soon?"

Al was ready to rob a bank before Milly called, but
it surely helped. He needed something astringent. He
could see what the army meant about his sinuses. Tension made him snuffle a little. Anything now—gunshot,
police sirens, torture by sadistic insurance investiga-
tors—anything to get that sweet, sighing racket out of
his ears. She never did tell him what she took. They
had a nice conversation and said goodbye. Al decided: Poor Milly, actually she's a bright girl. She's
just looking for an exceptional way in life, her way.
And I'm doing it my way. Poopie happens to be her
yukhy Peace Corps.

He drove back across the Bay Bridge and took another look at the Crocker-Anglo Bank on Market near
Grant. Just up Grant in North Beach, past Chinatown,
past the Broadway strip, was Milly's apartment, but
he put her out of his mind after he thought: we're
both finding our Exceptions on Grant Street. Then he
poked unobtrusively around the bank, noting sleepy

guard—a retired slow policeman with an avalanche of chins—and boy tellers with continental pants, girl tellers with beehive hairdos, spinster tellers of both sexes with lusterless nylon faces. Why wait? On the bank's Muzak there was muzak, I love Parr-ris in the springtime, played by the massed Lobotavani strings. It looked easy, so easy. Why wait? A guard with a meaty face rolled his eyes for the exercise, trying to stay awake. There was the patter of financial feet on marble.

Why wait?

He had installed his equipment in the trunk of his car. He drove out by the bay, under the Embarcadero Freeway, but this wasn't waiting; and in the cool beneath the elevated highway, he parked, and now this was no longer waiting; dived into the trunk, came up with rubber gloves, GI clothes, water pistol, note. He scrunched down in the back seat to change his clothes. Fortunately, a long life as a teen-ager, necking in automobiles, had trained him for this exercise. Al be nimble, Al be quick, he thought. Al will now get in his lick.

He dived up from the floor of his Volkswagen with bubbles in his blood and a new soul. No, it was the old soul, but equipped with GI surplus clothes, dimestore sunglasses, toy pistol, rubber gloves, cloth sack, and typewritten note, and that meant a new soul. He had new intentions and there was action ahead. He drove with authority. Right angles and long rhythms in his body. A reservoir of spriteliness fizzing through arms and legs. He parked the car in a no-parking zone near the bank. He left the motor running. A new soul in action. If he got a ticket, he would pay it. They

would not connect the ticket with the bank—not if he
was getting away—and if he didn't get away, well, the
parking ticket wouldn't add much to what was on his
back already. He sat in the car in that heavy moment
just before noon, when the lunch counters were beginning to fill up with those in a hurry. He waited for
the noon whistle. The first jet was spurting from the
mouths of buildings, a spurt of eager feeders. They
were running about and lining up. They would not
have to wait. Later feeders would have to wait. If you
don't have much money, you stand behind the stool
in a diner and wait. You feed like an animal. You're
caught like an animal. Al wished to get out of this
line. If you have money, you can buy privacy, comfort,
quiet eating, and respect. Cigars if you want them,
appointments with a barber, à la carte dinners. Well,
what can't you get?

He sat slumped, his hands sweating in the rubber
gloves, thinking. Then abruptly he peeled the gloves
off and let them drop to the floor of the car. He would
just not touch anything. The gloves were unnecessary.

Al grinned. This was not one of those perfect heist
jobs. This was an improvisation.

He put out of his mind the dream of what he would
do afterward. Now he would dream of his improvisation. He was riding with it. He would keep his eye
on the moment, the bank, the walls, the folks. Al
against the temporary enemy. Afterward no bitter
feelings, and he'd think—he'd consider—he'd be in
touch if he wanted anything.

And it began neatly, like a perfect improvisation.

Just after the screech of the noon whistle, he saun-
tered into the bank, past a sleepy guard cleaning his

ear with one finger, past a host of women shoppers and bill-payers, up to a window. There was a lank little lady on a stool there, watching life through the bars. He handed her the note. Her eyes turned black; the spreading iris took over. He hissed at her, "Don't press that button. I'm nervous. I'll shoot."

"I know," she said softly, with a sexy hoarseness. "I know, I know, oh I know." And the hands below that frantic face were deftly filling a bag with wrapped currency. It was as if the hands belonged to an efficient machine. It pulled and tucked. The face was perishing.

"Enough," he said after a few seconds.

"Don't shoot me." The aggravated hands went on packing stacks of money into the bag.

"I said move it over quick."

"I know, I know, oh I know," she said.

He took the bag under his arm and ambled toward the door, waiting for the scream. There was steel pounding in neutral gear in his knees. He planned to break into the crowd at the first sound. Not a murmur. But just as he passed the door and into the pushing crowd of Market Street, the scream finally rose up vertically, piercing the air. He leapt like a dancer into the crowd. One shriek, and then probably she fainted. She sprained her finger on the alarm button. He glanced over his shoulder and saw no stir in the crowd behind him. He held his pace to a medium-rapid walk. His VW was still there. The motor chopping nicely. Not even a ticket.

Into the car.

A good clean shift into first—second. He drove leisurely up Grant Street. A pink glint of rubber glove up from the floor mat in reflected sunlight. Two blocks away, he finally heard the police sirens on Market Street. He dropped his sunglasses out the window. A crunch under tires.

How fine to improvise, he thought.

How nice to break free.

And then his body just came loose, all the connections rattling apart, and he pulled over to the curb and fought to keep from soiling himself. He struggled, groaning; he left the bag of money on the seat of the unlocked car; he ran into a Chinese restaurant and used the Men's room. He came out gasping, but lightened and joyous. He had vomited, defecated, urinated, and now felt light as air, light as spirit. He was liberated at last. He would never need to soil himself with food again. He could live on air. He could live without Jarod, Ellen, or Milly. He could live on adrenalin, self-created. He floated in an adrenalin high toward his car, perfectly confident that the money would still be there, and it was. His luck, the luck of a happy improviser, held firm. He thought: Well, people don't steal so much anymore. It's an affluent society. And the blacks are keeping busy with civil rights and burning things.

He had not yet even peeked into the bag. But there was enough money inside—fifty dollar bills, hundred dollar bills, stacked and wrapped—to buy him a long space of power and freedom. Better than burning things, better than war, he thought.

He drove up Telegraph Hill and parked beneath Coit Tower, the smooth gray phallus said by San Francisco legend to honor Lilly Coit's passion for firemen. And there, in a parked car at the top of the city, with the cool yellow-gray sky above him, and the town with its lesser hills below, and the bay spread out around him, pockets of sparkling sunlight and blunt billows of summer fog, he at last looked into the cloth sack. Very light and calm, he counted. He had expected a few thousand dollars. But there must have been some kind of delivery from the treasury. Someone had forgotten the routine. Someone had neglected to put away the fresh cash. That teller must have been intimidated by his expression of determined improvisation. There was over sixteen thousand dollars in crisp new bills of high denomination, every one of them newly printed and smelling like metal, wrapped in crisp paper, crackling and eager to speed their way into the universe.

Al took this news rather calmly.

Then he looked again. The bills were new and untouched and the serial numbers were perfectly consecutive. At the bank they would have an exact record of the serial numbers. These bills shined up at him as if they could burn their way into the brain of anyone who looked at them. Each presidential hero seemed to be individually memorialized by a fiscal engraver. They were pedigreed. These were not good anonymous American dollars, civilized by much traveling in hands and pockets. They were mint examples. They belonged in galleries. They were goddam works of art.

Al was offended by the news. Good luck should be completed, but like bad luck, it's not rational.

The money suddenly seemed useless to him. The spell of improvisation had run out. He stuffed the money back in the sack and stared out across his steering wheel, like any other visitor enjoying the

view of San Francisco on a fine day. It was not yet one
o'clock. A few people with bag lunches were sitting
on the parapets. When he heard the sirens, and saw
motorcycles swinging like moths in a mote of light
up Lombard Street, he was sure that the bad luck
had begun to radiate toward him. He was the hub of
the wheel; follow the spokes. But it was only a fire. Al
was okay. Up on his hill beneath Lilly Coit's tower,
he waved abstractedly at the policemen following
the trucks below. He hoped they got to the fire in
time.

A girl with a motor scooter came up to him and
said: "I love a fire—anything—something doing, pops!
Say, what's that, your lunch in that sack? You like to
look at the city or the water when you eat your lunch?"

Al supposed she would like to share his sandwich
while they enjoyed the view together, city and bay,
but this was not one of his sociable times. He stared her
away. She shrugged and jogged her Vespa over toward
the telescopes that hunkered out at the bleak rock of
Alcatraz on its island. She put a dime in the slot and
the telescope was unlocked. Now she looked at Alcatraz.

Al put his hands on the sack of money. The little
bundles protruded sharply. It was like carrying a body
around with him. They were as useless as a corpse in
that bag, and as dangerous. With this sack on his
hands, he didn't need a telescope to see Alcatraz sharp
and clear in the midday sun.

14 The sun, the air, and the view also sharpened Al's thoughts. The sociable girl on the Vespa shared a container of cottage cheese with a young man in a Citroën 2 CV (plastic spoons and some welded sculpture on the back seat), and Al was flipping a little. Within the grand flip that had enabled him to take a bank and lose his breakfast, there was this little flip on the tourist's tip of Telegraph Hill. The money lay like a dead baby by his side. It was important, it was vital, something had to be done. But it was inanimate and his heart could not, at least for the moment, his heart could not take charge of it. His heart fled. His eye, his memory, his aching willfulness took charge. The Vespa girl was exchanging kamikaze looks of lust with the cottage cheese boy. Why couldn't he just play their games? Why need he rob the Crocker-Anglo Bank at the Corner of Grant and Market and get away with it?

Exhilaration drove him mad. He needed distraction, and here it came, like dexydrine in the blood, winding up the circulation and tightening the vesicles.

The cottage cheese boy was offering the Vespa girl an over-ripe banana and saying, "Nature is a good cook. I believe that."

The girl was thinking, I don't want to cure no queer

who don't know he's a queer. Again. One more like
that.

Al could read her thoughts. He could do anything.
She sat with lusciously spreading buttocks as she listened away the years on her saddle. Alert, intelligent,
in a fuzzy skirt, blouse hiked up, half-slip showing,
feminine, she listened. Nice girl. Wanted to be nice
to someone. Well, maybe he's not a queer. Maybe not
more than incipient. Maybe just a little *weak*. She
could help him. It's nice and feminine to help. It's
masculine to want to be helped. Do me, I'll do you.

Sometimes Al got a tickle in his finger when he remembered Milly's clitoris; turn it clockwise until it
went off—oh! oh! oh!—like an angry alarm; "clittie,"
she called it; trigger finger, he named the winding
organ. It knelled the toll of parting day, and parting Al.
Oh, oh, oh, she said; and he thought, She is feeling
something, she is feeling love; and afterward, wet
and panting, she said, "Thank you, thank you, Al. Say,
would you like some Chinese food?"

Well, why not, if it does both of them? Like Poopie
did for Milly and Milly did for him. Like Ellen and
Jarod. It went off like a bank alarm. Like Ellen and—

Al was aroused all at once. He shifted his weight
so his body pressed against the bundle of money. No,
not that. He had been getting away with things like
that since he first took Milly to the parking lot behind
the Frosty Freeze in Santa Barbara. No, no, no.

Fog through the Golden Gate. Gulls. The Affluent
Bank Robber Offers a Thought for the Day.

The weakness of diarrhea in his belly. Diarrhea
later. Heroes must have strong stomachs; otherwise

how to be heroic? Sad is okay, but loose bowels is unheroic.

Milly would wash her bottom in the tub, and then empty it of this insult to her divinity, juice of Milly; and then she would fill the tub again to wash her more sacred parts—elbows, ears, fingertips. Milly, being so clean, liked to be dirty. "I'm a soul girl, Al. Marry me just one more night." But she too needed something more than being married one more night. She met Poopie; she loved him because life was so hard for him. For example, when he danced with an older woman, which he occasionally had done in Reno and Vegas, he kept a cucumber in his pocket to let her know, as subtly as possible, that he was bewitched by her. In Tahoe, too. "And two tomatoes!" screamed one of his pals. Poopie, enthusiastic, had discussed an idea with Milly: "And a package of mayonnaise'd show 'em true pazazz—soul pazazz. Wow, vavavoom."

Jarod had explained to Al how all things bring benefits in the form of both gains and losses. For example, a nuclear explosion. True, it would wipe out millions. True, genetic variations. True, end of civilization, perhaps. But children not otherwise to be born would have the gift of life—perhaps new Socrates, Lincolns, Jesuses, Dizzy Gillespies. All prophylactics and other protective devices, creams and such, would be punctured, bubbled, scorched, seared. "No more precautions, boy."

Pill bottles would be smashed, y'know?

Poopie said, "Pig! She's a pig! pig! girl pig!"

Milly said, "Oh you're mean to me, Poopie. I won't put up with it, Poopie."

"Pig! Pig!"

"You'll hit me next!"

He hit her, crying "Pig!"

"Oh, I love you, Poopie. Don't hit me."

For health reasons, Al had once heard, somebody in Big Sur used to take a warm yogurt enema whenever he felt nervous. If he was just a little jumpy, he wrote home to Mother. But Al was not a faddist. When he felt a little nervous, he robbed a bank. Poopie beat a girl. The undergraduates smoked grass. We may seem inarticulate about our feelings, Al thought, but we don't know how to act right, either.

Poopie said to Milly, "Let's play the game where you let me do whatever I want to do to you, and I let you do it to me, too."

"What kind of a game is that?"

"That's a good game."

Milly edged away. But she didn't like Al Dooley to interfere. Code of the underworld combined with code of the masochist. "Code of the *Sado*-Masochist," Milly explained later, touching her black-and-blues with a look of abstract pity. (Eyes slightly crossed. Contemplation.)

Al had said, "Poopie. Poopie."

"Someone—not nice—will kill him someday, Al. I'm so afraid for him."

"You weren't nice to *me*, Milly."

"But Poopie is my old man." (Eyes wide, uncrossing, crossing.) "He takes me to the Fillmore. They'll kill him because they're so jealous, he's got talent and me and all."

"Someday, Milly, we've all got to go to the Great Rock Dance in the Sky. Yukh."

"You're making fun of religion again, Al. I used to be an Episcopalian—high church—remember that."

"You used to go skiing."

"That was a skiing retreat, Al. Schluss lessons, plus Bible. We would sit on our skis in the snow and contemplate. Discipline the body and the soul. The wind in the pines, the snow, and the presence of the Almighty. Our leader was from the Alps, where he had his visions the first time. Now he shared with us. Of course," she added, "that was the Santa Barbara way. The Upper Class way. Now we don't have to go to the snow line. Poopie and I have Fucking Retreats in our pad. He can spend the money on other things for the two of us—speed for him, for example. But it's all religious, Al."

"I like you a little better for having said that, Milly."

"I like you a little better for having said you like that a little better," she answered.

"I like you a little better for having said you like me a little better for having said I like you a little better," said Al. "For having said that."

"Sarcastic boy never won fair lady," said Milly.

"Hm. Righto. Say, did you hear I robbed a bank? Did I tell you?"

"No. Poopie will be home soon. I'm not sure you should sit on the bed like that. It musses up. He taught me how to make hospital corners—he learned before he got his Section 8. Unfit. He was in the army, you know, for many many weeks. Poor Poopie really suffered, really been around. You get much money there when you robbed that bank?"

"About sixteen thousand."

"Oh dear, that's a lot of cash. Better just smooth

down the blanket there—here, I'll do it. I know how a
woman's work is never done."

"I'm a little afraid to spend it, though."

"Well," Milly would say, dismissing him, "well, I
guess it'll all work out in the end. You are Pisces,
aren't you? Well, Poopie's Scorpio . . ."

There was a diamond glitter on the windows of
Berkeley across the water. Money money, hard cash,
and splinters of sunlight. Harder cash and be sensible.
As Al looked out over the bay, his racing adrenalin
receded, his deluded dabbling in reality receded, his
heart stilled now, even sleepy, he took a deep breath
and could almost hear the light music of that sunlight
breaking on those windows. He could hear the diamonds spilling over the white hilly city, all the way
up to the crooked line of Grizzly Peak Boulevard. The
bags of dollars sat lumpily by his side; the faraway
resonance of metal, the freedom and power of that
lovely glitter, was what he intended. What good would
it do to visit Milly for astrological advice and counsel?

He wished his eyes would not keep rolling down
from what he had done. He wished he could concen-
trate. Hard cash and there must be something next,
something more. Come to a stop on the matter at hand.
This was no time for daydreaming.

Why visit Milly when Sue Cody was a girl he really
liked and he would never see her again?

It was as if the daydreams of elsewhere and other
times, future and past and never, were intended to
inoculate himself against what he knew. A warning, a
cure, and where now? He stared at the bay between
San Francisco and Berkeley, the long salt river which

stretched out to the Golden Gate and split inward in two directions, toward Stockton and San Jose. Up close, the harbor sweats oil and feces, and beneath, the crabs ceaselessly eat the resenting suicides. There is no further west where they can flee; into the sea they plop. When the man whose wife mistreated him is hauled up—when the woman whose lover mistreated her is hauled up—when the jobless longshoreman or the sickly pensioner is hauled up—they have been given new careers in the bay. The pink crabs go moiling wherever flesh is exposed. There are denuded skulls, grinning, on clothed bodies, and weaving, working crabs, tugging at seams and buttons. The foot with its shoe on looks normal, a little swollen, wet; the foot from which the shoe had fallen is a skeleton foot.

An evasion from his dream of evasion. He had been there too long.

Al started the motor, backed out, and began winding down the road from Telegraph Hill. He would think about the diamond lives sparkling up and down the hills of the bay; he would forget the sea, the tidal muck, and the crabs. The skin of his skull had been stripped off by the winds outside and the parching heat within. The city glowed in sunset, hectic with its lights. There was the noise of city, the silence of no pursuit. Somewhere there was a fire, but here there were no police. Al was safe. He had been forgotten by everyone. Except that his skull was all bone, exposed by the crabs, he had nothing to fear for the moment. And nothing gained: he was merely Al Dooley again, racketing in his VV, needing some muffler work.

Now Al had another little improvisation. To bring

himself back to real life again: *Milly*. He would chat
with her about the overclean, consecutively numbered,
unusable dollar notes of high denomination. She could
help him find a remedy for the disease called Consecutive Numbering, Marked Bills. Now he was not just
working on his griefs—good sense.

He took the precaution of telephoning. Her voice
was unguarded. Poopie was not at home. He had
gone to Las Vegas for two days. "On business," she
said. "Do."

By *do*, she meant do come up. He did.

It had been several hours since he robbed a bank.
He was no longer the same man. It was one of the
finest banks in California, with outstanding reserves,
certificates of deposit, every account insured, and
guards trained by the Oakland Police Department, only
a little fat these days. This changes a fellow. He was a
bigger person than Poopie in every way. Certainly as
far as bank heists are concerned. He wondered if the
change in him was visible. He wondered if Milly
would see that he was a different man, Slim or Tex, a
sly, cool, and accomplished desperado.

She did see something.

She saw that he had the shakes and she put some
brandy in his coffee. "Mmm, hot, good," he said, hold-
ing his hands around the mug. "Ah, good."

She made a maternal grimace of pleasure. "You had
a hard day?" she asked.

> Spendin' cash, talkin' trash—
> That's how you find romance

"I like the AM stations," Milly said. "FM is for
creeps and phonies, dirty hippie creeps. I got my

KYA Kash Kard. I dig the KEWB Sports Scoreboard. But this spade station, they play a lot of Dusty Diamonds. Oldies but goodies. The Eberle Brothers, for example. Sam Cooke. Little Willie Johns."

"Turn it off," said Al, the new man.

"What?"

"Turn it off the radio."

> Dressin' fine, makin' time
> We breeze up and down the street

"I said off turn it the radio kid."

Click.

The new man sighed. "Now I'll explain," he said. "Wait a sec. But first thanks for the warm drink. Now more."

He watched her cleanest rump wiggle as she jumped up in her white Can't Bust 'Em jeans to get him what he wanted. She would jump to get it; she would thrust and squirm to give it. Now that he had been fulfilled, he could get what he needed to be fulfilled. When he thought of Ellen, it was as if a synapse were broken in his head. A little leap of dread; but Milly was different, fun and helpful.

"Gee," said Milly, "you seem to know what you want today."

"The radio off. More of that coffee."

"That's what I mean. It isn't like you, Al—the new you? Gee, you're out of sight. Nice."

He bugged out his eyes at her and said, repeating from some dim memory, "I like you a little better for having said that. It'll repeat on you sometimes, won't it? It must have been something we ate."

"What?"

"What what?"

"You're talking so funny, Al. But talk some more. I like it when you go crazy like this—I never saw it before. Poopie does it all the time. Usually you're so *rational*. Not Poopie. Oh no, not him. He talks crazy, and then he goes crazy, you know?—hurts."

"I don't hurt, do I?"

"Poopie is just so existential for me, Al, right? Right. He's my reality principle which I couldn't buy—my parents couldn't buy it—in my analysis. First I had a child analyst because I was a mere babe, an understanding lady it was, and then I grew to a woman's estate, right? So I had a man I could relate to and transfer and try to seduce. Failure would have been good for me—not the platonic form of failure, Al, but *existentially*, okay? Okay, so then I realized that nothing would help me but living out my conflicts and tensions in true neurotic expression of the agony and challenge of living. Which is what I'm doing now."

"Right," said Al. "He hits you."

"Right. Poopie is all my conflicts and analysts and parents and hopes and fears rolled into one. Plus a connection to pills. But I'm not a pillhead, I just chip a little, raise me up in the morning, bring me safely to port at night."

Al gave her his hardest look. He said, "You dramatize your life, Milly."

She sighed, she was happy. "You're so perceptive, Al. I'm a narcissistic show-off. But inside, I know true Heideggerean anxiety compounded with a deep sense of the lows you get when you come off methedrine."

Milly had changed since Al had known her at

school. Poopie had changed her. In addition to pinching, punching, biting, and kicking her body, and sometimes blackening her eyes, he had also softened her soul. Perhaps the pounding had produced relaxation. They pound abalone to tenderize it. She was sorry for Poopie. She was tenderized. Poopie brought out the maternal in little Milly Peck. And the maternal which Poopie Cola had brought out in Milly Peck now appealed to Al Dooley. Though he hated to admit it, he had never felt so close to a girl before. Nor to a tenderized abalone. But he needed someone—not crazy Jarod, not crazy Ellen. Exhausted, frightened, bewildered, rich and poor with new dollars in exact serial order, he wanted someone to take care of him. Milly. He needed Milly. He needed Milly's help. He also wanted her to rock him and protect him. Nice Milly should be good to bad Al.

Sensing something of this, her girl's intuition grinding in the void, Milly spoke soothing words and refilled his mug with coffee and Mohawk brandy. "You know that shoe you lost the night you jumped Poopie?" she asked him. "And I had to protect him because you're so big and strong, Al? Al? You know? How big and strong and brutal you are? But nice? Well, I returned it to you. The shoe. I did. I knew you'd need it, so I returned it to you. Didn't you receive it? I threw it out in the street after you, but I guess you didn't notice, what with the fog and all. Gee, and I wanted to return it to you."

"I stubbed my toe later." He cleared his throat. No whimpering. "That was a bad scene, Milly."

"Gee, well do I know how a fellow needs both his shoes, Al. So I returned it to you."

"Okay. It's the intention that counts—"

"The goodwill in a girl's heart, cause I certainly
didn't want you to go without shoes—bad scene, wow
—even if you did pile into Poopie like a wild man or
something, ooh, Al, I never knew you were such a wild
man, so impulsively instinctual and all." Al hunched
over the coffee mug, warming his hands. Milly gazed
proudly at him. This did more than the mug of coffee,
more than the Mohawk brandy, to restore his sense of
dignity and hope. The trust of a good woman gone
wrong. She continued fondly: "So how come you
didn't pick it up?" (She meant the shoe.) "I saw it in
the gutter the next day. Gee, Al, it looked like a person, all sad and beat-up and from the cars and the
wet and all. It just made me want to cry and take care
of it, Al. But I left it there because you know about
Poopie, he's so jealous, he loves me so. That poor, sad,
lonely shoe. Groovy. I covered it with a newspaper."

Al lived through the experience with her. It was a
little maternal thing she did. He understood. Insight.
He looked away, out the window. Insight plus modesty. He let the world outside the window cover for
his pride and embarrassment. Insight plus modesty
plus horny.

Downstairs, on slanty Grant Street, the beatnik's
Brooks Brothers was opening for an evening at selling
blue jeans, white jeans, tee shirts stamped KENYATTA
LIVES, peacetime surplus monaural bossa nova records,
posters advertising various political, pharmaceutical,
and *Kama Sutra* positions, souvenirs of the Barbary
Coast. A Chinese from lower Grant, walking his
butcherknife, bowed gracefully, with the age-old
courtesy of his race, to an Italian from upper Grant,

walking his switchblade. Who bowed with dignity, touching his fist to his inner elbow, with the age-old delicacy of his people. A café actor on a Vespa pushed up the street, his son on the jump seat scream-ing with joy. A flower child stood whispering in a doorway, "Got any spare change?" Two cops from the elite Tactical Squad studied him, figuring out the best way to ask him for his I.D. They stood under the Coffee and Confusion sign which bore, appended by chicken wire, an additional notice: Headquarters for Ethnics. The cops were getting ready to make their run. Floaters and tourists came strolling to look at the shopwindows filled with silver, marionettes, books, leather; and the girls in pairs, the boys in pairs, the girls and boys in solitary quest; the dogs and ocelots; the spitters, the gawkers, those buying and selling; all the Mediterranean street curiosity of North Beach. Down the way a bit, the display lights went on in a leather shop which specialized in disciplinary equip-ment, straps, spurs, and harnesses.

"Hey there," Milly cooed softly. "Say, anybody home?"

Milly was at home, having her salon. She appreci-ated a visitor now and again as eventide approached. She curled her toes. She went into the lotus position, which she had always used to get ready for homework or to do her hair or to really get to know a person. Once she had sat that way in front of Alan Watts and he said she did it really super.

"Hey—penny, Al?"

The early editions were being delivered to the grocery shop down the street. For some reason it dis-played slightly used paper napkins in the window, but

sandwiches to go, Gallo wine, and Mohawk brandy
were its real life's blood. The delivery man slapped the
bundle of papers onto a crate and snapped the wire
with his clippers. Al wondered idly if he had made
the two star advance final. He knew he should want to
read about himself, but he felt half melted into Milly's
floor; he wanted to stay. If only the world could just
be pushed by. If only it were all wide screen, super
Zenorama, everything flowing from the center.

"Say," Milly asked, "now that Poopie's gone for a
few days, aren't they doing a revival of a Charlie Chap-
lin at the Surf? Oh. Oh, Al. Oh, groovy, you had something else in mind."

She was on the right track. Insights galore.

"Oh but let's talk," said Milly. "Getting to know you
is the important thing, not technique. A girl needs security. A girl needs the sense that a man really cares.
Now take your technical types, you know, the lovers
who practice all that nasty stuff, ooh, you know, the
things I like, for instance—well, let me give you a for-
instance—"

It was agreeable to Al to discuss matters. Lust was
not the great issue at this crossroads in his life. In time
gone by there were these little problems with love—
who a chap is, finding out by making out—but now he
had a particular problem with bills of mint denomination. He sought advice, comfort, and contacts from
Milly. He would listen for a while, his hands would stop
their trembling and the heat in his forehead would go
down, and then he would explain everything to her.
No worry about himself. He had something to do. In
the meantime, as she talked, she might talk herself into
enlisting on his side.

The early afternoon had passed. The late afternoon also passed. Milly had brought her grandfather's clock, which stood on the floor, out of her father's house in Hillsborough. It ticked away the hours. The golden pendulum swung back and forth. The evening was passing. Milly spoke of her hopes and dreams, her need to fulfill herself, her fondness for Al. When she saw him grow listless over the cold coffee, she kept him alive with an injection of fondness. She lit up a joint and handed it over—good stuff. Carried over the border personally by a friend of Poopie's. Private stock. She hissed like a viper at him. He hissed like a viper at her. The little twig glowed. Acapulco gold. It diminished. Or Tijuana brass. She stared at the smoldering bud with smoldering eyes. All the philosophy in the world wouldn't sum up the philosophy in her heart. That fume of smoke. That hot little roach. That burn on her lower lip. All things that glow must burn and pass. But Al had a place in Milly's heart. He had a special place. She knew he was intended for great things, groovy things.

Al cleared his throat and raised his hand. He wanted to speak. Philosophy was great for monks and philosophers. The last light of sunset was streaming through the window halfway up Telegraph Hill on Grant Street in North Beach. Confused weather reports were fine for wizards and potheads. But Al had something else going now and needed a clear throat and a little attention. Business in Vegas had called Poopie away for a few days. Al desired Milly and also needed her help. Now seemed to be his chance, and it was: his chance to talk about Poopie. "Look at my teeth marks," she said. "Here. Here. And here."

Al looked. He was obedient. But he began: "I want to tell you what happened to me today."

"And here, too. Ooh, it still stings when I just *touch* it."

"It's not exactly what happened to me," Al said, "it's something I did."

"Ooh, Al, maybe? Maybe you would? Maybe you'd rub oil in my Poopie-bites?"

Al sighed and decided that maybe, with a loving, maternal, and gentle type of girl like Milly, a thoughtful person should take his cues from her and not try to tell her how and whether he robbed a bank until she was ready to listen. A mature man should follow a mature woman's lead and not just inflict himself on her, like some kind of wild beast in the zoo—wild beast in the wilds, tame beast in the zoo.

"Ooh, out of sight!" cried Milly when Al consented to rub soothing lanolin in the bites. In an instant she had her clothes off and was lying on her belly in a fluffy cotton rug. Rays of expiring sunlight through curtains made stripes on her sleek, small, slightly bitten back. Al knelt by her side with the itch and grime of bank-robbing still clinging to his body, but a bottle of medicated lanolin lotion in his hand. "There," she said. "Ooh, there. Around there, too. He bites me everywhere. It's got Vitamin D added. Yes. Yes."

He cupped his hands and rubbed lotion even where she was not bitten. She did not mention it, but her voice grew husky and she smiled and wiggled around and wrinkled her nose at him.

With a voice growing husky, she informed him that she was just looking for the courage to leave Poopie. He was nice, but mean. He was sweet, but nasty. He beat her and took all her money and sometimes hinted that she should go to work for him. Despite all his virtues, she was beginning to tire of him. "Yes, yes, yes, you do that so good," she said. "More."

She also told him more.

Then said, "Ooh, Al, what *are* you doing? Ooh, Al, but we're just friends anymore. Ooh, Al, but how did you know I still think of you that way? Ooh, Al, ooh."

Afterward, when the grandfather's clock had tolled the knell of parting day and the bites were eased, the itches were eased, Al and Milly took a bath. "Poopie wouldn't like it if he knew we took a bath together in our tub—*his*," she remarked. Al helped her clean the tub. As he bent to wipe it, she swatted him on the behind with a knotted towel.

"Ouch!"

She smiled maternally. "A little trick I learned from Poopie," she said.

Then finally, relaxed, clean, eating Rice Krispies with honey, nuts, raisins, bananas, wheat germ, and fortified skim milk—good health promotes healing— Al was ready to talk. Milly was right to make him wait until he was relaxed. She understood. He told her.

She listened in silence as he explained about his boredom with his studies, about the army, about his quest for meaning, about Sue Cody and the evanescence of romance, about the sense of uselessness in his career, about his need for exceptional action. He did not tell her about Jarod and Ellen. But then about the bank. And then about the problem with the bills: new, consecutive serial numbers, and he was afraid to pass them. Could Milly, without going to Poopie—somehow Poopie did not inspire his trust—make contact with someone to whom he might sell the money at a discount and get out clean?

Milly listened to this story in silence. She went back into the lotus position. There was a great deal of stock to be taken. Apparently there were depths in Al, though he didn't bite. Al had surprised her at last. Like a man in shock, he made no moral judgments. He was generous to himself. He did not say, I did wrong, help me. He said: I need help to get off, help me. That was nice of him. She appreciated a man with high immoral principles.

Narrowly she studied him to make sure he was hip, not just crazy; *in,* not odd. Well, he looked straight enough. She thought again: *He looks up tight,* but that didn't help too much, since she wasn't sure any more what it meant. Groovy, wow, she thought, because she knew what they meant. He needed her; the great earth mother was aroused. She could help him. He had called to her for help. Milly searched deep into his eyes, abstractedly scratching an old wound on her bare buttock.

Al watched in silence as her thoughts raced about the pretty little head with its thick undone coil of reddish hair. It looked kind of red in that light. At last she spoke: "Any better at it than I am, Al?"

"What?"

"That Sue of yours—she any better'n li'l ole Milly? you know? at it? Cause you say Yes and I'll scratch your eyes out, I will."

Al sighed. Spoken like a true-blue American girl in his time of trouble. She had rallied round him all right. He stood up to go. "Just don't say anything," he said. He was suddenly bone tired. "I'll figure out something."

"Ooh, Al, cause I'm a girl, you know? I care for you an awful lot is why I get so jealous." She followed him to the door. "Listen, I'm thinking, Al. Here, listen." She forced his head to her bosom. He stumbled and she caught him. "Hear me thinking?" He sprung his neck and rubbed it to get the circulation going. "Now I'm just going to worry over your problem, Al. I'm going to consider it *our* problem, ours together, how's about that? Just cause you were kind to me about Poopie and his bites and all. Rub-rub-rub, you were good to me, Al. You were. You still like me."

He explained that he would like to give her one of the new crisp bills, but he was afraid of passing them and being traced.

"That's all right, Al," she said. "I did what I did— you know, doncha? doncha?—only because you love me and you rub my bites so good and I *wanted* to. That bastard Poopie. Bye now."

But she did look longingly at the sack of money as he toted it out toward the car, concealed in a Macy's shopping bag which Milly had lent him. He promised to return it soon.

She stopped him halfway down the stairway by running into his arms. "Darling," she cried, "I know I'm a little ridick. I just want to tell you something—you trust me." A tear trickled from her eyes and made its way down her healthy rounded cheek. "Look, I'm crying, Al. See me cry? Little tearsie? It's because you trust me. I can't tell you what that means to me, somebody trusts me—"

But she began to sob, ran back, locked the door.

He looked up at the window from the street. There she was, all at once radiant, smiling and waving and blowing kisses. She stood waving as he walked the few steps down the hill to his car. Suddenly, in the San Francisco night, with a chill fog blowing over the town, he felt a movement of dread in his chest. Someplace he had made a mistake. He had made a wrong turn someplace. But Milly was still waving at him. It was probably fatigue. After robbing a bank and making love, he had a right to feel weary. Rest now.

He drove home to Berkeley, shaved off his mustache, tumbled into bed, and slept the sleep of the fulfilled and of the exhausted.

15 But Milly needed to fulfill herself, too. While Milly cast about for ways to fulfill herself, Al rested. Al could rob a bank, but Milly could not. It wasn't fair. When a girl does a thing like that, for example, everybody thinks she's kind of odd, crazy, lesbian, peculiar. Why, it should be just as feminine a thing—slinking in and knocking off a teller—as it is masculine. But people are hard on girls. As

Milly had decided many times before—not fair. But there are ways to equalize.

Al, doing his part, slept for the better part of two days, just dead in sleep, occasionally waking for a few minutes, staggering on rubber legs to the kitchen to draw on a bottle of milk and a handful of raisins, and then back to bed and down again. He was tied to the bed by invisible elastic. Once, practically sleepwalking, stretching the rubber, he brushed his teeth. During his few minutes awake, he hoped that Milly had figured out who might buy those numbered dollars from him at a discount. He would be a middle man. The profit would be passed on, shared. Poopie could be a middle man. Al himself was a middle man between Jarod and Ellen. Or maybe the end man. Or maybe no man. (Have another handful of raisins, keep up the sugar in the blood, he thought.) Soon perhaps he would be awakend by a call from Milly. With his knuckle he cleaned a mashed raisin from between his teeth and flopped down again. Tired he was now because he had worked before. Sleep he would now, and be awake when it again became necessary.

The mild Berkeley sun turned twice over his apartment. Twice the night dampness steamed off the redwood slats.

The Berkeley *Gazette* nestled against the Berkeley *Gazette* at his door. A young colored bandit had held up a bank in San Francisco. The branch manager had definitely identified him as a light-skinned hippie. He was an equal opportunity employer and he could spot them a mile off. The teller first thought he was, well, not really dark—a Mexican, a Puerto Rican maybe—

the light was sort of in her eyes. The note was sort of in
her eyes. He was a Negro all right. He was a black
desperado who said dirty things to her while he took
the money and she was too paralyzed to press the button.

Once the telephone rang; Jarod; he mumbled incon-
sequently and stumbled back into bed. It was as if he
had fought a long battle. The power circuits to life and
death were shorted. He had been in touch with reality;
now let him make touch with flight. Eons of evolution
tumbled through his head. Worm, fish, bird, lizard;
he was nimble, he was slow. He was hunter and pur-
sued. He murdered—but it was his own turn to be res-
urrected. How could *he* kill, and yet be the one to be
rewarded? No answer. Heaviness and swollen fluids·in
the body, and sleep. Light nerviness and sleep.

Deep in a dream of freedom and soaring in the air
—he was a bird, he was an eagle with a man's head, he
carried off his prey in his beak—a harsh electric sum-
mons filled his studio room. He struggled up from his
dream to answer the telephone: he flapped his wings
and lowered his heavy, stenchy, feathered body; he
brought the eagle down and opened a cruel eye. He
willed a man's body onto the eagle-man's head. Okay,
done. Okay, now attention to the phone. It was still
ringing. It would be Milly, it would be Milly with
news; he blinked open his eyes and it was not Milly.
It was the door. They were buzzing and pounding at
his door. Before he could shake himself enough
awake to answer, a shoulder splintered the door; four
cops came pounding through, with pistols drawn. Behind them, protected by them, lounged a civilian figure in wide-wale continental corduroy pants, loafers

without socks, and a tan Banlon shirt. This smiling, lounging person pointed his pinkie finger at the recent eagle—Al particularly remembered that he used the pinkie, not the index finger—and said, "Yeah, that's him. That's our boy."

"You willing to swear, Poopie?" one of the cops asked.

"Just look around. You don't need me to swear," said Poopie. He turned gracefully on his toes. "*There,*" he said, pointing to a bag which still sat on the chair before Al's desk. It was resting on a paperback edition of Wolfgang Kohler's study of apes and a book called *The Place of Value in a World of Fact.* "Them's nice pajamas, Al baby," he said. "Stripes look good on you."

Al felt very calm. His long sleep had revived him; it filled the nerves with electricity. He felt unsurprised and calm, though a little disappointed in Milly. He would really have preferred to be rich and free and powerful and successful rather than under arrest for bank robbery. Well, a young graduate student can't hope to have everything all at once. He might as well start at the bottom with a good long prison term. It teaches humility, also sewing and license-plate making.

"Don't make trouble, son," said one of the cops. "You be nice and we'll let you dress."

They even let him wash his face. They were sweet cops. For some reason, while washing his face, Al thought of the sadness of reading obituaries—the children and the grandchildren forever living after the honored dead. Al had no child and would be slow to create one.

Then the cops drove him with the siren working through the streets of Berkeley to the police station.

He was important enough to make strolling students
turn and watch. He was crowded between two cops;
his shoulders felt cramped in the back seat. Another
cop drove; Poopie slouched contentedly in the front
seat. Still another cop followed them on his motorcycle. I'm the prime minister of a new African nation,
Al thought. Emergent but underdeveloped. At the
crossroads of history. They're showing me the campus.
They're treating me so good. I'll give up being one
of the emergent unaligned states; I'll be a gallant
ally with missile bases, planning for my free elections
at some time in the very near future, as soon as we
get the army well organized.

Whoops, thought Al: mind wandering a bit.

The cop to Al's left considered himself a student.
He tried to suck in his gut and preferred to be described as a "social worker in uniform." He took extension courses in criminology at San Francisco State.
As part of a paper he was writing, he questioned Al on
the way to the station. "Why did you do it? What did
you hope to gain? Didn't you realize how anti-social
conduct gets you no place unless you got good connections?"

While he kept the sociology in motion, he gripped
the barrel of his pistol so that he could employ the butt
of it on Al's skull if the respondent tried any funny
business. Since he ran a little at the mouth, he also told
Al what had happened to him: "Your friend Milly
made him a little jealous. Our friend Poopie there.
Honey-fuggling—hey? Then she told him about your
problem. She made him promise to keep the secret, but
Poopie broke his promise."

"Yeah," called Poopie up front, "I broke the promise. Now can I just get at him a sec?"

"He's in the hands of the law," the sociologist proclaimed. He then settled back and explained to Al: "Broke his promise. There's the reward, you know? And the jealousy. The unwritten law. That word you used for doing it—pure East Oakland, isn't it? Linguistically speaking?"

That made it fair. After all, reward, jealousy, and Poopie just did his duty as a citizen. Al should understand.

"Oh, I do," said Al.

"The Code of the Underworld and all that jazz," said the educated cop.

Al came alert. It was like the old days, a seminar in a moving vehicle. Through narrowed eyes he asked his one true friend in that sirening police car: "But the Code! No squealing, isn't it?"

The cop took that under advisement. "Hm," he said, "that's a meretricious argument." He rubbed his nose. There was a rustle of applause—finger skin against flange skin. "You got a point there." After all, he didn't have his master's yet. He wasn't a real fast thinker yet. "But you're a non-professional," he decided at last. "They don't like that. Amendment to the Bylaws of the Code, buster. It's called horning in."

The police of Berkeley, California, were not accustomed to intelligent young graduate students in sociology who robbed banks. Therefore they treated Al with special consideration. They passed him across the bridge to San Francisco. There, instead of flinging him into a urine-stinking cell with no top for the toilet and

a curse for company, they flung him into a urine-stinking cell with no top for the toilet and a command not
to commit suicide for company. They took away shoe
laces and belt. His thoughts they left him. A man
might string himself along on thoughts, but he can't
break his windpipe just meditating. They made him
the precious gift of solitude.

Al found that he disliked Poopie more than ever.
Both in general and in particular. Poopie lacked merit
in Al's eyes.

About Milly, he felt resentful. He should not have
trusted her good nature. She had too much of it. Her
cup ran over, but all he got was the runover. Poopie
got the cup.

Sue came to mind as a true friend. He longed for
Sue—weird Sue with her impulsive feeling and her no
forwarding address. Good Sue with no afterthoughts.
He bawled a moment with self-pity, and then resolved
to face the future. The future would be something to
occupy the idle hours. He wasn't really a psychopath
—he felt sorry for himself. A true psychopath has few
feelings. Of course, sympathy for the self is one of the
few feelings a psychopath can have.

Having been slept out, Al sat awake, staring into the
blue aisle light and listening to the drunks moaning in
adjacent cells. A cop lounged under the bulb and
flicked his cigarette butt against the wall. Cabbage
smell from someplace. Smells of meat, spit, and excrement. Hopelessness of men who were not hopeless just
for the experience. No choices, no games, the destinies
of disaster.

Al remembered trees, woods, stars, birds, the Berkeley hills. He had never seen them. He had driven

through them, pushed girls through them, passed through them. There was a redwood house he had meant to admire. He remembered thinking he must stop one day and admire it.

He wished he had stopped to pity Ellen. The slight thickening and coarsening of age, and her misery thickening her. She should have enjoyed a maturing loveliness. He had neglected to pity her.

He tried to laugh. The past is different from the present in the same way an elephant is different from a mouse. More of it. God must have loved the past; he made so much of it. Al regretted the past. He had not lived it when it was the present. He was ridden through by time and events. He was locked away now. He was no different from the hopeless men all around him. Conjunctivitis coming, too. Just like a drunk, a nut, a larcenist. Sick at heart. What a bad time to get conjunctivitis.

Gray congestion of sickness in his belly. Brain working badly.

But I will live as a prisoner with burning eyes! I will wear boots and wool and lie muffled at night and my eyes will glow! In my memory I will recite poetry and compose a record of my humiliation, and they can never extinguish my eyes!

Al averted his mind. Instead he would see psychiatrists and do useful labor and his eyes would grow dull and stupid, like all prisoners, after a year of onanistic burning. At first filled with regrets and invented memories, his self-abuse, self-sweetness, would come to be quick and without fantasy. It would be a game to find sleep before the psychiatrist's pill took effect.

He wanted to weep with horror for his ignorance of

Al Dooley. His eyes itched. He was not sure how much he knew. He had been terribly alone and ignorant.

No he thought, no, no, no. I will read and study like Gandhi, like Trotsky, like the prisoners of genius! I will give up California and become a wise man.

Al understood at last, with grace and lonely clarity, that he was in trouble. He had been staring at the bare bulb and his eyes hurt. Probably he had touched the dirty money with dirty hands and then touched his eyes. When he thought of breaking the bulb and cutting his wrists, he thought of no one else, he thought only of oblivion.

PART

II

WORKING

IT

OUT

WITH

SOME

TROUBLED

MINDS

16 Suicide was the copout from fatigue, hunger, and discouragement; Al's good nature interrupted the fantasy of suicide. He got interested in things.

Late one night a man was brought in to the next cell. There was loud laughter and heels clattering and a heavy sound of dragging. When they picked him up and threw him into the cell, someone said, "How's the smart ass panther now?"

There was an answering voice which sounded familiar to Al, but he couldn't place it. By peering through his cell bars, straining sideways, he hoped to see beret and black jacket if it was really a Panther. But the body was already clanged in, breathing heavily, blocked with mucous.

A cop stood in front of Al's cell. "Hey, you! Stick to your own turf, got it?" His companion said nothing, but stood staring at Al with murder on a face striated and blotched like old meat. He was slightly stooped as if he had carried the main burden of the body they had dropped into the other cell.

Well, they'd have stripped off his Black Panther leathers.

He was alive. Al could hear him breathing.

When things quieted down again, Al went to the corner of his cell near the Panther's and said, "Hsst. You all right?" There was no answer. Al listened and thought he heard a quaver in the thick, mucousy breathing. "I'm Al Dooley. What's your—"

A clatter of heels down the hall and an enraged face exploding with the desire to kill: "You want trouble? You want trouble, Mister? You want your civil right to let us play on your kidneys a little?"

Al shut up. The man in the next cell didn't seem to hear, anyway, or had the good sense not to answer. It was better to live as if he weren't there. His neighbor was not there. His neighbor, whoever he was, was not there.

It seemed to Al that he was uncovering the first facts of his life again in jail. They refused bail; they held him for psychiatric examination, and indeed, he examined psychiatrically the world—glimpse of sunlight, jerk of nerves, taste of lumps in cereal, passage of time and leap of days. The world made some sense; only Al made little sense in it. Back to childhood, back to forever waiting. When he sat on his shelf in the cell and concentrated, time passed inching, reluctant. When he raced through memories and explanations, the hours fled by. And yet, when he recalled the inching hours later, they only lasted a moment; there was nothing he could cling to. And when he turned to the racing memories, when time had abandoned him, he remembered this and that and the other things—his parents shoring up mere details against oblivion in Santa Barbara—and there was an anchor in the world.

He needed something to do. Something to mean and be, something to do.

If he learned so much in the early days of his term of pre-trial investigation, what would there be left for the long wait and the long semester in prison? It frightened him that life fell so easily into place—meals, visits, questions, sleep, routines, daydreams. His dad cried a bit and found him a lawyer. His mother cried a lot and agreed with his father that everything possible should be done. He tested the other possibilities, the impossibilities, and found no great virtue in them. For the moment, he was content to ride. He felt safe against the world with the world all against him. He would probably not be beaten like the Panther next door. Poopie was a dream and so was everyone else. His mother and father ran a nice travel agency. He had just slid out of the draft. He had no risks to suffer now that he had lost the impossible risk he had set up for himself. Or so he felt. Calm settled over him. Sinus did not disqualify him for prison. He was cared for here.

Occasionally he wondered what would happen to him. He tried the elevator in his belly—no sinking at the thought of a term in confinement. The routine seemed to suit him. He had led his life that way. He would build his arms and shoulders with push-ups; he would build his character with meditation. The struggle was over. His mother and father would get used to the idea. Sad, but they still had each other. They had a good business, too. He would live through this day, the next day, the one after, and let the credit go. This flight to acceptance might have come after a long struggle, but in fact, he was in jail less than a month when the habit was already established and then, abruptly, broken. He had a visitor, Professor Jarod Howe.

The elevator shaking and quavering in his belly. A few weeks ago they had refused him this visitor. Nausea.

Jarod's skin looked gray beneath the healthy leather tan. Pale, thought Al; then I must be green.

It was nothing special to the police to have a friend come to visit him, just as it had been nothing special to talk with interrogators, lawyers, doctors, parents— mourning at his grave—and the gentle civil service employee, Mr. Jones, who issued him denim pants and shirt. They might have thought this Negro with the neat suit, hat, and briefcase (gold initials), was a lawyer. No. "Professor Howe to see you." Mr. Jones almost added "Sir."

"No."

But Jarod was already in the cell, smiling faintly. He peeked about and then sat on the edge of a bunk, leaning forward to keep from bumping against the unoccupied upper ledge. He studied Al with his classroom eyes, alert, amused, in control, in touch, not the crazy willfulness of the past months. With these clothes on, the suit in which he taught his large freshman lecture section, and with this obligation to visit a student in trouble, he was ready to talk to Al as he used to. Al felt happy. If being in trouble meant that Jarod became human again, in trouble was a good place to be. Jarod could calm him. He had not been brainwashed, but he had received a good rinse in fright and strain.

"Are you bored?" Jarod asked.

"There's not much to do here. I think I'm being observed. But it doesn't seem like a waste of time."

"Very good. Life is too short to make every day count. Learn to loaf and stretch a little."

Here, between the wall of this cell? Sink, bunks, concrete floor sloping toward the center. The drain was wet. It had been hosed down an hour before. A dank smell came from the wet pipe leading into the sewers. Al prowled sometimes, when he awakened in the middle of the night, and smelled this smell as if he were contemplating solitary sex. He was contemplating it in order to go back to sleep. He felt no desire to touch himself. He imagined it would leave him nervous, exhausted, and unable to sleep. That was only a guess. Since robbing the bank he had no desire to touch himself. Instead, in those midnight moments, lit by a bare white bulb protected by a steel lacing in the corridor, he would throw himself to the floor and do push-ups until his shoulders and his belly cracked with fatigue and floods of heat ran through his body, opening trickles of sweat under his arms and at his belt. And then he would sleep, dreaming of large shoulder muscles and nothing more philosophical than that. Dreams held in his fists. Hands clenched.

Jarod was smiling at Al with crinkly eyes—that handsome actorish look. "Listen," he said, "I thought of a joke. I was going to get you a silver bracelet for your birthday, like they do for diabetics or heart cases, you know? Only this would be for ordinary mortals. For bank-robbing normal just-folks. In silver. To be worn at all times: *I May Die.* Would you like that?"

"What's up, Jarod?"

"Well, we all need a cause. As you know about me. As you know about yourself—robbing, screwing old ladies, not getting your thesis written."

Nevada, the mute prisoner with whom Al walked in the exercise yard, was being led past his cell by a sergeant to a meeting with his court-appointed attorney.

"Pay attention, lad," Jarod said gently.

"I was."

"To me. To yourself now, pal."

"What's on your mind?"

Jarod sighed. "We understand each other, don't we, Al?"

"No."

"Right, we don't. Okay. But I hate to see you risk yourself where there's no possibility of winning, only getting trouble for yourself." He did not say: "foh yosef." He was speaking in his natural academic voice. "There should be another risk to take, other than women, chicks, and banks."

"What about you?"

Jarod shrugged and pressed his lips together as if to say it's hard, hard. "We learn from games, it's the American way. I got married, didn't I? And in my case it involved more than being a good sport about the girl I got in trouble—a demonstration to the world it was. I've only had two of my three lives so far. One as a smart colored kid; one as a chaser, getting my kicks; one as a success in whatever I try."

"That's three already."

"The one I'm waiting for is where I don't get what I want. I love some quiet girl who says No. I can't change the world. I want to live and die." He looked expectantly at Al.

Al did not answer. Jarod's eyes had the color of his voice, yellow, pleading, convincing, unconvinced.

"You're right to say nothing," Jarod said. "I'm on my way to that life."

Al listened to him, a stranger to his own life after it had been so briefly vivid to him. The sun speckled Jarod's clothes through the window with its distorted polish marks, his face was contorted, his tongue showed as he talked and laughed; and Al cared about Jarod and not about himself, about Jarod's fate and not his own. Who was this fluent animal with the pink tongue? He won everything without taking chances. Al was paying the price for no intelligent risk at all—for a joke, like having a bad sinus, for a game of shoplifting in a bank.

"I'm doing you a favor," Jarod said, "talking about myself like this. Otherwise what would you think about? You're having the day after a great joy—the unusable dead day of recovery."

Al watched the words emerge from Jarod's nose and mouth and spread over his chin like a sweet liquid. Being in trouble changed not enough. There must be a way to change things. Jarod was saying: after all that labor to find truth and act properly comes the madness of thinking you know what is good for you . . . He was talking about arrogance. Al was trying to listen.

"Where are we, Jarod?"

"In jail."

"In jail, good. You know what sadness is," Al said, "but you don't know what anybody else's sadness is."

"Do you? Yours, yes."

Al could not answer, not yet. But he believed that
Jarod would stay with him until he knew the answers.
A cockroach scampered and fell like a shooting star
down a gray wet wall; it hit the cement with a singing
pop. It scurried off, flicking itself; unhurt it seemed,
uncomplaining it seemed.

Jarod's lips were the color of rain. There was the
smell of a sick animal in the room—crime, urine, dis-
infectant, anxiety. There was the silent hurt man in the
cell next to him. The smells kept accumulating. Jarod
was boiling and steaming; his lips were cold and gray.
"Let me tell you what to expect," he said.

Al expected other smells from a sick animal. It was
Jarod and the jail and his expectations, and Jarod was
saying: "You'll see in the courtroom how the women,
listening, they open their thighs. I notice the same
thing when I'm doing the lecture. To let in a little cool
air, otherwise they'll come."

"You used to think about the subject. You talked
very well."

"What is the subject now?" Jarod grinned. "The
subject, topic A, was what I was thinking about, boy,
which is why I was a good teacher. I was black and
they listened. I did them, so they listened. I'm a
warmly sympathetic, deeply selfish man, and you must
get accustomed to me. The stickiest part of the Milky
Way is the part I'm standing on. What I want, I want
for me. When I was young, since you are young, I
used to wake up lonely in the middle of the night and
think: Someday I'll not wake lonely. Love. But I hold
girls between my elbows and hear them scream, and
it's their own pleasure they're studying. It's nothing
they share of my darkness. So now I no longer figure

that way. I wake up lonely and I think: Well, this will pass. I'll eat a melon, go for a walk. I'll make something of myself tomorrow."

"Dreadful," said Al.

"It's sweet when she gets up to find us a glass of water. But that's not opening the box. We penetrate body with body, but that doesn't open it either. The nerve is separate. The soul is caught in my black prison, and no white receptacle—"

"No black one?"

"No white, black, blue, or green body can know who I am." He turned his palms out—pink. "Therefore: nor can I. When she first told me what she wanted, I thought: Oh you white women, so that's all it is. I was a kid. I got started on the heavy road, pal. I could do up my discouragement."

"That's what it is."

"Now what I can do is be reasonable and fuck a lot. Whichever one I'm doing, the other thing looks better to me. Blowing my time, brother. I go to Washington. I yell my head off. But I really mean to do it, being reasonable or unreasonable, which is more than you've had on your mind these last twenty-four years?"

"Yes, okay. So then you decided to do something with the Muslims—losers—why not the Panthers?"

Jarod waited to see if he had something else on his mind. "Here we are," he said, "and we're still talking about me."

"Yes. And the Muslims."

"Exercise. Just trying out for size. Wrong size, buddy. After good practice, the Panthers are closer to it." He began to smile. He showed his teeth. "Which reminds me of another damned thing: you tried some-

thing on for size, too." He gazed into Al's eyes and
laughed. "So did you. Ellen."

"You know."

Jarod said, "I was meant to be crazy, but I didn't
have the time. I was supposed to break down. I passed
it on to her."

"You know!" Al shouted. "You knew, why don't you
do something about it?"

Jarod smiled and shrugged. "You take a little fug-
gling too serious, pal. I been trying to explain. My
whole life is doing something about it. You don't understand yet, it's *you* has to do something. It's your
turn."

Al stood in the steely light of confinement and
moved toward him.

Jarod remained in his place, eyes half shut, hands
folded on each other. He was figuring how to bring
him back, bring him down. "According to my wife, it
seem you say . . . after you've come, or rather, during your climax . . . you say: Spurt! spurt! spurt!
three times, like that. Spurt-spurt-spurt, more like
that? Anyway, she might not communicate it to me
exactly. Just listen, Al, and don't get all worried up.
Maybe you can help me." He raised his hand—*shush*.
In jail awaiting trial for bank-robbery, just told by
his best friend that he *knows*—and Al could help
Jarod? "Yes. Wait." Jarod turned his back on Al and
walked toward the little barred window. "Hall of
Justice," he murmured. Words to clear his throat.
"Others or myself," he said. "That closeness with
things seemed out of my grasp. Being black is something, you know, yet when you're brown and smart
and white like me, it is also nothing. People say I'll

kill you, yet you know that's, uh, inaccurate. People say you're an animal, and you know you're not. Blood? I call myself black, but chances are there's more your kind of blood in me than my kind. Funny, no? I think I loved Ellen, but how could I? Whirling like meat on an electric spit. Is everyone like that, Al?"

"I must have been—"

"Brains in a bottle of flesh—we *know* it."

"Yes."

"What you look at in the dark, when you peek inside, or when you can't sleep and you look out over the bay . . ."

Over the wind, sorrow, loneliness, grief.

"—what do you see? Brain says: This spurt is a hype. What else? What do you do when you know the end is coming?"

"I'm sorry, Jarod." He wanted to be forgiven. He didn't want to ask. "I'd like to do what I can, Jarod."

"What? Rob more banks?"

"I've always wanted to talk with you about that," Al said. "What I want to do and be. What I want to find."

"Hadn't you better first figure a way how to swing out of here?"

"Maybe I'll stay awhile. Give me some time for figuring."

"Boy," said Jarod, "while you're figuring in San Quentin, somebody behind you will be working over your rump. It ain't *conducive*, you know that?"

Jarod's ape grimace, teeth and curling lip, meant angrily to bar the way to the questions worth answering between them. But he knew this vast mood as well as Al did. The important questions were discarded by

the superior mental operators of the time on the charge
of deluding and distracting the human spirit. The artists wanted sensation, color, noise. Excitement and assault seemed enough facts. The philosophers wanted
science and the scientists wanted themselves, plus
government contracts. Only fools and the sick asked
for connections and meanings, and Al knew that he
and Jarod were still alike in this, still fools. They had
the state of being fools to share. Ellen was not what
they shared; neither of them possessed her. Sociology
was not a thing they took together; it was what Jarod
made out well in, what Al made out not so well in. The
world and Jarod had agreed that he was to be a winner,
but Jarod had changed his mind. Now Jarod and Al
were in the same boat. They had suffered a long collab-
oration in trying not to be foolish, and then in being
stupid. Now were they ready to pay? Al liked to believe himself ready to proceed and live in some part
of the real world. If he could enter his friend's loneliness for a time, they might go their separate ways in
peace.

"Funny," said Jarod, "if maybe you could get probation because of me. Wouldn't that be a gas?"

"How is she?"

"You didn't hear? I had to put her away. You
weren't listening. Committed."

"Oh, no."

"Here's exactly what you did. You screwed a crazy
white broad, Al. Ooh let me, she said. She dramatized
the whole thing for me. Dramatics is a part of the
disease—hysteria. Symptoms, so it's not my business."

"Poor Ellen."

"She was acting out, too. Lean close, tell me her

story, then tickle her throat and spill her dinner on me, the dinner and you, all mixed up. That blue devil blood of hers was like milk mixed with water—no nourishment in it."

The tears were flooding in Al's eyes. They were a stranger's tears in a stranger's eyes. Ellen's.

"She says she'll be good now. *Now* she says. No shock treatment. She thinks it's punishment. *Now* she says she'll be good, but they'll have to do the series. Breaks down the synapses—the memory cells—does a lot of good, they claim."

"It's too soon for that! She had good reasons!"

"I signed for it, boy. Generally they use drugs these days, mood-enhancers, but I got me a conservative man, he likes electricity. Another theory is you catch the psychosis fast, before it takes root, you rip it out by the rootlets." He studied Al's streaked face. "That's strange. I haven't been able to do that since I was a kid."

In his trouble, sitting in jail with a visitor, awaiting his trial, Al asked Jarod: "What are you doing next?"

"I suppose I'll try to help Ellen get well. She'll be out on probation. She lost the child."

"I didn't know."

"You should get out on probation, too."

"It's not much of a plan."

"It's our plan, boy, but maybe not. What do you want? You want out of here?"

"I'm scared. I don't know what I want."

"I spend too much time shucking and jiving. You'd druther I spent my time getting you straight out of here."

"I'm afraid of you, Jarod. I don't trust you at all."

Jarod showed his teeth. "That's not why you're here, soul brother. Don't try to tell me that's why you're here."

Al felt the shame flushing his face. No, he had no right to do that. "I didn't say that's why I'm here."

"Okay. I'll see Probation. I'll write some letters— okay, I'll make the calls. I have this federal judge—"

"What's he got to do with it?"

Jarod stood up, tapping his briefcase, creasing his face, smiling his smile. "He'll send word on down. He owes me plenty. This is word-on-down country, pal. I'll make them this friendly offer—help them with their law and order if they'll go easy on my good buddy."

He was laughing. He was happy.

Al wondered: Is he going to mess me up?

Jarod said, "Later, brother."

Messing with me?

"Listen!" Al shouted. "I don't want to go to the psych ward!"

Jarod started to laugh. "Trust in your friend," he said. "By the way, they showed it last night. They changed the title from The Affluent Negro to The Influential Black."

Jarod was standing. Al was still standing there alone a few moments later; no sounds in the hall, no footsteps; his face was still wet; Jarod was gone.

17 "You can insist on a lawyer being present," Detective Warren Brown, badge in his pocket, said to Al, settling with deep contentment onto the cushions of a naugahyde sofa in the George Washington Carver Felony Interrogation and Rehabilitation Room. "Or you can just talk to me like a friend and brother meaning to extort the truth from you no matter what the cost to both of us in agony and pain. That's a section of the code which I really love."

"So far you've been very nice," said Al. "This has been a lovely jail."

"Don't interrupt me, Al, especially to disagree."

"I didn't. You'd stopped already. And I agree, sir."

"Now you say," said Detective Brown, "you claim and assever, hum, let me just rattle these pages a little. You pretend you committed this here crime of unlawfully heisting a bank."

"Yes."

"You're sure you're not a dark-skinned man? Both the teller and the branch manager identified you as such. Here, lemme show you the composites."

Al examined the drawings. "They look sort of like anybody, don't they? Only spade?"

The detective sighed. "I guess you're not a nice dark gentleman from whom we can extract lots of Miranda-

type-case confessions. That branch manager, that
teller—"

"Well, maybe people isn't their bag, sir."

"The color of people is a problem people have, I
guess. Well, they're not the only one. You see the im-
broglios we officers are constantly getting ourselves
into—the composites are the wrong color, the wit-
nesses should give it to us in Braille."

"You can say that again."

"Please, Al. Heck—please? Especially to agree don't
interrupt."

"I was just trying to help."

"You criminals are always trying to help," Detective Brown said in a voice crowded with pain. "You
don't understand. You're all old-fashioned, that's why
you're our patients. You are looking for punishment,
my boy, and you have just got to get used to the facts;
you're sick. Treatment is what you need, not the gas
chamber or electrocution—not that I'm opposed to a
little electroshock series or two, say twenty-six treat-
ments in all, in cases of depression or insufficient brain
damage for normal survival. We try to secure you good
so's you don't break a spine. You're disturbed, Al. You
have a superior I.Q. but low tolerance for normal
frustration. But you seem to me, and I have all the
course work finished for my master's in criminology
reform, you seem to me, brainwise, a prime candidate
for what we like to call rehabilitation. That means we
patiently, kindly, with plenty of loving concern and
always listening to the client's point of view—"

"I know."

"Stop interrupting, stop it!" he cried out, and then
jumped nervously. He took out a notebook and wrote

something with a red felt pen. "I just self-graded myself a D minus for yelling and shouting," he explained,
snapping the notebook shut. "The reason I didn't give
myself an F is I restrained myself from using a rubber
truncheon on your kidneys. When I do that, I flunk
and have to start all over. Now where was I?"

"Patient's point of view," said Al.

"Thank you very much. Client. I'm a hawk, you
know, not a dove, but you have to be a hawk dovewise
if you want to get ahead in the correction business
these days. You heard of the weeping hawk? That's
me, buster. So I try to reserve my brutality for the little lady t'home and put it out in the form of mortifica-
tion. First for her, sometimes for me. Abuse and
self-abuse, you know, and a bit of leather. I tell you
this not to embarrass you or cause you any momentary
discomfort, any acidosis-type eating at the stomach
linings, but only to assure you that I am a human even
as you and others I could name. I am easy to the brain
linings. They call me Chapstick around here, ha ha, because you apply to a dry chapped brainwashed brain
and all is well shortly. Some of these other boys, let me
tell you, are worse than detergent. You'll get Excedrin
Headache Number One if you tussle with Detective
O'Baron. Don't provoke that man, he's ignorant. Okay.
Now tell me in your own words how you happened to
choose this particular neurotic act of defiance against
parental authority as personified in the federally regu-
lated banking system?"

"Actually," said Al, "I just thought I might get away
with it. I wanted to do something special. I thought I
could be someone special. I realize there is nothing to
substitute for hard work and merit—"

"That's the key to attainment in this world of rewards for achievement," said Detective Brown.

"You interrupted me."

"Sorry, sir." The keen-tempered lawman took out his notebook and wrote something. He snapped it shut and said, "Self-grading. The little lady will mortify me tonight, Al. Continue."

"It would be pretentious," Al said, "to ascribe my action to some thought-out rebellion against society. No, it was rather—"

Detective Brown could not restrain himself. "I am opposed with all my heart and soul to pretensiosity, sir! I also get grief and pain from repetitiousness and saying the same thing twice over. Oh-oh." He opened the notebook again. He wrote: Cat-o'-nine-tails at ten. Pick up baggies, coffee cake, witch hazel. He said: "Continue."

"After you," said Al.

"You're the fellow we want to confess, son. So you admit everything?"

"You caught me," said Al.

"No, I mean pride, shame, latentness, overtness, common vagrancy in the worlds of the imagination?"

Al blushed. It was the word Imagination which did him in. "Well, I'd say fancy," he said. "I'm too lazy to be truly one of the great imaginative minds of the age, such as S. Freud, L. Wittgenstein, A. Einstein—"

"Jarod Howe?" the detective interrupted keenly.

"I'm speaking only of the dead. Jarod is more a—"

Brown snapped his fingers. "I read that book of his someplace," he said, "the review of it. In the Sunday *Chronicle*. Someone mentioned it. Isn't it on my reading list over at State?"

"It's a well-known book in the field."

"Tell me what he's trying to say, Al, in your own words. I'm really interested this time."

"I very much appreciate your coming," Al said, standing up.

"He's a brilliant man, isn't he? Say, I bet he gets all kinds of special deals. Per diems, stuff like that."

"If there's anything I can do, please call on me again."

"Maybe you'd let me show you my term paper, Mr. Dooley. It's all on the tip of my tongue. My field experience is superb, but words lie, as Shakespeare said. They are not adequate unto our feelings and on-the-job training. Do you want to make a deal?"

"No."

"Of course we don't make deals. Let me explain it."

"No."

"Trying, Al. Trying to get you off this hot spot before you get in deeper."

"Goodbye," Al said.

Detective Brown took the hint. "So wish you had been more cooperative, son. When you're in trouble, you should learn to appreciate it. This is one of those times. Now if we can just identify the evil figures who twisted your fine young mind into the corrupted instrument of modern anxiety it is today, I will approach my inner conflicts a happy man. Until later, my poor dear friend." And he clasped Al's hands in his own two hot ones. He backed out of the barred room, bowing and distraught. Impulsively he sought to kiss Al's fingers, but Al pulled away. "It's not what you think," he cried, "I'm of White Russian descent. My father was a prince, he came to San Francisco from Siberia, walk-

ing all the way, across the Bering Straits, with only a
few family icons to give him a start in the new world.
He never thought his son would be a cop, Al. In the
old country he was a career prince, eleventh in his
promotion. On his deathbed I took a solemn vow to
become a social worker . . ."

The door was shut by a uniformed patrolman who
snapped at Brown, "Brown!"

"When?" said Brown né Bronofoffski. "Oh, when?"

Al put his ear to the door. He heard the low click of
Brown's notebook. Open, then shut. Mrs. Brown's work
would be cut out for her this night.

That, thought Al Dooley, was a nice diversion. There
was still a little St. Petersburg fog where Detective
Brown had sat so quizzical and perturbed.

But now, he wondered, why wasn't he returned to
the cell?

The naugahyde smelled peculiar. So many men
made of real leather had sweated in that fake leather
couch. He sat by choice in Detective Brown's chair,
although Detective Brown had sat by choice beside
him on the couch. He gave himself a few restful moments for having doubts about his psychic balance.
The world had tipped him one way and he had tipped
himself another. Al Dooley was not in a mood to criti-
cize Prince Brown.

But why had they left him alone in this interrogation room with no one further to interrogate him? They
were clowns, that's why. He could just as easily escape, cat-burglar bank-robber heist-job man that he
was.

The door opened in response to the thought and its

amendment: A bank-heist man is not a cat burglar. A cat burglar is a skinny fellow who climbs on roofs after jewels, or at least a lithe fellow like the young Cary Grant. I'm going out of the manic phase again. And the door was opening. Here comes the depressive. In shambled Poopie Cola in his jail-time blues. Al stood up. "You're a crud, Poopie," he said.

"I'm an informer."

"I'm just speaking in general, Poopie-crud."

"Don't insult me, Al. I do my work like a fine up-standing stool pigeon."

"I was only speaking in general, Poopie-crud. What else you here for?"

"To get straightened out. They give me what I ask for. I don't mind explaining. I dropped some speed this morning, it made me lean a little to the left. So I dropped some Demerol to cool me a few degrees. Then grass to lift it into the light. Some opium to sweeten it at the edges, you know, the icing. Then I put on some Thorazine to keep it bubbling nice and low. When I'm ready, I'll know what's good for you."

"You're programmed, aren't you?"

"I'm happy. I'm cool. I'm an astronaut."

"You're lucky," Al said.

Poopie motioned him to sit down. "Okay," he said briskly. "Hear me clear and roger over. Give the State very little trouble and the State, in its own turn, will give you little difficulty. Tell all. Explain. Sign the papers. You will get off by reason of, by reason of—" He paused, listening to the air as if for the high-pitched whine of a dog whistle. Al followed the specks across his eyeballs, but could not hear it.

"Insanity," Poopie temporarily concluded.

"Crud," said Al.

Poopie sighed. "There is something close between the police and crime. Take me, for example. It's my code, selling you, pal. They give me money and a nice handshake and Immunity One. They supplied me with confiscated Grade A drugs, but no LSD. I've committed some misdemeanors and felonies in my day, too. So it's not just to *your* advantage to cooperate, brother —it's to mine. So cooperate, hear me? Tell me what I like to hear."

Poopie was moving in on him.

Al stood up, but was sent back off-balance and down into naugahyde before his knees got straight. A nice short chopping stroke, spin left, spin right, top spin. Al tried to stand and the hand came down, pressing and hurting. He couldn't move. He was gagging and his heart was free and he was choking but it didn't affect his spirit and he could not stand. He was cut down into the chair.

"Tell me all, collitch crap-out."

Al was trying to get up, but could not. Poopie's hand was on his gullet and he was pressing. Blue fires dancing behind eyes.

"Talk if you can."

Pain. Darkness.

"When you wake up, try to talk. And if you can't, tiger, I've had some fun anyway. Call me anything you like—"

Al was trying to call him something, but he could not speak, could not speak, could not think. He thought he could still smell the sour flesh beaten into the couch.

"Aw, Al," Poopie was saying, "they promised me a

real great trip with Owsley blues if I got you to con-
fess in your own words what they dictate to you.
Come on, Al, you owe just one more little help to
Poopie. Try to listen to me now. Don't go out on me,
Al. Come on now, listen. Nice Paul. You paying atten-
tion or you doing a stupid crash scene on me? Al?
Nice Poopie, Al. It ain't a bummer."

Al wasn't certain just when Poopie left him. "After
all," Poopie said, "and I hope you can still hear me, we
both got Milly for a mutual friend."

He heard him say that, but he woke up in his cell.
He had twisted a foot. It must have been one man
dragging him by the shoulders. Mr. Jones, the nice
guard, was not on duty that day.

18 Stanford Mittance, Al's lawyer, thought
it best that Al understand some of the
elements of his defense, Al being so smart and all. It
wasn't like chiropractice or anything, where the mystery helps the patient cure himself. Faith'll do it every
time, but faith wasn't going to do it this time. Being
sociable while he unfolded his 'tatchy case into a little
beaverboard desk, he asked, "Where'd you get those
funny, uh, marks on your kind of throat, kind of blue,

and that look in your eye? Jeepers creepers, where'dja
get those eyes, Al?"

"Paul Cola."

"Oh cripes, they hadn't ought to do that. Oh heck, as
your lawyer I personally wish we could prove abuse."
He got a sheaf of papers straight and tapped the edges.
"Ah well, that's just mucous under the bridge. I'm
sure glad I'm not an incarcerated moral monster in the
hands of justice with none of the protection of the
law." He shook his head with sorrow for the suffering
of others. He had that little half smile, the sharp dim-
ple at the corners of mouth, which indicated that it
was the suffering of others he was concerned with. It
wasn't his own, thank God. A lawyer has to keep in
touch, but not necessarily in contact. He slipped off a
paper clip and squinted at his list of questions. There
was lots to cover.

"I know you're upset," he said. "I can see that, too."
He cleared his throat. "Okay, it's getting-to-know-you
time. Just as I need to understand you inside and out,
Al, your hopes and dreams and fondest wishes, so it is
relevant that you have the complete picture of yours
truly, the better for me to defend you with, my friend.
I assume you have the kind of broad-gauged mind
which is impatient with clichés and cuts straight to the
heart of the matter, whether or not it's relevant. So let
us proceed."

Mittance was a crewcut young man of fifty, tennis,
small sloop, berth in the Berkeley Yacht Club, who
liked to sit with a glass of bourbon on the deck of his
boat and explain how you only live once and he was
content to be a poor man in California rather than a
rich man in some Eastern firm. Of course, if he'd have

his druthers, he might could manage to be a rich man in California, too, why not? But the essential is to remain young, have a small sloop, keep the backhand steady, and receive the love of two or three loyal women, not counting offspring, female. Group dynamics was his other hobby—meaningful relationships. His calling in the Law was justified by the high interpersonal caliber of his clients—tax dodgers, insurance cheats, bribed judges, and now, at last, one fine young bank-robber with all the course work done for his M.A. in sociology.

Al's parents had found Mr. Mittance. He had colleagues in Santa Barbara who preferred practice in a friendly little town by the sea, where they would prefer to be poor, rather than riches and legal fame in the Bay Area, Berkeley, Oakland, San Francisco, the boiling incoherence of the metropolis. They preferred the sailing off the coast of Santa Barbara.

First Mr. Mittance flashed for Al's pleasure a glimpse of the legal uses of insanity—"that is, ha ha, far as I'm concerned, the whole world is a little nuts. Least I think I am, ha ha." But then he put on his thick black Swiss spectacles with the almost invisible line of bifocal. That line troubled him. He fixed Al with his youthful fifty-year-old gaze and really went into it. He said, "The M'Naughton Rule. The M'Naughton case (1850) established the defense by reason of insanity. You're insane, boy, if you can't understand natural consequences of acts or can't tell the difference between right or wrong. I looked it up last night in my notes. Seems to me, lad, you qualify on all counts, so I'm unfurling our mainsail—*non comprendi naturali consequenti*—and also our topsail, no diff between

righto and wrongo. That is, mains'l, tops'l. We're in
good shape, fair weather, sailing smooth."

"I'm darn glad of that," said Al.

"Let me explain the grounds of our case. The M'-
Naughton rule about insanity is going on a hundred
and a quarter years old. Shit, man, that's old-fashioned.
It says only a person with total mental incapacity to
tell right from wrong is excused from responsibility.
But such isn't your case, lad. In New York already,
they say 'substantial' incapacity. You get it—*substantial*."

"I got it."

"Important, that. They're ahead of us in New York in
the types of mind-zappings—socio, psycho, stupido—
but I think we still got a lead on 'em pharmacologic-
ally. Anyway, substantial, it widens the language from
know right from wrong to *know or appreciate*. Listen,
you *know*, but you don't *appreciate*. It's the times we
live in. I want to get up front and gut level. You're a
poor misunderstood boy of twenty-two."

"Twenty-three," said Al.

"I know and appreciate that," said Mr. Mittance.
"It's you didn't know and appreciate the nature and
consequence of your conduct. That's the broader use of
the term. It's you're unable to conform your conduct.
It's the army, it's the struggles, it's all that dope in the
streets, and your glands—you're overworked—you're a
brilliant student—you're really offbase—you had these
bad friendships—"

"I want to plead guilty," said Al.

"Huh? Sure, you mean not guilty by reason of insanity."

"No," said Al, "guilty."

"You're berserk," said Mr. Mittance. "That's crazy not to plead not guilty by reason of insanity."

"I changed my mind. I knew what I was doing."

The lawyer narrowed his eyes and gazed at Al. "Your mother. Your girl friend. Your other friends. Your many years behind bars." He had forgotten something. "Your father's travel agency in Santa Barbara."

"Maybe I could get probation."

"Maybe you could get a lot of prison. Buggered in the rear, lad. Mistreated in San Quentin. I must remember to show you some pictures of the handsome young prisoners injured from behind by the hardened criminals who didn't know how to plead not guilty by reason of the M'Naughton rule. I wonder," he mused, "if they'll let me bring in my album of photos. Probably stopped by the guards. Come on, Al, don't come on like a mad dog ravening in the streets."

"When you think of all the people get away with things," said Al.

"That's right. Good thinking." Mr. Mittance beamed. "Now you're getting to the nitty-gritty. Do your thing—feel sorry for yourself."

"When one considers how the penal system doesn't resolve anything—"

"Oh yes it does! Don't put it down like that!" Mr. Mittance cried. "Don't forget the sado-masochism! The rampant homosexuality! The need of guards to have something to guard, of wardens to have something to ward."

"I'll do whatever you say," Al said, "but—"

"But you'll keep your own independence on the inside. That's right. Good boy," Mr. Mittance said, gentle, crooning, and patient. "Be crazy mad character disorder psychopathic personality on the outside, but on the inside, heart-of-heartsy, be just plain you. That's how I want it. That's how it should be. Shoot?"

"Shoot," said Al.

"Roger and over. Now here's how we proceed, lad —" He puckered up and gave his long-burning, group-dynamic look, but then went on crisply, "According to the 'mad dog' rule, that's one way they refer to it on the pejorative side, you don't need a saliva test, however . . . Say, by the way? You under the influence of methedrine, speed, heroin, downies, uppies, sideways, LSD, mary jane, morphine, cough syrup, the peace pill, dexies, Dexamyl, Seconal, glue—?"

"*Glue?*" said Al.

"Sorry about that. Didn't mean to put you down."

"Glue is for kids."

"I said I'm sorry, Al, I regret, don't you ever forgive?"

"Okay."

"Make up? Friends? Okay, that's just up-tightness under the bridge. Benzedrine, opium, hashish, Diet-Rite Cola?"

"No."

Sigh. "Well, we'll do our best, Al, for that's all we can really expect of ourselves, isn't it?"

"I don't like turning my head around. I like to know who and what I am. That's my quest." He was falling into Mr. Mittance's automated gibbering.

"For that's your quest," Mr. Mittance murmured. "An idealist. A thinker-type of philosopher. A truly lonely freak from way back, much influenced by the things around him . . . Pure pathology. You voluntarily messed in your brains with ideas, isn't that right? —the worst kind of tampering. A confirmed solitary. Oh, you're a difficult case, Al. They don't show up on litmus paper, urinalysis, tap the knees, dilation of pupils. You're a hard one, Al, but I really respect you to the utmost for it. I do."

It was as if he were pronouncing a marriage in and around the two of them. Al knew pure fear. He had fallen into the hands of a citizen. He was normal and they are relentless.

"Look outside!" said the lawyer. "Look!"

Al was about to be struck about the head—not in the face as if in a fight, but about the head, as a man beaten. Mr. Mittance had something to show him. This was the lawyer and counselor talking. Forget the long wet pauses and the puckered lips. This man knew what he was long wet pausing and puckering about. "Look!"

Al went to the window of his basement cell. It gave onto a drain cut into a well beneath the street. He was lucky; it was only the basement, not the sub-basement. By twisting he could see shadows, legs, shoes. There was sunlight. There were the bluish reflections of buildings, shadows within the damp shadows. Perhaps the really mean cases, not idea freaks like him, but bad chaps, victims, were kept in basements beneath his basement. He could still see shadows, and sometimes living soot would drift comfortingly down between the grates at foot level.

"All right!" said the lawyer. "Those shapes will become like girls. You'll dream of them—freedom to walk the streets. Try to help me!"

"Those *are* girls," Al said.

"Help me to help you, Al . . . ! Where? Which girls?"

"What can I do?" Al asked.

"Be M'Naughton rule for me! Be crazy a little! Help me, boy, I'm just a Boalt Hall Graduate in law, not Law Review material, not Supreme Court justice clerk stuff, but I want to do you out of eight to eleven or worse. We live in a tough state. You heard about the mugger, he rolled down the hill with his victim, they got him on the state Lindbergh law—kidnapping! A life sentence!" He paused to do justice to the threat. He was an honest man. "Course, that was an inner city type, y'know what I'm telling you—a public defender. I'll do much better in your regard."

"Thank you, Mr. Mittance."

"Caw me Stan. Your parents are picking up the tab. You poor poor boy. But not in public." The glasses had come off, the eyes were watering, the eyes were wiped, emotion receded; Mr. Mittance was back on true course. This married sailor was emotionally stirred. By Al Dooley. It probably meant better service, but Al felt glad to be in jail, with policemen all about in case he needed help from sudden attack by tender-hearted, emotionally stirred, group-dynamic lawyer. "I shall try to explain, Al, with words of art—that's the legal term for stuff we don't like you laymen to understand. But you're a smart lad, intelligent, cultured, handsome, charming, blue-eyed, uh, where was I?"

"Water under the bridge."

"Right! You can understand me and I'll explain it all to you. Refreshed myself last night, reading my notes from school and the sunset rose over the Berkeley hills with pink and violet and God it was beautiful, Al. First item: the hearing to establish *present* sanity. Can you understand the charges against you? Can you participate in your own defense? Those are important questions, Al, and I implore you. Excuse that. I'm a bit nervous."

Al said, "I think I follow so far."

"I'm a little nervous because this is a new type of trial for me. We're going to get in the newspapers together, Al. You represent the youth of our time, troubled, uneasy, rootless, striving. And so do I. I hope you believe that."

"I do."

"Oh I do, too."

"I know you do."

"We both do, Al. I'm only forty-nine, very healthy, not too old for getting in touch. Well, fifty."

"That's really young, sir."

Mr. Mittance—Stan—gave him his burning reproach look. That Sir really cut him to the quick. Sometimes Al had his brutal ways, like many of your kids under thirty. Stan was trying to be up front and gut level all the way. "I'm into all kinds of awareness," he said softly. "Right now, for example, I'm a little up tight because I'm due for a special weekend stew at Bolinas. I'm overdue, Al."

Al was sympathetic. Once he had known a girl who was overdue.

"It's the mind-zap stew for professionals, doctors, lawyers, social workers, wizards, and of course your top Bay Area writers and artists. We really lay it on the line, Al, and there isn't an ounce of phoniness left by the time the weekend is over. Forty-eight hours of

utter frankness and no smoking. It's nothing but basics
—hostility, aggression, and love. But I had to take a
raincheck this weekend, Al, in order to prepare your
case."

Al bowed his head. The man had a point there. If
he weren't here to do good for Al, he wouldn't be here
at all. He could attend his stew.

There was a long space of silence and the gathering
of psychic power. Essentially Mr. Mittance saw his
role as that of helper. He would have liked to put it
simply—a kind of truth-telling interpersonal legal
love-gypsy, only with profound human connections
and a chance to get a fresh start. The trouble with
putting things simply like that is: they are not simple.
He tried to express it with the language of the eyes, as
they do in South Korea, Tahiti, Acapulco, and the
Haight-Ashbury. The moment might have been
sweeter, were it not for a clang of doors and a thud of
truncheon in the adjacent interrogation rooms. Just
next door a couple of weary policemen were huffing
and puffing and punching and kicking and explaining
to prisoners their constitutional rights.

"And now," Al asked encouragingly. He didn't want
to waste his parents' funds.

"And now," said Mr. Mittance, "we must at last
come to consider the trial itself, if trial there be. Because you can be found not guilty simple and pure or
you can be found not guilty by reason of insanity. By
virtue of insanity they call it. It's a bifurcated trial. Oh,
it's really a hearing—they consider all sorts of goodies.
The first issue is guilt or innocence of the act, and
the second has to do not with your actions but with
your state of spirit. That's your insanity. It's an ego

trip. Sometimes I feel that way, too. Do you think you could ever learn to care about others, really care?"

"I'm kind of involved with myself just now," Al explained.

"I know. I know," said the lawyer. "I understand. Girls in Berkeley, girls in San Francisco, and a possible twenty-year term. It cuts a fellow off. I'm sympathetic to the plight of the young. I'm into that little deal, too. I like to blow my mind whenever I can work it into my schedule. But remember: only I, your attorney, stand between you and a long, unhappy sentence. Your California state prisons tend to be non-creative and anti-life. Just get in touch a little, Al."

"I'm trying."

"You're thinking. You're working it out in your mind. You are striving to get your head straight. I realize all that. If I didn't have insight, what kind of an attorney would I be?"

"Tell me more," Al said, "about my chances to avoid nine to fourteen years in prison."

Mr. Mittance sharpened a finger at him. "Naughty, naughty, to be so curious. Oh, shame, Al. You've met Detective Brown. He's on your case and he's a pussycat." He took a noisy sucking breath and thrust his pelvis back into the pelvic socket. Not many lawyers had this freedom about the body which he learned from Esalen, Synanon, one LSD trip under strict supervision of a registered chiropodist, a little structural integration in La Jolla, some sensory awareness and gestalt awakening in the classrooms of Grace Cathedral, Yoga classes from Swami Sidney Cabot at the Berkeley Yacht Club ashram, and the complete series of intermediate and advanced sexual freedom lessons.

He was no hick like this kid might think. He didn't
believe in freedom to rape, for example, but everything
else was okay by him if it's done with a real religious
sense of experiment and wonder. Of course, freedom
to rape is carrying things pretty far libertarianwise,
even if you do want to ask yourself sometimes, Why do
some smart girls have the privilege of just dangling it
there in front of you and then they say No?

Well, let her do it; that's an ego trip. Stanford Mittance remained a moderate in the field of sexual freedom, though he had passed the course with flying
colors. He made distinctions too fine for minds which
were not yet polymorphous perverse, educated by encounter groups for consenting adults only in the Berkeley hills.

However, Stanford Mittance was not just a healthy
person who happened to be a legal love-gypsy; he was
also a member of the Bar. He went on briskly; it was
his job. "In some cases the mental condition of the defendant might negative the required mental element.
That's the general category denoting the mental part
of the crime which indicates a felony. Do you understand me?"

"No," said Al.

"I thought as much. I'd better explain it in further
detail. Without conforming to the M'Naughton rule
about insanity, there is also the Miranda case and other
contemporary precedents. You confessed, didn't you?
But who knows what you were *really* confessing?" His
eyes narrowed and he nodded twice. Only he knew. It
took many kinds of therapy to put together all the
pieces of the puzzle.

"There isn't much doubt," Al said. "I recognize my

plight. My mind wanders, things don't seem real, but I know what I'm doing."

"You say you're in touch?" Mr. Mittance asked.

"That's my opinion. Sometimes not enough, but sometimes more than I seem to be."

Mr. Mittance shrewdly shook his head. "That's your opinion and it's your right to have it," he said. "What a wondrous thing is Man—any other questions?"

"How should I behave at the hearing?"

"If you wear a coat and tie, the sentence is usually lighter."

Al wondered what he would do without a good Berkeley lawyer.

"And another thing." Legal firmness recompressing the corners of Mr. Mittance's eyes. "I know you're a beatnik with principles, Al. But usually the only one in the courtroom with the long haircut is the defendant." And he winked.

"Do you want me to cut it?"

"Not that it's greasy. It's nice and straight. It's clean. It's neat. But I want you to be my cub scout, Al, a veritable, well, poor unhappy upper-middle-class kid from the world of no firm values."

Al had thought he might be guilty of primitive thinking. Either he would get away or he would be caught. Evidently he had been caught. But now punishment seemed further away than ever.

"I might want to stay inside and think awhile," he said.

"Yes, think of the disgrace to your folks who sired you and hired me," said Mr. Mittance. "Think of your work in the world. Think of how horny you'll get in a prison full of psychopaths and pederasts made that

way by the condition of their lives. Oftentimes it's not
a matter of free choice in their cases, Al. They are
twisted that way."

"I'm not sure."

"You're stubborn."

"It's all moving so fast."

Mr. Mittance put his hand on his arm. "Let me slow
it down for you. Let me tell you first of all you can't
trust Professor Howe. I know. I may be your only true
friend through all this."

"What do you mean?"

"I *know*," said the lawyer. "And I'd hate to see you
sent up, your young life blighted, because you're not
thinking good these days. Of course your synapses are
flooded by the excitement. Naturally there's been a
little breakdown here and there. You've gotten to be
arrogant, an individualist, up tight. Poopie and all that
ugly, ugly abuse didn't do you too much good, either.
Oh, ugly. But try to take a good option on reality, Al.
It's all we've got this side of madness."

So many people on Al's side. So all alone with all
these friends. So few enternities in the passing days. Al
wished Mr. Mittance wouldn't pucker his mouth that
way when he made a good point, though it was true, he
did make some good points.

Mr. Mittance stood off and fixed Al's face with his
gaze. He touched Al's bruised neck, just brushing it
with his finger, not hurting him, and made a little face.
He was trying to make interpersonal contact with his
client and trying to make him cooperate nicely and
appreciate what might be done for him. "I need your
help," he said. "Al, I can't carry this burden all by my

lonesome. You might think this so-called Professor Howe will work things out for you—"

"No," said Al.

"But this time he won't. And if I can't either, it's assault in the shower time, Al, it's a lot worse than that convicted felon Paul Cola, it's you hardly get a chance to say, No, I prefer not to swing like that. Those brutes are on you like elephants. Those guards look the other way." He got his eyes focused for gut-level contact and put his face near Al's. Onion in the sandwich within the last two or three hours. "Those are Mister Baddies in there and it's an evil scene for a clean-cut like you. They don't ask if you're a consenting adult. I want you to think it through and don't blow it with me."

"I'm trying to think," Al said.

"Listen to me."

"I'm trying to feel."

"Do what I say, Al, and start drifting a little with the tide and let's see if we can save you from the torment of being a loser, a jetsam, a kid growing old with shame in his heart and a lot of hurt in the parts of his body."

Al was silent.

Mr. Mittance shook his head. "Trouble with you young folks under thirty these days is when do you take things seriously? When, Al?"

"Right now," Al said. "I'm trying."

Mr. Mittance said as if he hadn't heard: "Try."

"Is this the right way? I've gotten off so many ways. My life has been like that."

"Good thinking, good thinking, Al. I'm happy that you're learning to have emotions, even if it interferes with a modified M'Naughton Rule judgment. Just don't let on is all I ask. And always remember," Mr. Mittance was saying, "no matter how blue you sometimes feel, Al, in this stinking hole not worthy of a hippie lad of your fineness and delicacy, as you rot I suppose in this *Les Miserables* of a sewer, no matter how many appeals fail and whatsoever torments of the damned, I'll always be sitting on my sailboat in the springtime sun of the San Francisco Bay, trying to understand you. I'll be there. Let me lay it on the line for you—fifty-two springtimes, but firm. Count on me. An appreciation for youth's foibles which is pure, fine, and extra-judicial."

"Thank you," said Al. He was studying desperation. He was learning fast. Life and other people slip out of reach.

Clang.

The nice guard, Mr. Jones, wearing a star on his blue chest, said, "I believe your time is up, sir."

"I wish to appeal that," said Stanford Mittance. "Caw me Stan."

"Okay, Stan, it's dinner time for the psychologically disturbed and the criminally insane. Everybody's got to go to chow."

"Are you hungry, kid?" the lawyer asked.

Al nodded. Tonight there was bread pudding. He had seen them crumbling the bread and fumbling the raisins.

"Then I'll depart." He shot a look at Al which said: No manly clasping before this facetious blue-clad linear-thinking minion. We'll expand our fraternal awareness some other time.

Clang.

Farewell to legal counsel for now. Oh, he was right, he was right about the ego trip. Al's zapped mind lay curled up someplace inside. He would have asked Mr. Jones to wake him from the dream, but that would be taking a chance on the dream into which he might be awakened.

19 Smiling and neat, as if he were making rounds, a minister or a salesman, Jarod returned. The cop who ushered him in wore respect in the sirloin grain of his face. Dr. Howe was a citizen, a person, and a non-felon. "Hello, friend, you may wonder why I'm here," he said.

Now he's a pitchman, Al thought. *Hi, friends out there in used-car land, it's Dodgerama time again—*

"You may wonder why I don't need to smile, shuffle, and carry an old oilskin shopping bag. Well, don't need to yell either, citizen—"

A permanent carburetor? battery additive? tune-up for the soul and spirit? What's he selling this time?

"Jarod, please, what's the joke?"

"—but I mutter jes' a little cause Ah loves it."

Down into the watermelon patch.

"I don't mind," Al said. "You've got something going against me. But I wish you wouldn't."

"How's Poopie? How's Milly?"

"Just fine."

"—Ellen and my kids?" Jarod smiled sweetly. "I came to talk a little. I see they put us here in a nice visiting room. Hey, you with the monitor, you hear me? Should I speak up? He paused, winked at the wall, pouted, waited for the non-answer from the planted transistors, and turned back to Al. "You got an A for the seminar, although normally we expect a paper to sum up the field work. However, your data will be tabulated—"

"Shut up," Al whispered. Silence. Jarod shrugged indifferently. He decided to make a new start.

"First me," he said, "then nobody. And then all the rest. But I really like you, Al, that's why I talk this way." He peered at Al and shook his head. "Heard about that gullet of yours. Al, that is one award-winning abrasion."

"Okay. I wish I knew what you had in mind."

"I have something in mind."

"I know."

"What is it?" Jarod was delighted. He grinned.

"I don't know."

"It's up to me, isn't it?"

"I've been waiting."

"Stop waiting," Jarod said. "Isn't it time for you to speak up?"

"Think of all the poets who died in prison," Al said. "If I were a poet. For politics. So maybe I can do some prison, even if it can't be clear-cut politics and I didn't burn my draft card. It was my sinus. It's politics, too, in a way."

Jarod smiled. "Your way, boy."

"I wanted to do something for myself."

"Those poets had causes."

"So do I."

"A poor cause. Yourself."

"That's all there is until I find a better one." He thought of losing Milly, but that's not a cause. He thought of losing Sue, but that was the sacrifice of a prize he had never earned. Something must be real, there must be something to be remembered in history, something must feel like loss.

Jarod puzzled over him, squeezing his eyes so that red and purple and whitish lines appeared. "You're not taking this seriously. That's what the shrink means about lack of affect. Is it what you're thinking? You playing games with me?"

Al shrugged and turned his hands out. "No more'n you playing games with me, Jarod."

"Um. I see. You're going to miss things." He knew how to make Al listen. "Take Ellen. You'll miss all the chances. Love, and then it's over and nothing can be saved. She hates or you hate. Or nobody hates, and you've got nothing at all. No feelings, it seems. So you start again—this time for real and another little lady and not there either, of course. Heartbreak, pal. I'm forty."

"You're young to be so tired."

"I'm forty-two."

"When a girl puts her arms around you, how old are you?"

"It means she'll take them away later. Cramps. She'll

want to or you'll want her to. And so." Al was horrified by his face. There were mummy crinklings. The air would strike him in this gray tomb and he would shrivel to nothing. "Don't feel sorry for me. Here you are and here I am. These are selfish tears." But there were no tears. "If what I've been going through is the crisis of turning forty, then the human race is composed of heroes, all those who survive to be forty-one."

"That's the famous Tony Curtis comeback, due to vitamin pills, exercise, health—"

"And the sweet breath of young girls—classic. You can't beat tradition, the distance time gives to suffering. When a girl puts her arms around you." He grinned. "I have simple needs, pal—to be surrounded by a few people who will soon hate me." He pushed out his legs in the chair with comfortable fatigue after this display, yawning as if ready to doze after an afternoon's ramble along the bay with a dog at his side. Al thought: Like a comfortable animal. Al thought: He has perfect discharge of emotion. No animal is that comfortable. He's a sieve.

But why is this sieve making it all his problem? I'm in jail, and we're both thinking about him. That's what a leader does. The people get in trouble, and they worry about the leader in his palace.

Jarod said, "I'd like to be a lover—of white people, of these California hills and deserts, of the sea, of America, of my students and colleagues, of my work and living out my time. Instead I just like taking care of myself and a few Miss Twenty-twos. Which is a part of taking care of myself, man."

"You tell me this—"

"Because I'm trying to take care of you. You're a

smart one, honky. Ah don't like that word. You're a smart one, pal."

Al raised his hand like a boy asking permission. "Then maybe," he said, ignoring the new accent, "maybe you should take care of me, if you're my guide and mentor."

"Um. Okay. I know you might not get off, so I'll tell you a little about prison life. If you're sent to jail, practice self-pleasure. Masturbate a lot. Refuse to be buggered if you can. It leads to future difficulties. But don't fear jacking off. You can make it very refined and amusing. You won't be able to curve your back as much as you'd like to. You'll find new resources. But think about women and you'll be okay when you come out."

"Well, thanks for coming," Al said.

"Loneliness won't leave you alone."

"I think you'd better go now."

"Been nice talkin' to you," said Jarod.

"Playtime," said Al.

"Conversation City," said Jarod. "It's your friendly Tupperware salesman, here for the installment."

"I have no idea what you're up to," Al said. "It's all under the shit."

Jarod smiled. "Thank you."

"Well, goodbye."

Nothing done. They had spoken of important matters and nothing had been said. There was a vision of another way, a life of truth-telling and gentleness, and they did not believe in it, and yet the vision of it troubled them both.

"Wait!" Al said.

Jarod turned to look at him. He was carrying a tattered manila envelope instead of his briefcase. It was like the confession of some deep disarray in the trivial disarray of his habits. "I'm waiting."

"Don't you have any more?"

"Well, maybe," Jarod said.

"Why don't you tell me? You said you wanted to help me. I need help now. I'm desperate, I'm in trouble, I need help."

He wanted Jarod to tell him the truth, any truth, so long as he meant it. Maybe only that we are all terminal cases. No matter what we build and consume, the end is near. Despite California living and vitamin pills and heart transplants, anyone now alive is heading in just one direction.

He believed Jarod knew the truth. Something more.

He wanted Jarod to speak.

"Remember," Jarod asked, "remember how I said I'd try to get you off? Remember about my friends, my federal judge, those owe-me and word-on-downers?"

"I remember what you said."

"Well," Jarod grinned, "well, well, the news is peculiar. They don't trust me. They don't want to do for me. So I guess maybe you're on your own."

Al shrugged. Relief.

"Almost. I got a few trickerations left, though. Hey, brother, don't give up on me, y'hear?"

"Fine. I appreciate that."

"All right," said Jarod at the door, ringing the buzzer that would get him let out. The buzzer was stained like a beetle's mottled back. "You jumped my wife, you wanted to jump me, didn't you? Was it because I'm a nigger, honky? or your teacher? or your old man?"

Al began to laugh. It felt hilarious. He was floating on grass. Jarod was too smart to be so stupid. He had something in mind, but Al would no longer play with him. He was making Ellen a silly tool, like Al, himself, like everything. He was the enemy. No, he was nothing. Al believed he was laughing, but then he listened and he was not laughing. A deep and impenetrable silence between them.

The guard, Mr. Jones, was there. He opened the door. He stood respectfully waiting for the important black man to move.

"Let me go my own way," Al said.

"No. No you don't. Man, in this world, it's science, not romance."

"From now on stay out of my way," Al said.

"Man, I won't let you," Jarod said. The guard moved toward them, puzzled by what it seemed he might have to do—protect this innocent black professor from attack by a crazed probably dope fiend killer bank-robber kid. Jarod put up his hand. He could take care of it. Mr. Jones shouldn't worry, so he took a step back to do his worrying. Jarod said to Al: "I'm not going to let you hide in jail, Al. Drop on out like the rest of us and face the music. It may not be soul music. You might have to face Lawrence Welk."

"I mean it. I don't want you anymore."

"I might could not be able to do anything."

"That's fine. That's what I want."

"I'm going to try."

"Jarod, if you'll just leave me one bit of friendship for you, you'll stay out of this."

"I don't mind if you kill me, boy. I'm going to shake you loose from this particular dream if I can."

"You can't."

Jarod shrugged. "The new governor doesn't listen to me."

"You can't."

"The people in Washington, they're new, they don't like me. They think I'm shiftless."

"You can't."

Jarod was grinning and waiting for something more. Call him nigger. Call him cuckold. Call him fool.

"Get out," Al said. "You're no friend or teacher of mine. I don't know you."

"You've given me what I needed. Thank you," Jarod said.

The door clanged shut. In a moment Mr. Jones would reappear to take Al back to his cell. Al pressed the mottled beetle's back in case he forgot. They weren't very careful about escapes in this county jail.

20 During the next few months Al was in a kind of nervous state, sort of jumpy. His mother pointed out to his father and his father pointed out to the court-appointed psychiatrist: It's only natural that our boy Al be a little nervous, you know, not crazy, just jumpy, just not guilty by virtue of insanity, since he was betrayed by his close friend Milly and she was small comfort to him because she was engaged to this untrained musician, Mr. Cola, her fiancé at the time, and those bills were so new and clean and consecutively numbered and growing up is such a problem, a true dilemma, growing up mature, anyway.

Even his lawyer anxiously instructed Al about preparing for the future. The criminal case did not make him a criminal for others, it seemed; it made him interesting. Because he was a college boy from Santa Barbara, the city and county toyed with his crime as he did, ambiguously tolerated him, hated to take him seriously. If he had evaded the draft or refused to go to Viet Nam, maybe they'd have grown irritable. But robbing a bank? Well, he'd only done it once. In a world devoted to ideas these things matter less than they used to.

A letter had come for Al at home and his lawyer handed it over.

> *Needle Park*
> *Ur-Frisco*
> *4 Aquarius 4*

You still thinking about thinking about someone else, Harry Krishna? Me too. I caught it from you.

> Your sickning but friendly,
> Cody.

Somehow, although he did not recall her using the word, he had always known she would pronounce and spell it "sickning."

"Who's that from?" Mr. Mittance asked.

"I don't know her," Al said.

Mr. Mittance made a face. He rubbed the crick in his neck from reading the letter around Al's fists. "I'm only trying to help any way I can," he said, "but I guess I caught you there. Some girl, I'll bet."

"Doesn't matter," Al said.

Mr. Mittance continued his face in the dimension of time, stretching the look of Okay I Won't Touch. "I didn't say it did. Try to think of me as just your lawyer, priest, and spiritual advisor and we'll all be a lot happier, Al."

Al made the effort.

"Nothing to tell?"

Al shook his head. Mr. Mittance swallowed, trying to overcome spiritual advisor's chagrin. "I have some other questions," he said.

Somehow Al had to come part way through his isolation. He was using it to get an edge on things. It was making him high, like methedrine; it helped him float, like grass. Well, he had to move someplace, think things through, and if that didn't help, act things through. But that's what leads nice kids from good families to bank-robbing if they don't like what drugs do to their heads.

Robbing a bank was only a gesture, it seemed, like so many other bits of gesture or luck. It didn't change him all by itself. It didn't even define him anew as criminal.

Well, let it work in him awhile.

Jarod had said: "A chance to do some great field work in the cultural anthropology of prisons. There's a good group of Muslims and Panthers. They got an old friend of mine in here."

"They keep me pretty much in isolation. I walk in the yard."

"They're protecting you from harm. Well, fewer clues, but pick up on the ones there are."

The clues here were: clangs, noises, shouts, smells, and sorting out his anxieties. His body getting refined down by jail food and not eating and sore dreams— sheriff's macrobiotic. And now that he expected letters from Sue, he didn't get any more. And didn't care, either. And the loneliness that did not leave him alone.

Poopie, on the other hand, carried his head high in a rare mood of contentment. "Does like I say, that girl," he informed his friends at the Minimum Daily Requirement, proud of his lady Milly, though he did splinter her guitar and beat her up a bit after she confessed that she had been weak in the flesh with Al. Poopie was afflicted with an outmoded moral code. He tended to forget that he had been away from Milly for a whole weekend.

Also.

Also there were lots of other complications. Dr. Bessie Frisch, who had his own problems, fiddled with the hearing aid attached to his horn-rimmed glasses while he listened to everybody. The hearing aid led both to his ears and to a miniature transistor tape recorder built into the Phi Beta Kappa key dangling from a chain interlocked with his vest buttons. Dr. Bessie Frisch had been teased so much about his first name as a child—he was named after his mother's favorite sister, and had worn bangs until he was fourteen—that he was given his choice by fate at the age of twenty: Become a psychiatrist or remain nervous, jumpy. Well, it was sensible to give a look to psychiatry. He gave it a look. He took it up.

Now, handling other people's problems in the mental health field, he oftentimes became nervous, jumpy. Also he suffered from swollen glands under the arms. But he was shrewd. Shrewdly he asked Al, "Do you think you developed a criminal mentality out of protest, hm? against the name Al?"

"Hm?" Al asked cagily.

"It's short for Alice, I presume, hm?" asked Dr. B. Frisch. (He was called "Bea" by his close friends, who sought to avoid embarrassment whenever they could.)

It turned out that Al was short for Allan. Dr. Bea Frisch tried another approach to this curious problem in psychopathy. He interviewed Milly, Poopie, the police officers, including the talkative one who went to extension courses, and the bony little lady who had been teller in the bank. Recently she had left that job to work at the notions counter of a Woolworth's. She reported on Al's behavior when he had been robbing the bank: "He looked like a fine young man, well brought up, intelligent, kind, and considerate. Only he seemed a trifle nervous, jumpy. I would say temporary insanity, Doc."

"Hm," said Bessie, arms akimbo.

"No, let me express it one more time," said the lady. "Temporary insanity. That's what I would say."

The bony little ex-teller wore a heavy tan. She had just returned from an all-expenses-paid trip to Acapulco. She ascribed her error in first defining the bank robber to the police as a dark-skinned colored Negro person, a spook, to the fact that it was Tuesday and she was wearing her brown contacts. Now she only wore her green contacts and any bandits at the Woolworth's notions counter would be juvenile delinquents from Mars.

The wheels of justice ground away against the evidence. No power on earth could stop the march of American social work. With the exception of Paul Cola, most thoughtful citizens seemed to agree that it would be a shame for such a fine young man, adventurous, far-sighted, ambitious, and nervous, to be locked away among criminals, rapists, bank robbers, anti-social types tending to exert a bad influence on an innocent young psychopath.

Poopie, on the other hand, argued for the gas chamber. He had always found strong punishment a deterrent to crime. He had friends in the Minutemen who advised him on sociological matters. When asked if he was a member himself, he put forth an objection. "I ain't gonna tell you," he said. "But we got our stash someplace—and it ain't grass, which would be illegal, bein' a hallucinatin' drug and all. Guns are for sport and killin' the foreign subversives."

Most people around the San Francisco Bay came to have opinions in the case. Information was generous, passionate, analytic, and concerned. The San Francisco *Chronicle* did its duty by its critical readership. A reporter who specialized in hippies, drugs, topless dancers, and school riots—the education beat—did a first-person interview with Al Dooley. How did you get that way, Al? What troubled you as a youth, Al? Do you feel you have struck a blow for something, Al? He had to figure out the answers to his questions him-

self, since the authorities wouldn't actually let him in
to see Al. The San Francisco *Examiner* went out to
talk with the concerned relatives, teachers, and con-
gressman of the twisted mind, and then rewrote the
Chronicle's interview. The Oakland *Tribune* covered
the story as news, but finally responded more emotionally with an editorial urging the closing of the
university if this was the kind of product it turned out.
Al's nihilistic over-intellectual rationalizations, as
quoted in the *Chronicle* interview, indicated an over-
intellectual and nihilistic individual, probably involved in the conspiracy to tear down the very fabric
of American civilization.

The radical underground press rallied about the
cause and set up a fund for The Berkeley One, as they
named Al. He had struck a revolutionary blow against
the money economy. Under the headline PIGS THWART
THOUGHTS, they informed the public that a copy of
Chairman Mao's little red book, addressed to Al
Dooley, had been stopped at the front office of the
jail. A Bible, however, had been let through, and this
proved once and for all that Church and State are not
separated in the military-industrial complex. The hippie underground press published anguished reports
about the inhuman deprivation of drugs and sex in jail.
That was how they treat martyrs in this country—no
grass. Without grass to counteract that greasy jail food,
Al was sure to get cancer. They also rewrote the
Chronicle's interview with Al the Bank Freak.

Al Dooley was coming to be celebrated. There was
anger, there was pity, and there was puzzlement. A
public nerve vibrated with the contemplation of this
taciturn young man who must have suffered a great

deal. He had pale eyes, poor posture, and metaphysical angst. He gave the media something to do other than wars, sports, and disasters. The Question Man stopped six people and asked them, Would you rob a bank? and they all said, in their various individual fashions, No, not necessarily. The *Chronicle*'s interview was so successful that the reporter who wrote it did another while on his vacation in Acapulco. This one was highly sympathetic to Al Dooley. The reporter composed some fine lines about the puzzle of life, early toilet training and late weaning, the Spock generation. From Acapulco he asked the Al Dooley in his head, "Would you do it again?" And imaginary Al Dooley answered, "No, it was the wrong way to approach my problems, I know that now."

The reporter happened to show the article to Al's dad before he gave it to the newspaper and Al's father said it was so well-written it made him want to cry. This made the reporter want to cry, too, because he hadn't taken a girl with him to Acapulco.

When the investigation was completed, it was time for a legal hearing. Mr. Jones, the non-civil-service guard who liked to talk to Al about his children and the school problem, led him into court. Judge Harlow, robes flapping, pounded for silence. Particularly his sleeves flew. All interested parties were questioned. Al explained how he had really meant to go on a freedom ride or join the Peace Corps, but he just hadn't thought of it in time. He had wanted to do something exceptional. No one had invited him to be an astronaut. He would have liked to explore inner and outer space. That was what was in his heart. No one had shown him how to float a new electronics stock. He would

have liked to abscond to Brazil. Later on he would
have returned home to face the music. That's the kind
of embezzler he would have been. Colonel Glenn had
written his memoirs for *Life*. This kind of irritated Al.
He had wanted to break out of his routine. He, too,
could be an exceptional man. He had wanted to get
rich quick, plus famous and distinguished. The judge
interrupted: "That's enough out of you, Accused!"

His defending lawyer, Stanford Mittance, leapt to
his feet in protest: "Your Honor! In this modern world
of today! The misunderstood youth of a troubled urban culture!"

"Objection sustained," said the judge.

Milly Peck, wearing a black veil, lifted the lace
with one finger in order to shoot Al an apologetic,
heavily shadowed look. The spiritual projectile of sadness shot all the way across the courtroom to where Al
waited in the witness chair while his lawyer engaged
the judge in a duel of wits. Milly was in mourning for
her swollen features which were distorted by grief
and being beaten up. Her look said to Al: I hope you'll
always care for me in the future as you did the month
before yestermonth. Poopie forced me.

"Objection!" shouted Al's lawyer in response to a
fine point of jurisprudence.

"I already said sustained!" cried the judge.

At last Al's lawyer was satisfied. He could not de-
mand an abject apology from the presiding judge. He
had received simple justice and that would have to
suffice for the moment. He pinched the bridge of his
nose where it had been pinched by his gold pince-nez
glasses. "Step down," he said kindly to Al, and offered

him an arm. He whispered, "Wasn't that sweet of the judge to sustain my objection?"

Milly kept on shooting look after look at Al as he walked unaided to his chair. Al's trouble had matured Milly. She was grateful to him. Poopie had discovered the undiscovered depths in her, thanks to Al. She didn't really care so much about the guitar. When Al settled himself in his oaken courtroom chair, she lowered her veil and the looks of apology subsided. Also Poopie's ire was being stimulated. He sure did make demands on a girl.

However, Poopie remained in good humor. He enjoyed getting on the side of law and order when the opportunity presented itself. He was still smiling, with just a little bit of ire, when Al's lawyer called him to the witness stand. Poopie declared: "I just asked her and she tole me. Does like I say, that chick." Then he had a surprise deposition to make. "But seems to li'l ole me like Al never intended for to make a bank heist. He was driven out of his skull, you know, he flipped . . ." He caught Al's father's eye. "Your Honor, I would say he was nervous and jumpy because he didn't feel so good."

Poopie also had a nice tan.

Then Milly mounted the stand as a character witness. "I was mean to him, like for instance, I did everything he told me to, Your Honor. A man needs some resistance, some challenge to his manliness in this our culture of modern rootlessness. Did I forget anything? I feel so nervous and jumpy up here on the courtroom stand."

And Al's parents also were invited to speak at con-

siderable length. It turned out that Al had always
been foursquare behind the American Constitution
and carefully selected numbers from the Top Ten Bill
of Rights, in favor of firmness in Asia, tempered by
mercy, and spent many a fretful hour with accompany-
ing sinus attacks at the thought that the Communists
might someday succeed in their design to take over
the Sovereign State of California and use it as a base of
operations against Arizona and Nevada. His worries
about the role of youth in the future of America made
him kind of—

"I know," said the severe but kindly judge. "All of
us here in these chambers believe in tempering justice
with a bit of largesse, do we not? don't we? But I'll
make the decisions around here. So much talk makes
me jumpy," he declared, looking about him nervously.
It was a legal hearing, not a trial, but still a fellow
can't be too careful. He toyed with a small set of copper
cuff links which he had just brought back from his recent vacation in Acapulco.

Dr. Bessie Frisch tamped out his pipe and summa-
rized his report. "Good, good," he said to the judge.
"As it emerged in my examination, the name 'Al,' for
this particular patient, awakens nightmares of feminine
disturbance in his childish oedipal frustrations. Now
if we take the name seriously, 'Alice,' say, or 'Alberta'
. . . Somewhat jumpy, even nervous," he concluded.

Al wished his parents hadn't said that about Asia. It
did not fairly represent his convictions. But the point
was simple when you come to think of it. They wanted
to get him off and he wanted to get on with it. They
always told him to get along with people and the old
boy had a point there. He was confused about where

and what to get on with. He had sickened in the world with a little help from his friends. In prison he might have other kinds of help he didn't want. Prison isn't supposed to be the good life, either. The old boy had a point there, too.

His father was winking at him across the courtroom. His mother was snuffling a little, and reaching for the Kleenex in her purse, and hoping that maybe he would come into the travel agency business in Santa Barbara when all this silly business got cleared up. You can recommend a stay in Acapulco to people without fearing they will regret it or catch intestinal infestations, the so-called Montezuma's Revenge, contrary to what some people think. She'd never even heard of the Aztec Two-Step. Those were filthy rumors spread by the rival agency, which sold Royal Hawaii. Little did people know the danger they ran eating all that poi; sometimes the trouble doesn't show up for thirty years. Al would be really wonderful at handling group arrangements if he'd only come into the business—always good with people.

And now it was Dr. Jarod Howe's turn on the stand. Al's mother couldn't take her eyes off him, but Mr. Dooley studied the flags at the judge's right and left hands, California and the U.S.A., and then his nails, and then the flags again.

Jarod testified that Al was a serious, imaginative young man who did his work carefully and tried to draw the logical consequences of his studies. He blamed himself for Al's troubles: for urging Al to take things seriously. He was a normal man, Jarod said, in an abnormal world. (This did not sit well with the judge. Fortunately it came from a black man and he

couldn't blame Al.) "I misled him," said Jarod, and
that sat better with the peers. "I made him want
things the way we minority peoples do, crazy things,
immoral things. *Mea culpa.* I think it was my fault."
He evoked the four golden autumns of college and
draft evasion, and when they are finished and the de-
ferment is made permanent, then what? After the four
acrid, leaf-burning seasons with the books and the
girls, the smoke, the coffee, and the talk—then what?
No military service at all, and four more years of graduate study, or maybe five. "Take the Haight," Dr.
Howe said, "take Telegraph Avenue, take the East
Village. They're America's first teen-age slums. We
have to find something else for our youth to do."

Fortunately, as he spoke, there was a tiny little race
riot going on across the bay. The National Guard and
the police were busy. Not all the young people were
hippies and beatniks. Fortunately for Al, Oakland
blacks were carting television sets (color ones) out of
the fifty-pay shops, to replace the black-and-white
sets from the riots of two years ago. The new color
jobs hadn't been in yet. Fortunately perspectives were
changing all over America, and also in the halls of
justice. That boy was not much more of a criminal than
anyone else, it seemed. After Viet Nam, another new
way might have to be found.

Judge Harlow listened to all this with a knot of rage
gathering in his heart. The courtroom was hot and
stuffy and he wore nothing but shorts under his judicial robes and kept an electric fan blowing between his
legs, blowing like blind justice, first on one side and
then on the other, but nevertheless he felt nervous and
distracted by so many people getting away with so

many errors (loose talk, bombastic assertions, crimes against nature and society). What right had this nice boy to be such a bad boy? What right had the irrational and rational to triumph against the irrelevant? And he knew the doctor was right, he had to cut down on the cholesterol, it was doing things to his thought transferences. Arteriosclerosis would be a problem for a clerk, a lawyer, or even a defendant (the one with the long hair), but—and Judge Harlow smiled sneakily —thank God it doesn't affect justice. Those little globs of spongy sticky fat in his arteries made the blood do a little turnaround, a little double reverse twist, spinning dizzily into his heart, but it didn't interfere with the march of truth unto the gas chamber. Well, capital punishment isn't so bad any more, either. They give the star of the show a bit of tranquilizer to prevent his dragging his feet and scratching and screaming. They just usually went mild and philosophical down the long, long trail, and stoned out of their nuts. Judge Harlow believed in mercy, too. And progress. And revenge against the wicked. He was saying: "People like you ruin nations, epochs, the best of families!"

Oh dear, the voice of morality. That usually means no probation and lots of road repair or, in the South, the picking of the sheriff's peaches.

"People like you are no good to the world, no good to yourselves!"

A stab of insight or how did he know?

"You remind us that it's all there for the taking— fun, kicks, freedom, power—but lemme tell you something, boy: it isn't. It isn't! is the answer, just in case you're asking any questions. And yet you have idealism, it is not all quenched, you remind me of myself

when I was young once and human. Poor lad, if only
you can be saved. Will it help to be abused by the
perverts and criminals who sometimes work their way
into the otherwise outstanding prison system of the
state of California? If only there could be a junior
prison system, like there's a junior college system. For
unconfirmed intellectuals they got the junior college
system, and what do they have for unconfirmed criminals? Nada. Reformatories is another kettle of fish.
Youth Detention, but don't contradict me, I warn
you."

On occasion Al was learning to have good sense. He
neither contradicted nor interrupted. Judge Harlow
continued soothingly.

"I respect you equally with Detective Brown. I respect him, too. I respect the stool pigeon folks who give
us law enforcement personnel in the judicial division
such helpful advice. I have respect for *people*—that's
fundamental. I intend to recommend Detective Brown
to higher office for Devotion to Duty. Devotion is a
must in our chosen field of endeavor. Many's the time
Detective Brown has been selected for a disagreeable
task. It's not all just patriotic stuff, riding a motorcycle,
escorting visiting dignitaries, putting down student
riots, you know. Sometimes you go to wait quietly in
the interrogation chambers, too. It don't make no
never-mind if you get varicose veins from just standing
there. Your own innermost feelings don't matter, how
you feel about violence on people. You're just doing
your job. You got to treat our criminal class with
the only kind of treatment they understand—firmness
within the limits of what the law allows, nothing showing on the x-rays. Incidentally, it's been proven you

get just as clear an x-ray from the inner city as you get from, oh, a kid with a good stable home. Harken to my words, boy, but don't let your mind wander. You look all shook up. That way lies anarchy. You don't have any call to be such. Obey! You think you have the right to make up your own mind, but look at the ants and worms crushed by the bodies of lovers in the park! Look at the birds made into a really sad goo by the propellers of prop-jets."

Al looked.

"Not there, fella, here." The judge was frowning and stern. "Try to pay me the attention I deserve."

Al said nothing.

The judge winked and kicked a leg of his chair, narrowly missing the fan. It was a way he had of kicking it, like a habit, irritably. "Don't interrupt, defendant, especially to disagree with me in your heart of hearts." The court reporter was beaming and writing. He was so happy the judge had these gestures which gave him the time to catch up. But the judge was a little cross, because he couldn't really kick the chair without hurting something, his toes, his fan, the feelings of the bailiff or the defendant.

He proceeded with the examination. "That witness of yours stuck his nose in the air and he's a—just a—a big, um, *professor*. I'm not saying he's not as sensitive to x-rays as your next person. Don't misunderstand me, son. And that girl let you do those fun things to her and she dresses so nice and neat. And you look like a good old boy and you robbed a bank, didn't you? Well, this sort of destruction of our basic values has got to cease in this country."

Some of the crowd in the courtroom came to their

feet (scattered applause), but he shushed them with
an upraised hand. He was a Mendocino circuit judge.
He was a North Beach Marconi & Columbus Society
nominee. He was a man of feeling. "Do you repent?"
he cried.

"What do you think, Judge?" Al asked.

"Don't interrupt, especially to agree, Al."

Al kept his peace.

Judge Harlow waited approvingly. Ten, nine, eight,
seven . . .

"I think you repent," he said.

"I do, I do."

"That's so nice. Thanks to God. Oh, praises be! Our
Lord is a highly talented, emotionally unbalanced individual Himself. He makes mistakes, too; long hair
and a beard. Threw the first stone. Set that lad free,"
he cried to the bailiffs, "and give him compensation."
Six, five, four, three . . . "I was only kidding, boy. No,
keep that guard on him." He leaned forward and examined Al's face. "I just wanted to see if you would
take advantage of me. Start to run and make your
getaway. You didn't move much, I'll take that into
consideration."

He stopped talking. It was as if the rattle of wings
had ceased. Al knew he was insane, but he knew he
knew, and this made him wonder if maybe he was just
overtired. Oh dear, that's judgely thinking. He's done
it to me.

"Quiet in the court!" someone cried. The judge was
that someone. "Quiet down, fellas, I asked you in a
nice way."

The judge said ptooey into his fingertips. *Ptui!* He
rubbed his hands.

He said: "Okay, kiddo, I'll tell you what I'm gonna do. You committed this here crime while our country needed you not to do it. So I can't let you off. But on the other hand, you're not one of our average numb-skull neurotic kids with those student riots, non-negotiable Negro demands—I'm not implying anything against our black citizens and voters, of course, their kind of radicalism and no firm values. On the contrary, it's a tragic thing which occurred to you, sick and pathetic. I'll have to be good to you, because you're crazy, see? Ill in the head which is turned around funnyways because of God knows what self-abuse at a tender age. Psychiatric. Not necessarily an attack on our basic institutions, just a little bank snatch. Would you promise to be good henceforward, Al?"

"What?" Al asked.

"Just for supposing's sake, supposing I let you off —promise? promise to be good?"

Al saw his father and mother nodding and smiling. Mr. Mittance, his lawyer, was triumphantly but modestly examining his cuticle. Dr. Bessie Frisch was conducting a little in the air with his pencil.

"Send me up!" Al cried. "Oh, God, I don't want it! I don't want your favors! I don't want your rotten time!" He got up and ran to the swinging aperture which led from the abstract legal terrain of justice to the humane arena where the spectators were spectating. He saw Jarod grinning and nodding as if he had done just right, he had done good. "Let me out!" he yelled. Of course, by this time a guard had him secure —blue arms, a badge cutting him in sudden embrace, cutting his heart like a cookie into the shape of a silver star. Another guard with another cookie cutter gleam-

ing on his chest watched to see if he had any concealed weapons, razors, suicide pills. "Let me out!
Take me back!"

Imperiously the judge lifted his arm. "Wait," he
cried. "This is very inneresting! Don't think I won't
take this into consideration, accused."

"Take me back to my cell!" Al pleaded.

The judge called in a deep and commanding voice,
"Listen, buster, when anybody leaves this court first,
it's me. It's got to be that way. It's a must. But don't
think I'm blind to what has just occurred."

And as if blown by the electric fan, he picked up his
robes about him and dashed into his chambers. He was
wearing a detachable snap-on bow tie. It fell and lay
like a small bird on the scratched, polished, re-
scratched, re-polished floors.

Jarod was bobbing and smiling at Al. There was the
blotched reflection of the flag of the state of California
on his shiny forehead. He turned—the flag of the U.S.
of A. on his forehead.

Al sought to awake into the world and make good
contact with his trial. Surely it hadn't all happened in
his macrobiotic head. He should have listened more
closely. But the hearing was over and Mr. Jones led
him back.

21 Al returned to his cell that afternoon to await consultations, deliberations, and verdict. It wasn't like a trial. Things had to be taken into account. Justice must be blind, but nice about it; a bandage about her eyes, giving the weights to this criminal and the scales to that.

The habit of not talking with the man in the next cell had been fit into the pattern like all jail habits. Not making contact is an action which requires no action. A simple style of incarceration frees the moral imagination—this seemed to be the theory—and stimulates the proper regrets. Alone—leave them alone. Now Al would have liked to change the pattern, but the other prisoner did it for him. Al was just resting after the social rigors of his hearing. It had been a busy day for a closed-in fellow accustomed to four walls and his own thoughts. He lay on his bunk with his knees drawn up and his eyes deciphering the message of the ceiling.

In the next cell there was a sudden yelling at dinner time, a lot of yelling from the spade cat, normally a silent Panther, who was recovering from resisting arrest. The doctor had come in and said, "No, there won't be any scars. Yeah, he'll heal over okay," and so they had taken away his dime and weren't letting him call and they were waiting for him to heal over okay before his actual trial. The Panther wasn't a kid. He used to be Wilbur X, but now he had shifted over, religion was too slow at bringing the millennium, and he was a squad leader for self-defense of the Black Panther Party, and he had just discovered the strangest thing about himself. And so he was yelling. If it had been just himself who was hurt, he would have cooled it, kept it quiet, but it involved others—five children for openers.

The guard, Mr. Jones, who brought him the usual greasy dinner, tasting of tray, used to tell him about those kids. "Number one boy, I really love him . . . That girl eleven of mine, she sits in my lap and I really love her . . . My baby, he was the baby for two years, he's only nine, I really get a kick out of him but he's sort of, well, retarded. You know, the bag of water broke. Fever. Things went wrong. She didn't give birth for a whole day afterward—dumb docs. Then there's the second girl, she might be the smart one, make it up to college, y'know. Then there's . . ."

And then the talkative friendly guard, Mr. Jones, felt a stabbing pain in his arm, in his shoulder—it was killing him—and he fell nearly dead. And the former Wilbur X in his solitude discovered this thing about himself, that he didn't want the nice white guard with one defective white child to die, and so he yelled. The black bastard recovering from his resisting arrest yelled and yelled. Yelled. They could hear him fine out in front. Ha, it really gets to him. The solitary was doing him some good, or the broken ribs were itching, or something normal like that. Black Panthers, shit. Muslims, shit. They heard him yelling up at Control Central or whatever they call it and they drew on their cigarettes and sagged in their chairs and fingered their sidearms and looked, as best they could, with the help of black cop boots, like stringy healthy Western cowboys. Only they were fat cops with thighs stretching the seams.

The nice guard with the four normals, one defective, had too much cholesterol in him and too much anxiety about raising a kid on this funny non-civil-service job. He had taken the exam for a better one. Another twist to the arteries. It was the same job, but it paid, there were benefits. And he had been eating and worrying and his plumbing collected these bits of clinging creamy fluff. Arteries deep inside, running the show.

The nigger was yelling and screaming. And discovering. He didn't want the guard to die with his chin in the remains of the mush—corn mush spilling onto gray jailtime floor . . .

Yelling. Yelling.

Finally they came to slam him (no scars) and shut him up (no marks) and all he wanted to say was, "Mister Charlie there got heart-heart-heart-attacked."

Or a stroke or a clot or a damn lightning down from non-civil-service heaven. They dragged Mr. Jones into the guardroom, where he could die like a man and a guard, but he was already dead. Nevertheless, the ambulance came, and before it pulled up, they ran across the alley for the doctor who had examined the former Wilbur X. He just took one look at the guard and wagged his head, "Unh-unh." He was no coroner. This was coroner's work, but he should have been called sooner, why didn't they?

Well. Well now. Well, now the yelling came from the nigger back there, he remembered the one—

Oh yeah. Well, they're shifty, they're untrustworthy, and sometimes they yell a lot when you least expect it.

They didn't slam the former Wilbur X for this deed, but they were irked. Because if he had been a white man, say, they'd have ambled over a little sooner, buckling their belts, thumbs easy, and that poor guard—wife, five kids—might have been saved. A veteran of World War II, a Democrat, a Catholic, and a Cholesterol.

The whole experience made the former Wilbur X nervous. Mother-fuckers—but, from his Muslim days, he really didn't prefer that language too much. Then, in the middle of the night (he kept on stirring, the light always bothered him, bare bulbs and no old jockey shorts to put over the bulb), he found himself smiling. In that way of jails, he knew about Al Dooley, the smart ass bank-robber, next door. The blood could hear Al shuffling around, wide awake. Well, if they both stuck out their hands, his hand could see Al's hand. Al's hand could see his hand. Al had liked that guard, too. Talked a little, kidded, told him about his family.

So, sleepless, nightmarey, spooked, Al swung over on a vine, like Tarzan, and spotted the smile on the former Wilbur X's lips before he could wipe it off. Big fat smiley lips with thin, drawn activist lines of cat seeking his way in the jungle. They would soon speak the same language, wouldn't they?

Lord Greystoke?

Tarzan?

Cheetah?

Al Dooley?

Oh, he had a contact prison high from seeing so clearly the truth-telling black nameless yelling liar in the next cell, picked up on a loitering and resisting. Maybe ex-Wilbur X knew more about it. Jarod sure didn't know. Maybe Wilbur was in touch. Al wasn't learning fast enough.

"Poor Mr. Jones, to die like that," Al would have said if he could only have swung over on a vine through the jailtime jungle. But of course, no matter how clear he could see it, he still couldn't do it. He was cut off from the yelling nigger, just as he had been in the Muslim temple when Jarod had spoken and this very Wilbur X had leaned him against the wall and pinched, tugged, and patted him to make sure no weapons and to assure him of plenty spite . . .

Jail food had given Al a thin, sallow, Mandarin head of thinness, sallowness, Oriental depression. Of course, if he ate the bread and potatoes with gravy, he would be blown up and farty and depressed. He ate what it was in his character to eat—picking at the tray. He ate what this time in his life called for—sliding the seventy-three cents per day menu back through the slot. And then low sugar in the blood during the night, and his liver sapping the proteins, and doubts about reality. His fantasies when he dwelled in the nice straight campus world of beat and hip and academic reality had now given way, in this impossible jail, to abstract visions. There was a drug culture going on here, in his body, too. Low sugar in the blood and peculiar adrenal spurts and cerebral manifestations.

Dawn a long time off.

Breakfast further away.

Vibrations of larceny in all these hearts, and sugar-quake in the blood, and who am I?

Thinking big? small? Categories shriveled to a point of mote in the air. Dust. The loneliness that won't leave me alone. The clatter of guard and tray to cement floor and that insane yelling, *Save him! help him!*

Al lurked in silence because he didn't know what it was all about.

Oh, who am I, hoo, hoo?

Coffee madness with no coffee, no drugs, no torture, no electroshock metaphysics. Al knew that this churning of cosmic ambition had gotten him in trouble before—asking too much of Jarod, of himself, of the world outside and the world within. *Who am I?* is the boy's question, who gets money from home, who gets a fellowship, who thinks who am I and slips a stupid note to a bank teller. *I am I!* he thought, and then: *But who is that?* And what name could he give this flooding pity for poor dead Mr. Non-Civil-Service Jones?

Madness. Cheerful absence from himself. And these midnights of horror, self-meeting, self without mirror or pleasure or a girl's hand of oblivion (who were they anyway?).

Do guards get pensions?

Do non-civil-service guards' widows get pensions?

Jarod and Al were both pure-blooded seekers from way back. But way forward, were they also finders? Probably not; the seekers, contrary to what we are told, usually are not. Seek, multitudes, and one or two of ye shall find. And if more, it's a con, it's a shuck. What's the way back, way forward?

I've been locked into myself, so I do nothing. It's all

been happening to me, around me, inside me: I'm not a part of it at all. And that man died! Everyone I know, if he lives long enough, will drool and dribble and use a potty chair again. Jarod will be dead, and Milly will turn dry and withered, and Poopie will scrunch along the street with arthritis. If I live, I'll have an old man's visions of Sue Cody, maybe—but what else? A scrapbook about my bank heist, but what else? Cacklecackle, little explosions of fun. What else? I'll drop like Mr. Jones. What more? What else?

If only he could swing over on a vine to Wilbur X and tell him and discuss and just talk.

They could be *friends!*

(Al was trying to think like Al, like former Al, but as the floating motes floated through his head, he was thinking about the guard. Why couldn't it have been Al instead? He was worthless, a college creep, a nothing nobody nowhere draft evader with a plugged sinus. And this time . . .)

"Wilbur! Wilbur!" he called. "Do you remember me? I saw you on campus, and remember I came with Dr. Howe to your meeting?"

"Man, I wish you wouldn't talk to me," came the low careful voice. "Man, I really don't need no more trouble."

Al waited to hear if he would change his mind. He didn't.

(And this time, just now, it was getting to be a habit, Al was thinking about someone other than himself. The guard. Wilbur. Some whose names he would never know, and some he had known blindly—Jarod, Ellen, and that former Al Dooley for whom, once upon a time, everything had gone just his way . . .)

22 Al awakened from a long sleep—*are they drugging me?*—to find a familiar presence on the opposite bunk, leaning thoughtfully into his face. "Oh, ah, what?" Al asked. He closed his eyes to give the question time to take effect, but the dream didn't go away.

"In general, I shouldn't be here," said Judge Harlow. "But there are many precedents for my action—sometimes it's called Taking a View. Jail conditions, the state of the accused, little deals like that. I cleared with Counsel. Your lawyer is really happy about it. The Prosecutor doesn't mind, either. I gratify my own conscience, too, by making a well-rounded study of the legality and the human significance. In Western justice there are these little bitty exceptions to the rule about having counsel present at all times, Al. They'll never get me on turpitude again. Think of me as a probation officer, for example. Anyway, here I am, and I did much enjoy talking with you, and certainly just carrying our little chat forward another step or two won't prejudice me against you. Or you against me, either, I hope—Al? I just wanted to ask your opinion about something very near and dear to me."

Al sat up, scrubbed his cheeks with his knuckles, and said, "I'm morally sick, but I'm guilty and in my right mind. I hallucinate a little, but I'm responsible. I should be sent away."

"No, no, no!" the judge cried. "You certainly are a monomaniac about your case, aren't you? Don't you think about anything else? Isn't that a little selfish of you, Al?"

"Am I dreaming?"

"Al," said the judge reproachfully, "Al. Isn't an experienced administrator like me on to those tricks? At your age! Shame!" Well, true, if it was drugs, it wasn't a tranquilizer. It was a psychic and a moral and a metaphysical and even a political energizer. Why would they give that to jail inmates awaiting sentence? Judge Harlow crossed his legs in his robes and sighed and said, "I wanted to get your expert sociological opinion about a little book I'm taping. You see, I don't plan to spend all my life deciding guilty or less guilty, as the case may be. That's too depressing, Al—human and inhuman iniquity. Bribery, perjury, and influence —it's not pure, Al. What I really want, I want to make my way in first-person journalism by Judge George C. Harlow as told to George C. Harlow. I use an Ampex 428 with a Fuji playback. Listen, Al, here's the scam. Most judicial memoirs are kind of dry, but I was a juvenile court judge those many years, had that crisis that tried my soul, so how's about I call my book, 'A Girl with a Wayward Spirit'?"

Al bowed his head in his hands.

"Ketchy title, don't you think? Actually, I'm putting in a lot of good strong law and order, too, but I make it the personal touch like that, my own feelings and weaknesses, moments of doubt, tribulation, and how grabbing this thing in chambers messed up my whole

marriage and career as a juvenile judge. She was a
runaway, white, fifteen, blond hair, blue eyes, maybe
wearing tennis shoes and pedal pushers, unarmed, answers to the name of 'Cindy.' Oh, she was armed all
right. They moved me over to senior citizens court like
you as a result, but the whole nasty thing is on my record, anyway, so I'll never make Circuit Appeals—"

Al looked up to see if he was still there. Psychic
energizer didn't erase him.

"It's not an elective office, Al. Your goodwill or the
reverse is irrelevant, but I guess I haven't made myself clear. Your opinion is valuable to me. You're a
trained sociologist and you're under thirty and you're
in contact with the degenerate public of today. You
can help me, Al. 'Juvenile Offenses in My Life'? 'Poor
Lost Kids I Have Known'? I really plan to ring the bell
on Dr. Spock. I wanted to ask you about that, too. Do
you think they spared the rod and spoiled the child in,
say, your personal case? I've seen many a lousy criminal kid like you come from really outstanding families.
Your parents are solid people, inside and out, Al, as I
hope you appreciate. All I ask is for you to come to
my aid with your mentality. I'm going to put in my
own little ethical turpitudes, so this book could really
be a humdinger. Turpitudes be darned, full speed
ahead. How about 'The State Versus Wayward Spirits'?
You think that's kind of long for a title? That Cindy
really lacked responsibility. That's all I can tell you
right now. 'Wayward Spirit' has a lot of dignity, but it
just doesn't tell the whole story as it happened in my
life."

Al looked at his own hands and saw that he was still
there. Psychic energizer kept his criminal hands at-

tached to his law-abiding body, or perhaps it was the reverse.

"Aren't you going to help me, defendant?"

"I wish I could."

"You *can!*"

Al shook his head. It just didn't seem ethical for him to give sociological advice and counsel to his judge. It didn't seem possible. If he were to try to open his mouth, he might not be able to, but he didn't want to try. His stomach was unhappy about the whole thing.

"That's all right," Judge Harlow said, "I won't let it interfere with my primary duty, which is to measure you fairly and evenly for the psychopath you might be, and render a verdict in keeping with the best interests of this republic and of the state of California."

Al saw it coming.

It had been looming up since the beginning.

If he didn't stop it now, he would never know what it was to enjoy consequences for acts.

"I can see it coming," Al said. "Sir, please don't throw me out of prison."

"Of course not," said Judge Harlow. "It's as plain as the hairy mustache on your face you're a menace to society."

"I haven't learned my lesson. My mind is mashing around with the facts and"—His fingers groped for his sandy dropout mustache. It was gone. He had shaved it off as a love-offering to society—"and I slip and fall in reality. Things don't have any meaning, and what's worse, meaning doesn't have things."

"Sure, I get you, you don't want to be helped by that high-yellow professor who has done you a lot of harm, do you, hm?" asked the judge. "He claims he's, um, up tight with his good buddy, but you and I know different, don't we? Come on, tell me, Al. What's *really* been going on between you two?"

"I've been ungrateful to him. I'm irresponsible. I can't be beholden any more."

"I know all that," said the judge. "More, more, more. I'm not just the kind of political hack who would let you off in order to make time with the permissive liberal community of Northern California. I have a higher duty in mind. Southern California."

Judge Harlow suffered from sudden excesses of anxiety, bird-wing flights of frown across his brow, that worried glare and concern of the old-timer. He was not senile—after all, he was still a judge—but he tended to forget pleasant and unpleasant things and remember the things in the middle. Then when he tried to recollect the powerful moments he had forgotten, all he could find in his crowded brain was that America is going downhill fast. That wasn't it, that's not it. But it was true, too. "About this Little Chairman Book of Mao," he asked. "Now I'm not from Orange County like some judges I could name, really bad reactionaries, care for nothing but fundamentals. You can tell me if you've read it, come on, tell me, Al."

Al shook his head from side to side very slowly, indicating that he hadn't really read it, but he carried it around a little, like the Panthers; he had heard a good deal about it, of course; he might just wait for . . . no, he wouldn't be funny . . . the picture. "I didn't like it," he said.

"Detective Brown has given me a pretty fair report on you," Judge Harlow said. "Says here you're not a revolutionary, you're more like a"—he stared at his notes—"lyrical sociologist? Can that be?"

"That's okay," Al said.

"That's right?"

Al shrugged.

"Don't even read the Red Mao Book, just keep it around?"

"Oh, I used to dip into it," Al said, "but I'm doubtful about the style. It doesn't have a relevance in this country. It serves as a totem for the blacks and some of the kids on Telegraph, but—" He blushed. He had fallen into graduate assistant pedagogical habit. Kindly Judge Harlow had seduced him away from his depression and abstraction. "Carrying it is a hustle," Al said, "to get a certain kind of girl."

"I wish you wouldn't use those words," Judge Harlow said. "Make it a lot easier for me."

Al had no idea which words he was referring to. He wouldn't ask. He was not only a philosopher, thinker, lyrical sociologist, and bank-robber, but also he had one of the finest under-thirty vocabularies on the West Coast, plus an outstanding ability to remain silent. He hoped he didn't seem sullen. People sometimes thought he was sullen when his head was only turned inside and far away.

The judge was humming softly. He, too, had a head filled with elsewheres. His own book would cover them. That was a right-wing frown that flitted across his brow, not a bird-wing frown. Again he was giving birth to a thought. "Status quo," he croaked.

"Sir?" Al asked.

"He has an investment in the normal way of the world, which means getting along."

"Sir?"

"Professor Howe. He may be a colored Negro gentleman, but he has something to lose. You think he's a weird person, kind of far out? that what you kids call him? But to me, I see right through to the heart of things—that's my chosen field—it's just for fun he's like that. It's pleasure. When you're weird, son, really weird, wildness and abandon and all that, you give up, you have nothing to lose, you don't care about your life. You haven't gotten used to anything. I've been talking to him—I hope he doesn't mind my saying this, and I know he won't, since he's not here listening. You may think he's your fine colored friend, but he's more my kind than yours, Al. He's no kid. He's over thirty, too."

"I'm not sure I understand you, Judge."

Judge Harlow sighed. Even right-wingers are sad and need to be understood, especially when they explain how and why they happened to be discussing the meaning of life with a colored Negro gentleman. Well, this isn't Orange County. "He's a part of things," the judge said. "How can I say it better than that? I'm not sure you're a part of anything, defendant."

"I'm a student. There are a lot like me. I'm a part of them."

The frown could quickly change to a kill look. Judge Harlow was keeping a firm grip on himself. "You're going to be thirty someday, too, and in forty years from then you'll be sixty, like me, and then ninety. You'll be a non-student. Maybe you should learn to get along with the fundamentals. Crime in the streets and perusing that Red Chairman Book gets you nothing but trouble." Judge Harlow was tense, tight-lipped, in

touch; blood in his head counteracted the artery problem; he was in a reactionary groove where he felt grim,
sober, and secure. "I suppose you need a lesson, Al.
This state university system has been a problem ever
since the war. If we could only put all you dropout
kids in work camps for a while, that'd teach you a lesson."

"Sounds like socialism," Al said.

"If we only do it one at a time," the judge mused,
"then it's disciplinary training. Got you there, didn't I?
In my day 'non-student' wasn't a profession. We
learned how to contribute to the free world—accounting, engineering, medicine, and law. Oh, we had our
Greek scholars, too, and some boys who were a credit
to their respective races. But we didn't have all this
surfing and rioting and those different kinds of Communism and so much sex at the movies. Things were
simpler and somehow better, son. You'll find it all in
my new work, 'Young Wayward Spirits,' plus some
personalized moments of fallibility. Some might call
it turpitude, I call it human frailty. That Cindy was
like you in many ways, a snare and a delusion."

"I agree, sir. I wish you a lot of luck with your
book."

Judge Harlow looked deeply into Al's eyes, and then
at his watch, and then back to the eyes. "You weren't
much help," he said.

During the thoughtful pause which followed, both
of them focused on the near future. Al found it within
his power to offer something different to consider. "I
wasn't really a dropout or a non-student. I was more
like a graduate student. That's not the same thing,
sir. I could have gone on to get a B.A." But Al himself

was thinking about a new life. The chapel was a new idea. He hadn't considered the chapel at San Quentin.

"As Socrates said, one of the great judges—you remember, he condemned that fella Hemlock to death for a crime not much worse than yours—*be what you wish to seem.* Of course, if you don't know what you wish to seem, you got a problem there, Al." So much for classical jurisprudence, which was suitable for a time when people used to know their places. The judge was sad—right-wing sadness, but kind. "That Dr. Mao really spoiled you," he said. "You're a mixed-up person."

Al hoped that Judge Harlow might be able to straighten him around with another word or two. Some of these right-wingers were surprisingly human, and this fretful man seemed to be one of the human ones, a credit and a plus to the fundamental race.

"What does working in the chapel involve?" Al asked. "Does it have anything to do with your faith? Should I become a believer?"

"In prison?" Judge Harlow asked. And sure enough, he was surprisingly human. A joyful smile looped across his face, revealing teeth, gums, creviced tongue, more teeth, and perhaps a bit of gratified sadism. "In San Q? the chapel? religion?" He was shaking his head incredulously. How out of touch can a kid get? An old man forgets things, but a kid doesn't even know them. "I think you better seem what you wish to be, Al."

"Thank you, sir," Al said. "If I can count on you, I'll learn a useful craft. I really mean it this time."

"Promise?" said the judge.

Al stopped a moment and looked at his soul and tried to decide if he really wanted to say it. He couldn't see his soul, but he knew it was there. He really wanted to say it. "If you let me out," he said, "I'm going to get into more trouble. I haven't learned enough yet."

"Told me that already—"

"I've got to get in touch. Oh, it's not really to prove anything, sir. Be a decent person and responsible for my acts, that's what I really want."

"Okay. You could have helped me in what I asked you—a practical matter."

"I'm infected with the virus of metaphysics, sir."

Judge Harlow twisted a fist into his palm. "Okay, that's enough," he snapped. "I have heard enough already. This is a dirty rotten kid who tries a man's patience. I've listened to enough of your filthy talk, boy. Looks like license-plate time for old Al Dooley."

"Thank you, sir." Al fell to his knees. The judge stepped backward, disgusted. That sort of thing cut no ice with him. He recognized a phony baloney when he saw one. It just confirmed him in his view that human beings are no better than colored people. He waved as he went out.

"See you later, kid. Be sure you show up in court for the verdict, hey? Trouble with being a wayward spirit and delinquent like you and that sociopathic girl I used to know—okay, her body was firm, but her character was weak and she talked too much—trouble is, kid, you don't build a secure relationship anyplace. You tend to just get put away . . ."

23 The day of the deciding dawned clear and cool. After the weather report, between the dusty diamonds and the sports scoreboard, all the local news stations carried word of the forthcoming news. The case had implications from one end of the universe to the other—from Berkeley to Sausalito and down the peninsula—implications and reverberations and it was something to do. A crowd of friendly hippies gathered in front of what they called the Hall of Square Justice, a crowd of unfriendly protestors gathered in front of the Hall of Injustice, a crowd of gawkers and watchers gathered in front of the Theater of State Reality, a crowd of pals and relatives and the truly concerned gathered in the streets and byways of downtown legal San Francisco. Al Dooley, they felt, was clearing new ground. Just like Alyosha Raskolnikov, the Russian philosopher and murderer, Al Dooley, the American graduate student and kleptomaniac, was telling it like it was. Like Herman Hesse, the Marquis de Sade, and Alan Watts, he would leave the world just a little different. Naturally there was a mob to participate in the holy rite of sacrifice.

Also the Mission Magic Mile shopping district was having its annual warehouse sale and those concerned

with Al Dooley's fate were admixed with those concerned with getting thermal underwear, Metrecal, and
Winchester hunting rifle refills at factory prices. Al
could hear the cries of the mob outside. In his heart
he knew there were tumbrels rolling. He could be forgiven a moment of egotism. Charlotte Corday was only
seeking thermal underwear.

An amplified flower-rock band which now called itself the M'Naughton Rule was belting out Al's favorite
tune to console him. Milly had told them it was Bobby
Dylan's "Sad-Eyed Lady of the Lowlands," because it
reminded him of her, but since they didn't know that
one, they played one of their own favorites, "You Made
the Sky Turn Pink," in the hopes that it would become one of Al's favorites, to be hummed by him in
his cell until he received transistor privileges. Their
leader was planning to send him a Bible with pages
soaked in LSD—an old trick but a good one. You can
get pretty happy munching on the Lamentations of
Jeremiah. Their masked girl singer, Miranda Case,
shook her blond fall and her satin rump and screamed:

> "You taught me how to think!
> You made the sky turn pink!"

"Hum, hummable," said Judge Harlow to the bailiff.
"Say, what kind of person does that girl singer look
like? Anyway, tell the officers to clear that plaza with
a little carefully chosen police brutality and let's get
this show on the road."

In a jiffy there was a fine typical San Francisco scene
of flailing clubs, raining bottles, screaming girls being
dragged by the hair, cops pummeling through the

mob, trying to sort out the minority groups with their
clubs. You'll find that your average rowdy trouble-
making black citizen has a strange sensitivity to a can
of mace in the face. Your hippies show a likewise symp-
tom. A forty-five-year-old Mexican lady on her way to
find some thermal underwear against the damp San
Francisco daily winter got bashed on the chest by a cop
who just couldn't stand beatniks. It wasn't his fault;
she had long hair and couldn't get out the words, "Sir,
I was just on my way to the Mission Magic Mile for the
sale at Bert's Surplus," before justice was done. Oh
well, thought the cop as he saw her fall, them Spics
is used to it. Good pair o' tits on her. Most of the
veterans of the Viet Nam war protests and the Haight
Street drug busts had skinny, nimble bodies and
scampered away in time to fight again. Pretty soon
cooler heads prevailed and the police riot was under
control. Judge Harlow sent out another bailiff with the
message, "The right of free assembly is guaranteed
by the Constitution or maybe it's the Bill of Rights.
Please leave enough audience for the media."

A holiday atmosphere prevailed along with the
cooler heads.

A lonely guitarist, moaning with the wisdom of his
race, crooned, "Sad-Eyed Lady of the Lowlands." His
name was Jimmy Wing and he was a beatnik folk
singer from Hong Kong who had somehow survived
in North Beach until the hippie movement put flowers
in his hair. "Sad-eyed rady of the row-rands," he sang,
"sad-eyed rady flom where no man comes . . ."

The cop who had clubbed the Spic lady smiled
benevolently at Jimmy and thought of his mother. See,

if these kids are just nice a little, we can live with them.

The holiday atmosphere continued to prevail.

The coolest heads went away to wash their eyes and try to prevent corneal damage.

Inside the courtroom, the interested parties gathered—Judge Harlow, Al Dooley, Al's mother and dad from Santa Barbara, Milly Peck, and of course the newsmen. Where was Poopie? Al wondered. Al had this continuing sense that he was a little bit bland as a type and maybe Poopie was the sort who lost interest easily. Inside he was vivid, Al Dooley was a giant inside, capable of desperate deeds at noon, but how was Poopie to know? He couldn't even keep a bank heist firmly in mind.

"Order in the court!"

Before the bailiff could cry out, "Judge Harlow, Fifth Circuit Juvenile Emeritus, is in session," the judge reminded him that this was just a hearing. It wasn't really like a real trial. It was just, aw, sort of an effort to get at the essential reality of the impulsive criminal act. "So don't say Order in the Court," he said, smiling and twinkling at the bailiff in that unself-conscious manner which had long endeared him to the blind news vendor in the hall.

The bailiff raised his staff, pounded on the floor, and said, "Order in the Hearing!"

Judge Harlow smiled and nodded in his mild and sweet way which had so pleased the blind mint-man (Chockies, Milky Ways, Mars bars) from whom he usually bought his candy and in whose hat he always placed a bet on the numbers. The blind news vendor was the driver for the blind Chockies and numbers runner. He used to take him to Oakland for the accounting work in his pink Cadillac.

"Will the prisoner please stand?"

Al shuffled forward.

"Do you have anything to say, prisoner, before I pass the verdict?"

Al had the cunning idea that he might have different things to say after he heard the verdict, depending on what it was, but decided that this was a good opportunity to keep his mouth shut. He did so, uttering only the words, "Nothing, sir."

The judge smiled approvingly. "That's nice," he said. "Of course, I can't let it affect my verdict. However, I'll take your behavior into consideration when I say my prayers and make out my will, haha."

He beamed so that his tongue could be seen in his cheek. A ripple of laughter spread through the court— Milly, parents, newsmen, bailiff, blind Chockies and numbers salesmen. Judge Harlow really dug appreciation, so he raised a hand to wave at his fans. Then he raised his other hand for silence. He now had both hands over his head and it felt kind of funny. He lowered them. "Okay prisoner, it's horror verdict sentence time," he said. "Well, not so bad as all that. Hear me out and listen carefully."

Al Dooley had been listening carefully all his life. He had been trying to discover reality by listening and it was making his ears ring. He was willing to try once more. He was young, wasn't he? And though he wanted to choose, he was finding the choices limited. "Yes, sir," he said. He would hear him out.

Judge Harlow controlled his impatience. "All the

good affidavits your teacher there gave you was very favorable for you, son. I have to admit they really respect your talents and neuroses over there at the University of California at Berkeley. At least the dark-skinned gentleman over there sure does. He likes you like you am. However, I have to defend"—he glanced at his notes—"society. We can't have you mad dog radical kids running around talking filth and using dope and robbing banks with impunity. You get away with this, you get away with that, pretty soon you're trying to get away with the other thing. Life isn't so simple. I've talked and I've listened and I've talked some more and I just can't seem to get it through my head what you're after. Everyone tries to tell me you're looking for the meaning of life. I don't mind that so much. But why can't you do it like the other fellows? Hang around those Singles bars and meet a better class of female. It's been clearly established that you're a white male adult, I.Q. in the superior range, but you act stupid and your mind is peculiar. Smoke marijuana—not that we're accusing you of that, son. Carry the Little Red Chairman book, though our records of you sitting in and picketing and rioting are kind of lacking. Dream and fuss around like you was a kid in a small town on Saturday morning (I was that kid, too, son). There's been enough coddling of the likes of you and me. It's time we learned a lesson. If I let you get away with this, get off scot-free, go to Acapulco and have yourself a laugh at the expense of justice, why, every Rufus, Leroy, and Floyd would think he can rob a bank and get off because, oh, he feels up tight. Do I make myself clear? Am I speaking to you, folks? Well, I'm going to say it loud. I'm a

traditionalist and I'm proud. This white male adult Al
Dooley has had all the advantages the twentieth cen-
tury could buy. He has looked into fires and seen the
apocalypse. He has dreamed of disaster and wondered
who his real father was. What good were such won-
derings? His real father is sitting right there in the
courtroom with us, a puzzled, unhappy, disappointed
man. Where did he go wrong? His real mother—well,
he didn't have so many doubts about her. Nevertheless,
she must ask herself some questions, too. What was she
doing when this boy cried out silently in the night for
guidance and counseling? Why couldn't she hear him?
Was she playing golf? If so, why didn't she invite him
along?" The bailiff whispered to Judge Harlow. The
judge nodded briefly. "I see," he said. "I am informed
that the Santa Barbara Country Club links have no
facilities for baby-sitting. The principle remains, my
friends. This boy is responsible. His parents did everything they could. They couldn't do very much. But is
loneliness and isolation a reason to rob public institutions such as the Crocker-Anglo Bank? Is it any reason
to exhibit yourself before a minor, female, white, and
ruin a whole career in the aid and reform of juveniles?"

Al wished he could hear the judge. He knew what
solipsism was. He wished he could hear the real judge
and not make him up as he went along.

"Something can't allow it," said Judge Harlow. "It's
on the tip of my tongue." He snapped his fingers,
glanced at the note on his desk, and it fell off the tip of
his tongue. "*Society* can't allow it," he said. "Is a de-
prived spirit and a sickened imagination any reason to
hold threatening notes onto a poor spinster teller and
scare her within six to eight inches of her life? Can a

kid from a good family do something the law clearly proscribes for our black but equal citizens and get away with it? My friends, the answer to all these questions is, and must remain, a resounding Maybe. Therefore I find," said the judge.

Well, Jarod wasn't in the courtroom. That was discretion. Someplace he was shucking and jiving.

"The defendant," said the judge.

No, there he sat. How could Al have missed him? Hilarious Jarod, squinting at his briefcase as if everything was locked inside.

"Not Guilty by Virtue of Jumpiness!"

A roar of approval went up. Justice blind once again! The judge might vindictively have declared Al a sociopath, a psychopath, or a lower-class criminal, but once more he had set a precedent in legal history. Rod Raskolnikov, the well-known Russian murderer of pawnship keepers, had also sort of gotten off for jumpiness, didn't he? Even new precedents have to have some kind of basis in history, don't they?

The mob rushed forward. Kisses, hugs, and embraces. If Al didn't catch a cold out of this, he was just plain lucky or resistant to viruses. Judge Harlow ordered the courtroom attendants to push the little group back. He had a few more things to say, but he would sum them up briefly. Al was put on probation, ordered to consult with a qualified physician (Dr. Frisch ready with a referral), and, in general, told to eat lots of wheat germ, celery, and Thorazine in order to calm his nervous feelings. A young man should watch the physical as well as the psychiatric parts of his character. No more shoplifting or boosting, even on impulse. Counseling the patient against violence or moral epi-

lepsy, kindly old Judge Harlow stated, "It is far, far
better to abide by the law than to waste your time on
illegal pursuits."

He beckoned with a finger to the blind numbers
salesman. Blinkie took off his sunglasses, put down his
white cane, and followed the judge into chambers. Al
had no chance to bid him farewell.

Milly flew into Al's arms. "I'm so proud!" she cried.
"Of you! You're so *interesting*, Al."

"Don't jump to conclusions," he said. "All I did was
rob a bank and get betrayed by my moll because she
was neurasthenically bound to a crooked, double-cross-
ing pimp, was all I did."

"I don't care," said Milly through her soft, buttery
lips. "I forgive your frustrated aversion to a girl not
worthy of you. Thank God I've changed! Now I have
found a purpose in life—caring. And I care for you.
You're unusual, Al."

"That's nice of you, Milly."

"At last! It's about time!"

"Thank you, Milly. I think I've gone insane."

"And Poopie has offered to step aside. He says I'm
too much for him. He says you're twice the man he
ever was."

"That's nice of him, Milly."

"I'm afraid he's pretty sad, kind of distraught. But
oh well, it can't be helped. I got you under my skin, Al,
and I just had to work out some of my problems."

"That's really nice of you, Milly."

"And you know what? Your nice daddy says he will
send us to Acapulco for our honeymoon if we promise
to be good. Let's be really good, Al."

At last Al was on the right track. Married, settling

down, he could quickly get off probation, write a dissertation on the criminal mind, and find a job teaching in a quiet little school, a small but distinguished liberal arts college. A record as a bank-robber marked him off as a bit different from other young instructors in sociology. In a world which admired slight distinctions, an occasionally dreamy and melancholic character, this could only work to his advantage. There would be that *je ne sais quoi* which always helps. "We'll have adventures together," Milly promised him. "Life will be our adventure."

And of course, if he got bored with Milly or his job in a small but distinguished liberal arts college, he could vary the routine. He might take off after Poopie in a typical underworld act of revenge. A bit of insurance right there. He could break the monotony. The murder of a stool pigeon by a handsome young sociology professor would lead to a bigger job in a better school, a larger but more distinguished university, still more forgiveness by wife and family, and a sense of pride that Al Dooley brought some variety into the steady hum of the American routine. Two feet firm, Al knew how to stand tall with all the power of desperation and vanity, working the machine. This throbbing, this spinning and thrumming, these fiery explosions were what it was about. He had found his own way to hit the jackpot.

Detective Warren Brown (Bronofoffski) was weeping. He had gotten emotionally involved. His father, the prince, would have found some feet to kiss, but there was no room for Russian charm in the population explosion of this courtroom.

Jarod was smiling and waving in the crowd. He was

mouthing a word. He wouldn't push his way forward.
He didn't blame Al for having complicated feelings.
That's how it is. He was saying the word again. He
winked. He had responsibilities. He would catch up
with Al later. He would leave him alone in the crowd to
work out this hour of disarray. He lifted his briefcase
in a victory symbol, not a boxer or a warrior but a
triumphant professor. He shrugged. The word again:
Ellen. He was on his way to see Ellen. He lifted his
briefcase again in farewell, and then Al saw the tall
hurrying body in a devouring confusion which opened
around him.

Jarod was riding again after his time of hesitation.
His book on Classless Poverty was to become the
totem work for radical young intellectuals, a group
which included almost everybody. It replaced Herbert
Marcuse, who had replaced Che Guevara and Frantz
Fanon, who had replaced C. Wright Mills, who had
replaced David Riesman, who had replaced Monopoly
and Miniature Golf. It revolutionized thinking about
race, sectionalism, work, leisure, the new eroticism, the
old Big Stick policy, Europe versus America, the im-
portance of the classic cinema, permissive child-rear-
ing, homosexuality as a means of social protest,
homosexuality as a way to brotherhood, the measuring
of social distance, the interrupted time-space con-
tinuum, the normal as abnormal, nausea, anguish, the
Freudian backlash, the Marxist revival, the death of
God, the resultant responsibility to communicate, and
the need to find privacy amid the population explosion. A thousand copies of the hardcover edition were
purchased by Youth Sell, a marketing organization

devoted to the hopes and dreams of the under-twenty-five consumer. Several hundred thousand copies of the quality paperback edition were purchased by the Southern Leadership Council, the B'nai B'rith, the U.S. Air Force, and other concerned organizations. Because of its lucid style it was adopted for experimental use as a freshman English text at the University of North Carolina, Greensboro campus.

He was becoming the director of a program which encouraged ghetto dwellers to invest in their own property. It was based on a new economic theory which demonstrated how black people could get a piece of America by renting slum housing to each other. He turned down an ambassadorship to Nigeria on the grounds that this was a trouble spot and a black man should not be asked to take over a job doomed to lack of success. He would have liked, instead, Mexico, Brazil, or Greece.

Only Ellen seemed to have lost her way. Did so many have to draw an empty machine so that some could hit the jackpot? If Jarod hadn't been a black man, her illness might have put a limit to his political aspirations. As it was, no one could refer to Ellen without expressing sympathy for the husband, bravely carrying on. Pat Livard now worked as his housekeeper. Taking care of unbalanced women was a recent form of enslavement for many men, black or white.

Al Dooley was alone once more with his intentions and plans, his making out and his asking what next he might draw out of his luck. When a man doesn't pay the cost, he pays the price. But it was not the end for him, either. Jarod pressed chance and courage toward the jackpot; so would Al. America was the prize they claimed, turning and clicking the wheels into lucky place.

He walked down the long white steps of the court house, blinking in the sun, surrounded like a politician by his little knot of guards and therapists and attendant reporters. He had a position to sustain; he had a public. A television camera turned its ferocious eye on him, borne on the back of a sweating cameraman who averted his own eyes so as not to be redundant. A green light was flashing. White teeth were flashing. "Hey, pal," said the commentator behind the camera, "you plan to join the Peace Corps if they'll take you, like your little lady here says? Vista? Job Corps? Poverty? Work your way to the top in a modern mental facility for the criminally insane? A truly Now program for today?"

"I," began Al, "who—? who's my girlfriend, you say?"

Sue Cody was waving to him in the crowd of well-wishers. What did her smiles mean? What did her tears mean? She was moving toward him with her face shining and righteous. He was moving toward her.

"Hey, that's beautiful," said the commentator. "Okay, if you want to reach for each other, that's beautiful. Go on, do it, do it, *do* it."

Just like a celebrity, Al punched him straight in the face. "Hey, I'm Marvin, why'd you do that?" Marvin said as he went down to one knee.

Al did it partly for Sue Cody, more for himself, and perhaps also because the man from the teevee seemed to require a touch of California spontaneity for the Special Six O'Clock Report. But Sue's radiant face did not understand Al any more. She waited for what he would do next.

The red eye was flashing. The lens had zoomed in close. Sue and Al. Al smiling. Al troubled. Al rubbing his fist. Al helping the man from the teevee to his feet.

The grateful mouth of the recently grounded commentator: "Hey, thanks for that at least, plus what's the little lady's name, Al? Hey, don't you remember me, Al?"

"Sue Cody," she said, "that's like in Buffalo Bill."

"Pleased to make your acquaintance. We got a great take on the whole scene. Al, say you remember and don't knock me down again. It's all clear in your mind now, isn't it? You remember?"

Al was looking at Sue and wanting to ask her questions. Sue was looking at Al and wanting to answer his questions. Al was ripe to ask the questions. And if Al wasn't ready yet, he would do his best to get ready.

The mob was shouting and shoving and pulling at them.

"You remember, Al—Marvin? *Marvin?* The Affluent American and the semantics of it all?"

Sue and Al pushed through the crowd without answering anyone. Sue had this old hearse she'd just bought and it was waiting for them.

ABOUT THE AUTHOR

HERBERT GOLD has written eight novels, including *Fathers, Salt,* and *The Man Who Was Not With It;* a volume of stories, *Love and Like;* and one of essays, *The Age of Happy Problems.* He has taught at the University of California at Berkeley, at Stanford, Cornell, and Harvard. He has received numerous literary awards, has published essays and stories in many magazines, and his books have been widely translated abroad. He lives in San Francisco and is working on a book about the conditions of American life in the sixties, *The Magic Will,* and on a new novel.